I0700209

ENGAGED TO THE EMT

PIPER RAYNE

This book is a work of fiction. Names, characters, places and incidents either are products of the author's imagination or are used fictitiously. Any resemblance to actual events or locales or persons, living or dead, is entirely coincidental.

© 2018 by Piper Rayne

Piper Rayne® registered in U.S. Patent and Trademark Office.

All rights reserved, including the right to reproduce this book or portions thereof in any form whatsoever.

Cover Design: Angela Haddon

Line Editor: Gray Ink Editing

Proofreader: Shawna Gavas, Behind the Writer

———————————————
ABOUT ENGAGED TO THE EMT
———————————————

Luca Bianco is a jerk. There I said it.

He thinks he's so suave and sexy, walking around in his paramedic uniform stretched out by all his hard muscles and saving lives every day. I swear he thinks every woman in the world would kill for a chance to be with him.

Men like Luca are good for one thing only — a one-night stand — not commitment. I don't care if my friend did pay good money at a charity bachelor auction for me to go on a date with him, I refuse to do it.

That is until Luca offers me a deal I can't refuse, and I agree to be his pretend fiancé.

The heat that's simmered between us for a decade ignites and I'm not sure even Luca will be able to kickstart my heart after I call code blue.

What's that saying? Love is blind?

Not true. I can see this head-on collision coming a mile away.

Engaged TO THE EMT

CHAPTER ONE

Luca

"Guess what, Ma?"

My mom's soft smile appears first, her unconditional love-filled eyes set on me.

"My baby?" She lightly smacks my cheek in a way to ask, 'what am I doing here with Lauren?' Even Mama knows I'm no saint and until last night I was far from having a girlfriend let alone a fiancée.

Maddie finds her way to Mauro and Vanessa to Christian, the four of them staring at us like we're aliens who just descended upon Earth.

I raise our linked hands together, sparing a quick glance at Lauren who doesn't look as enthusiastic as me. "Your baby is getting married," I announce.

I understand the question marks filling their eyes, we've been at each other's throats for as long as we've known each other.

All of their mouths are open and I kiss Lauren on the cheek. We need to up the PDA on this endeavor to make it believable.

Newsflash, the engagement is fake.

How did we get here you ask?

Months ago, I volunteered to be auctioned off for a date for the First Responders Fallen Heroes Bachelor Auction—I'm a paramedic. It was a sure thing that some sweet piece of ass would bid on me and a big fat donation would be made to the charity.

After witnessing two women wrestling on the floor over who would win me, I was eager to see who won the right to be on my arm for a night. Until I found out a girl from high school and two of her friends decided to switch up paddles and place each other's bids for fun. This left me with Lauren Hunt. And yeah, it may have hurt my ego a bit that Lauren didn't bid on me herself.

But in order to understand why I've decided to deceive my family, we have to go back to last night.

Scratch that. We need to go back to Friday, so you can understand why Lauren agreed to my crazy request in the first place.

CHAPTER TWO

Lauren

"*L*auren!" The little girl's voice even puts a smile on grumpy Jeremy's face, who's been clear to everyone today that he doesn't want to be here.

"Polybriana." I open my arms and she wobbles over to me. Her signature fire engine red braided pigtails swishing from side to side.

She falls into my arms and I hold the nine-year-old tight to my chest.

"I brought you something." She steps back, her eyes taking in the room around us and landing right on Jeremy.

Jeez, is it instilled in girls to want the bad boy from birth?

Her cheeks flush and she pulls off her backpack, pulling out a red, black and white thread bracelet.

"A friendship bracelet?" I've gotten lots of drawings during my time as a pediatric physical therapist. I have a shelf full of coffee mugs, thank you cards and I love every single one. A bracelet is a new one though.

"Well it's just a bracelet," she says.

Gotta love kids and their ability to tell you the truth.

"I love it," I say, clutching it to my chest.

"Hawks colors!" Her little eyes sparkle as she looks at her creation.

"Did you catch last night's game?"

"Kane was amazing."

I sit down on the exercise ball, bringing the bracelet around my wrist. "Help me tie it?" I ask because it will only help her fine motor skills.

We manage to get the bracelet on working together and I figure I'll cut the extra long strings off later.

"Perfect fit." I smile down at the sweet girl whose had such a hard road. She had developmental delays that were found much later than they should've been.

"Hi, Jeremy," she says as the thirteen-year-old boy walks by on the beam, trying to keep one foot in front of the other.

"Hey," he mumbles, not even giving her a fleeting glance.

"Briana, love the braids." My boss and Jeremy's PT, Peter, smiles at the little girl and then winks at me.

Briana giggles and shoots me her usual look when it comes to Peter.

"Come on girl." I stand from the exercise ball, moving it out of the way and pat the mat for her to lay down.

"He likes you," she says, handing me her foot. I take off her brace and start bending her legs.

Since it's our warmup, she doesn't wince. The side of her face is pressed to the mat facing the direction of Jeremy as Peter tries to get him back on track after a horrific car acci-dent. He's come a long away despite his attitude. Peter's been way too nice and hasn't shown enough tough love, in my opin-ion, but that's his personality.

"He's my boss," I tell Briana with a shake of my head.

"When's Jeremy done?"

She changes the subject away from Peter, thank goodness, but moves onto a topic I always hate discussing with her.

She's been here for five years now and has seen many kids come and go, knowing she might never be the one to finish her therapy.

"He has at least six more months I'd say. Enough about boys." I tickle her ribcage. "Tell me about school. What are you learning?"

Briana laughs and tells me about learning Spanish and starts saying a few phrases I know from my own years of taking Spanish during school. She thinks it's funny when I can respond back to her. We finish our physical therapy set a half hour later, Jeremy already gone, so Briana's attention has thankfully been solely on me.

"See you in two days." I hold up two fingers.

"Don't lose the bracelet," she sing-songs, walking out to her mom in the reception area.

I wave to her mom, who adopted her five years ago and literally saved her from a life spent in a wheelchair.

Once she's gone, I see I have five minutes to grab a quick snack before my next client, so I head to the lunchroom. The first thing I notice when I walk in is the red piece of paper with white writing attached to the front of the refrigerator.

Ugh, the Christmas party. I'd forgotten about that.

"Are you going?" I turn to find Peter in the doorway. His arms crossed over his chest, his shoulder leaning against the doorframe.

"I have to check my schedule. I completely blanked." I open the fridge, take out my apples and peanut butter and sit down at the table.

Peter steps in and sits down across from me.

"Did you see what the company is doing now? A talent show." He crosses his legs, his eyes following the apple dipped in peanut butter to my mouth.

"Well, for that reason alone, I might have other plans." I crunch down on the apple.

Peter's familiar creepy smile appears on his face while his eyes fixate on my lips as though he's thinking about something other than an apple being in my mouth. Oh God, please tell me I'm way off base.

"Come on. It'll be fun. Gives everyone a chance to show their fun side."

I swallow my bite of apple. "Still, I think I'll pass."

"That's a shame." He straightens his back, linking his hands on the table, leaning toward me.

Please, Jesus, NO! I telepathically try to tell him not to do it. I know Peter likes me, but he's my boss. No way should he cross that line. Then again, I don't remember anything about non-fraternizing in my contract.

"I was thinking that maybe it'd be fun if we went together. You know. You're single. I'm single."

"And you're my boss. I'm your employee," I gently remind him.

He chuckles, leaning across the table farther, the legs of his chair sliding along the linoleum of the floor.

"I've checked and there's no problem with us dating."

"How could that be? It's twenty-eighteen." I eat another piece of my apple because it will keep me from blurting out something I can't take back. I don't want to blow the best job I've gotten since graduation.

"We're small. Truth is I think maybe when they started the company, they forgot to add it to the policy manual." He raises his eyebrows.

By they, he means Ollie and Reba Garfield who started this company. There are three buildings in all and Peter manages this one which is located close to the pediatric hospital. Ollie and Reba seem like the types who would hire a lawyer to make sure all the t's were crossed and i's dotted, so

I'm not sure what's more disturbing—the fact that the policy doesn't exist or that Peter has looked into it.

"That seems unlike them."

He shrugs. "Ours to take advantage of."

My stomach twists. He can't be serious. How do I turn down my boss and still keep a good working relationship? This is exactly why good ol' Ollie and Reba should've triple checked to make sure the 'no fraternizing' clause was in the employee handbook.

"So?" he asks. "Come with me. We can meet up on Fridays and practice our routine."

"Routine?" I choke out, a little bit of apple falling out of my mouth onto the table.

Anyone else and I might be embarrassed.

Peter stands up, grabs a napkin and cleans it up for me.

Damn, I thought maybe I grossed him out and he'd lose interest.

"We could do Sonny and Cher, or we could do a skit if you don't want to sing." There's hope in his eyes. This has to be a joke.

Just then my co-worker Cindy knocks on the frame of the break room door.

Thank goodness, my next appointment is here.

"Hey, Cindy." I stand, disposing of the rest of my apple and peanut butter into the trash. Is it bad if I just ignore his request?

"I have a package for you." She walks over to me while her gaze is on Peter.

I inspect the small white box with my name on it.

"A courier delivered it." Curiosity is all over her face, but I can't assuage it because I have no idea what this is or who it's from.

"Weird." I sit back down and open the box.

In it is a slew of Brach's candies. The ones I used to eat at the grocery store in my high school days. A bunch of us would stop there to grab a drink and snack after classes.

"Oh, there's a note." Cindy's arm appears from across the table and points to said note.

"I thought you were single?" Peter asks from across the table. The smile has left his face now.

I'm not sure what to say.

"Open it!" Cindy's practically jumping up and down, biting her lip. You'd think the package was for her.

"Don't you have work to do?" Peter asks Cindy.

Her gaze shifts his way, then back to me, her lips tipping down. "After Lauren reads the note, okay, Pete?"

Cindy is always pushing the limits and Peter always lets her. Hence her being the only one who shortens his name.

"Fine," he lets out the exasperated word.

I slide my finger along the seam, and I have to admit there's no small amount of giddiness inside me. I haven't received a package in…forever. The last time was probably my boyfriend, Cody, back in high school when he'd leave notes in my locker.

Inside the envelope, there's a note scribbled in male handwriting.

Dig under the sweetness for your real *surprise.*

I drop the note to the side. Cindy picks it up and reads it. Sliding the candy away, I blink to make sure my eyes aren't teasing me.

A Blackhawks ticket.

I gingerly pick it up to investigate whether it's real.

"Oh, a sports ticket?" Cindy's voice is filled with disappointment.

Clearly, she doesn't know me at all.

"To the Blackhawks!" I say, raising it into the air. "Man,

who would have sent me this? It's not my birthday or anything."

"Check the note on the back." Peter sullenly points to the ticket as I'm doing a little dance in my chair.

I'll be in the same building as Duncan Keith. I hope they have good security.

I turn the ticket over to find there's a Post-It note attached.

Stipulation to accepting ticket: you have to go with me. One date. Your friend paid a lot of money to the charity. I picked something you'd enjoy. Somewhere we don't even have to make conversation. Text me your answer.

Luca

Even his note is full of attitude. The way he scribbles his name reminds me of a serial killer or something.

"Cindy," Peter drones.

"Going. Going." She leaves the room.

I unwrap a royal caramel and bite off a piece.

"Not many guys would do something like that. I didn't know you were seeing someone." Peter stands up, peering into the box and the ticket next to it.

"Well..." Just as I'm about to correct him, a brilliant idea forms in my mind.

"I guess you already have a Sonny for the talent show." He nods his head and starts to walk out of the room.

"Peter," I call out, and he stops, circling back around.

I shouldn't lie. It'll only make things more complicated. "I...I'm sorry," I say, the lie burning in my throat. Though technically I didn't say what I was sorry for so I could have just meant I'm sorry that going out with you is the last thing in the world I want to do. Who's to say?

"Don't be. I should've asked you sooner. Your next appointment is probably here."

He leaves the break room and I finish my caramel, the taste not nearly as good as it usually is knowing I just lied and acted like Luca was someone I'm actually interested in dating.

I stare down at the ticket. Blackhawks. I've never been and he's right, Vanessa paid a lot of money for a date at that Bachelor Auction. If I don't go, it'd be like throwing her money out the window. Money she worked hard to earn at that stupid gambling club she was involved in. Plus, he's right, we don't have to talk much if we're cheering on the team.

I pick up my phone and go to his number.

> **Me:** Pick me up an hour before game time.

Three dots appear immediately.

> **Asshat:** You like the candies?

> **Me:** I like the ticket.

> **Asshat:** I'll pick you up an hour and a half before game time.

Ugh, of course he has to dictate everything.

> **Me:** I said an hour. I'm not wasting my time alone with you. Actually, I'll meet you there.

> **Asshat:** Fine an hour, but I'm picking you up.

I waver because I don't really want to take public transportation and he's right, parking will cost me a fortune down there. But it's a tough decision on spending time with Luca Bianco or paying for parking. I'm good at ignoring him, and it would be more economical if he drives.

> Asshat: Still weighing the pros and cons of being in my company???

> Me: Fine.

> Asshat: See you then. ;)

I drop the phone, pick up my box and hurry to my locker before meeting Kyra for her session. I'm not about to share Brach's assortment of candies with anyone—even if they are from Luca.

CHAPTER THREE

Luca

I'm taking Lauren Hunt to a Hawks game. For most women, this wouldn't be a panty dropper so much as something to bitch about. One good thing about Lauren is that she's as much into sports and competition as I am. So, the Hawks game is to butter her up. Butter her up to accept my marriage proposal. Not that we'll ever end up at the altar or anything.

"Please." I hold my hand out, motioning for her to head down the aisle to our seats first.

After all, I am a gentleman.

Her eyebrows crinkle because she's trying to figure out my end game.

For those of you who don't know, Lauren Hunt and I find it difficult to be civil to one another. What her issue is with me, I have no fucking clue. My issue with her is irrelevant to this conversation.

We take our seats in my designated season ticket spots. Not the best but not nosebleed either. Hey, I'm not an executive like any of my NYC cousins. Give me a break.

"Beer?" I ask, raising my hand for the guy walking up and down the aisles to stop.

Regardless if Hunt wants one, I need about ten to get through tonight. Then I remember that I drove so I'm gonna have to stick to my limit. Damn.

"Buying me one?" she asks, crossing her legs.

I ignore the dick twitch in my pants. My body can't deny she's got amazing legs, even covered in dark denim.

My male anatomy hasn't gotten the message that we only need Hunt for one thing and it doesn't involve him getting any pleasure.

"It's a date." I shrug, handing down a twenty while the friendly people of Chicago pass the money along to the vendor and then the beer back to us.

Great city. Great people.

She sips her beer and places it in on the floor in front of her. Her eyes on the rink down below us. I won't brag like I normally would about having season tickets because I need her and I'm smart enough to know if I come across arrogant, she'll get pissy and deny me the teeny, tiny favor I'm going to ask her. Yeah, not so tiny, but hey, I like to think I'm a prize.

"Thanks," she mumbles.

Either Americans have gotten fatter, or they've narrowed every seat in the United Center because we're close. Like arm to arm and her perfume is overpowering the usual sweat smell that permeates in the arena. There goes my dick again thinking he might get a say on where we end up tonight.

"The least I can do. Your friend was the highest bidder from the auction."

"Why don't you print it on a ribbon and pin in it to yourself like a prized pig at the state fair?"

A laugh rises up out of me like the bubbles in the beer I

just sipped, so the fluid dribbles out of my mouth and onto the floor.

With any other girl, I might be embarrassed.

"Here you go." The girl next to me hands me a napkin from under her nachos.

"Thanks." I nod, and she smiles. She's here with some guy who's busy talking to the guy next to him. I could probably steal the hot blonde from behind his back with one flirtatious comment if I wanted. Which I don't.

"Ahem." Lauren tears my attention away from the other woman. Back to operation get myself a fiancée.

At this point, you're probably wondering why I'd ask a girl who clearly hates me to go along with this fib. Yes, I'm using the word fib. The answer to your question is this—Ma likes Lauren. Plain and simple. And Lauren won't get attached like some other chick would. When the gig is up, she'll be done. No stage-one clinger status for her.

"I can't help the admirers, but if it makes you feel better you have my sole attention tonight."

She turns to glare at me for a second and then looks back at the ice. "Until you drop me off."

"Maybe if you let me tuck you in, you can have me until morning." I grin.

Her mouth drops open and she turns to stare at me.

I'm a firm believer in giving women what they want, and Lauren *wants* me to be an asshole. It makes it easier for her to deal with the chemistry between us. She thinks I sleep with women and discard them multiple times in a weekend. But Lauren doesn't know shit about me.

"I love the Hawks, but I'm not sure this is worth watching them in person." She uncrosses her legs and pushes up off her seat.

The lights around the arena start flashing, and the music becomes louder so the team can be introduced.

"Come on." I reach for her elbow and a shock courses through my body.

Of course, it does. She probably ran a helium-filled balloon all over her body tonight to make sure I get shocked anytime I touch her.

I could take that as a compliment, but…who am I kidding? I am so going to take it as one.

She sits down. Based on her outfit tonight, the girl loves the Hawks more than the Bears. Her Hawks socks, old school with Hossa's number on them means she's been a fan for a long time. And her jersey is ratty as hell which means she didn't buy her outfit especially for tonight.

"Another comment about you in my bed will result in my knee to your balls," she says with a fake smile.

The intro starts and we each stand and clap as the starting players hit the ice. Once the players are all out Lauren's screaming 'GO HAWKS!' right into my eardrum. I catch on to the fact that she's a 'let me tell you how to play' girl right from the start. She's screaming at the players so much you'd wonder how they earn their salaries without her to guide them.

"High stick, ref. Get your eyes checked!" she yells. She turns to me as I try to sink down into the seat. "Did you see that?"

A guy two rows behind us who happens to be wearing Blues garb chimes in, "You need the glasses."

Lauren whips around, one hand on her hip and another finger pointed his way. "See you in St. Louis."

Now the big guy stands up. Shit, he's really big. Either I insert myself now or later.

"Still riding the 2015 championship? Here's a hint, not going to happen again," he says with a smug look on his face.

Lauren's face morphs into an expression I'm pretty familiar with—her typical, 'I'm going to kill you' expression.

"Let's just enjoy the game." I tug on her jersey.

Now that look is fixated on me.

"Or not." I shrug.

"She's a little ball of fire, huh?" the guy whose girlfriend keeps eye fucking me says. The way he's looking at Lauren suggests they might be looking to swing or some shit.

I like experimentation as much as the next bachelor. But I don't share. Ever.

I half smile back at him.

"Let's have a chat after the game. When you lose!" Lauren spins around back to face the ice.

The guy must realize that Lauren isn't the type of girl to back down from a challenge because he returns his attention to the game.

Lauren raises her hand for the hot dog guy going by.

"You eat hot dogs?" I ask, digging cash out of my pocket.

"It's a game. I always eat crappy food at a game. It's half the experience." She shrugs.

Her hand lands on my hand that's stuffed in my pocket.

My dick twitches in excitement at how close she is to it.

"I got this." She smiles.

A rare smile from Lauren Hunt directed my way.

And it's beautiful.

Hell, she's beautiful. Not that I'll ever tell her that.

"It's just a hot dog, Bianco." The tone of her voice pulls me back from whatever la-la land my mind drifted to.

Fuck, what was that?

"Thanks," I choke out when her hand brushes mine again as I pass her the hot dog.

"Well, these tickets must have cost you something."

"They're mine. Season."

The hot dog is still resting in front of her lips when she turns to me, eyes wide in amazement. "You can afford them?"

I shrug. "A few of my friends and I go in together."

I act like it's no big deal, but it's a luxury that will probably vanish with a wife and kids.

"That's awesome. The plus of having friends who enjoy sports." She raises her eyebrows and takes a bite of her hot dog. I shift in my seat watching her chew, lips spread and wrap around the extra large wiener.

"Maddie and Vanessa not into the Hawks?" One look at them and anyone could figure out they're not sports fans.

She takes another bite. "What gave you that idea?"

We share a laugh and it strikes me this is our first real conversation. Well, not our first, but probably our first alone. I mean, take away the thousands of fans and we're alone.

For the rest of the game, we cheer and high five for the three goals the Hawks make. Her energy is addicting. The guy behind us doesn't say much since Hawks kick the Blues' asses. We dance and scream with the people around us and by the time the game is over, I have to get out of the fog induced moment that I had a great time with her. So good, it wouldn't be a huge upset if I had to do it again.

"Want to go to the bar for a drink or grab some dinner?" I ask her once we're out of the single file line of people fleeing the arena.

"Um...sure. The hot dog didn't really satisfy me."

"Cool." My hand instinctively touches the small of her back.

She scowls at me over her shoulder and I promptly remove my hand.

"You good if I pick the place?" she asks.

I'd wanted to take her to a bar where I knew people would tell her what a good guy I am, but I'm trying to be agreeable so lady's choice it is.

"Sure."

"Great."

We make our way to my car and I open the door for her

because, again, I'm a gentleman. She slides in and for some reason, she looks better in it than she did on the way here.

I slide into my own seat and start the ignition. "Where to?" I ask.

"Native Foods Cafe."

She shoots over a sweet smile in my direction, but I see the wheels in her mind working. It's her own twisted form of punishment by suggesting that place.

Two can play that game.

I smile just as sweetly in return and throw the car in reverse. "Sounds good."

CHAPTER FOUR

Lauren

o I feel bad for taking Luca to a vegan restaurant? I do.

Take your two fingers and make a space. Now make that space smaller. Smaller...smaller still... see that sliver of space? That's how bad I feel.

I don't want to be a bitch, but one Hawks game in exchange for calling me a tomboy since I was fifteen doesn't make us even.

His car is impressive, but I'll never tell him that. Other than the God-awful color that is.

His music taste is similar to mine, but I'll never share that fact with him.

It's nice to have an intelligent conversation about sports with someone since none of my female friends are sports fans.

All of those good qualities about Luca Bianco make the ride tolerable, not enjoyable.

He parks his car along the curb across from the neon sign of Native Food Cafe.

I rub my hands together. "Ready to try some new foods?" I open my own door because in my mind this isn't a date.

"Do you think I've never eaten vegan before?"

I tuck my hands into my jacket pockets since winter is fast approaching. We've been lucky to have nice weather this far into December. I expect January through March to be freezing.

We walk across the street, Luca wearing a leather jacket that if he was anyone else would get the girl parts going, but it's Luca, so they stay dormant.

Okay, that's a lie. A small one.

"Tell me one vegan dish you've had and where from?"

He opens the door to the restaurant for me. "I'd tell you, but then you'd think less of me."

I shake my head at his absurd way of thinking.

We walk up to the counter, Luca's eyebrows scrunched as he reads the ingredients. I'd put money on the fact that he's never eaten vegan before but I think he'll be surprised at how good it is.

Why do I even care?

The kid who had to stop mopping the floor when we came in, washes his hands to take our order stands impatiently behind the register. He shoots his co-worker an annoyed look since we're coming in right around closing time.

"Want to get it to go? I think they want to close," I say.

Luca glances at the guys who are having a silent conversation with each other. "You don't want to go to my house and it's too cold to go to a park."

"Cool, then we'll just grab the food and eat at our own houses." I step up to the counter. The teenage kid flings his head back to move the hair out of his eyes so he can see me.

Haircut might be an option, buddy. "I'll have the cauliflower bites and an order of sweet potato fries. To go."

Luca joins me at the counter, his hand sits firmly on my hip, almost locking me to him. "Burger with fries. To go. One bag." He hands over his credit card and the kid takes it from his hand and swipes it.

"I was going to pay." Leaving Luca's side, because his hand on my hip feels intimate, I grab the number from the kid and slide onto a stool at an empty table.

The two kids go off to work on our order and most likely spit in our food.

"Are you inviting me back to your apartment?" I ask, tapping the plastic number on the table.

"No, we're going to your place. Vanessa lives with Cristian, Maddy and Mauro moved in together, and that leaves you alone. I figure you don't want to eat your cauliflower with my roommate Ben drinking beer, watching you while he picks his belly button lint." He laughs. "Disgusted?"

"What the..."

"My reasoning sold you, didn't it?"

For the millionth time tonight, I shake my head at his antics. "I hope to never meet your roommate."

"He's not that bad. He'd wrestle me to the ground if he knew I told you that."

Ben isn't one of Luca's friends I'm familiar with. He must be someone he met after high school, or maybe it's his EMT partner.

"The secret is safe with me. I don't see any reason why I'd meet him anyway."

Luca looks away, concentrating on the guys working on our order behind the counter. Diverting eye contact. Interesting.

Not that I know everything about him. The only string that ever bound me to Luca was his friendship with Cody

Gillard. Cody and I dated our entire junior and senior year until we had to leave for college and I decided I didn't want to do a long distance relationship. We broke up before that final summer, and Cody wasn't happy. Rumors circulated about Luca and Cody spending all their time at Summerfest in Milwaukee, sleeping with girls everywhere but a bed. So immature.

It had grated at the time, but Cody was free to do what he wanted by that point.

"Do you still talk with Cody?" I ask, trying to make it sound like I could care less what his answer is. Truth is, I don't really care. Only in the sense that anyone does when their ex's name comes up.

Luca's head snaps back in my direction and he appears to want to slice me into pieces. Then the cool, easy smile that's practically branded on Luca Bianco surfaces on his lips.

"Yeah. He's in California now."

"Really? Still trying to be a wine connoisseur?"

His deep chuckle floats out across the table.

I continue tapping the plastic number on the table. "Married or kids?" I ask.

Luca pulls his phone out and I wait for him to show me some picture from Facebook or Instagram. Cody didn't take our break up well, so we never kept in touch through social media. I wonder if he still has me blocked from seeing his social media profiles?

"No," he answers, still staring at his phone.

Guess I was wrong about pictures.

I'm surprised Cody isn't taken. Before our break-up and the appearance of a completely different Cody, he'd been someone I thought was meant to be a husband and father. You know the type—coach the mini-me, date nights with his wife, matching pajamas for Christmas morning photos.

"That's cool that you still talk. You guys were inseparable."

He nods.

So...that's a dead subject.

"Is that how you knew to send me Brach's?"

He glances up at me from his phone in a dead stare. "Your love of that candy wasn't exactly hidden knowledge."

I bite my cheek to keep myself from smiling. He noticed those things about me?

Thankfully we're interrupted by the worker bee dropping our paper bag on the counter with a fake smile and hand out for the number.

"Great." I hop off the stool, but Luca beats me to the bag, grabbing it before I get a chance.

He's so damn competitive.

"Have a nice night," I say sweetly to the guy who's probably going to flip me off on my way to the door. "Hey." I swing back around, walking backward. "Maybe good karma will go your way and you'll get laid tonight." I give him two thumbs up and circle back around as Luca pushes the door open.

"Yeah, he's flipping you off right now." Luca laughs, finding his keys in his pocket.

"Seriously, I get that we were late, but we're still customers who have Yelp at our fingertips. What is wrong with today's youth? Don't they care about being a good person?"

Luca opens my door and I slide in the car.

It isn't until he's tucked next to me with the food behind us that he responds. "Not everyone can be a paramedic and want to help people."

There is a list of adjectives that one could use to describe Luca Bianco. On the top of that list would be self-centered.

"Hello, I'm a physical therapist. I help people too."

The engine roars to life and he pulls away from the curb, breaking immediately when a cab flies by. Luca mumbles words I'm thinking were Italian curses and continues toward my house.

"I save lives," he says with smug satisfaction.

"I kind of do too, you know."

He glances over at me, his dark eyes taking me in for a moment before he responds back. "We're talking coding in the ambulance. Rehabbing a torn ACL isn't the same thing."

And here I thought we could co-exist. His brothers are dating my best friends and I'm going to see him at every damn wedding, baby shower, baptism, first birthday, second birthday. My head hurts just thinking about how entwined our lives will be.

Why did I ever bid on Mauro for Maddie?

Because you're an awesome friend who gave your bestie a chance at her dream guy?

Damn it, I hate it when my sentimental side wins.

"For your information, I've saved lives. I help children live a life without canes, crutches or wheelchairs. I push them to better themselves and I make miraculous things happen." I huff, cross my legs and stare out the window.

"You're right. What we both do is important. We shouldn't argue."

Wha...wha...what? "Who are you?"

The light from the street reflects the humor shining in his eyes. "I'm just sick of the fighting."

"Fighting is what we do best. It's basically how we communicate." Then all the puzzle pieces join together in my head. I'm so stupid. "You want something."

We pull up in front of my house just as I realize what a fucking moron I am.

"Nope." He takes the keys, grabs the bag of food and gets out of the car.

He's totally playing me. I might not be a psychologist who can quickly spot a liar, but Luca, I know too well. Not well, but when it comes to our interactions—I know him. And this nice Luca, taking me to a Hawks game, buying me dinner, wanting to eat with me...this isn't the Luca Bianco I know.

I climb out of his car, the slam of the door echoing down the dark residential street. "Tell me what it is you want."

His lips remain straight, not even a hint of a smile or smirk.

Another clear sign that this isn't the Luca I know.

"Come on. Let's eat." He nods in the direction of my house.

"By prolonging whatever it is, you're just pissing me off, which means if you need something, I'm more than likely going to say no. Or we could play a little game..."

"How about we eat?" He waits patiently as I insert the key into my door, disengage the alarm that Cristian, Luca's brother insisted we get installed.

Police officers. Jeez.

We step inside and he's the one to shut the door and flick the lock.

"Planning to have your way with me?" I'm not serious as I walk into the kitchen to grab us some drinks, utensils, and napkins.

The sound of the television blaring drifts into the kitchen seconds later.

With my hands full, I head back into the living room. "Feel free to make yourself at home," I deadpan, handing Luca a Vitamin Water and a napkin.

"Thanks." He lifts the napkin and drink. "And thanks."

We sit on the couch because although our house is nice and newly redecorated thanks to Maddie's mad skills, the family room area is small and the best place to see the television is the couch. No worries though, there's still a cushion between us.

I open up my box of food, a little bit of steam hitting my face. "I can't just sit here and watch soccer with you and not know what you want."

I hate that I've had to resort to being sincere in my request.

He opens up his own box and I'm a tad jealous I didn't get the burger. It smells and looks delicious.

Luca doesn't respond, just stands and heads into the kitchen.

He knows our house way too well thanks to his brothers always suggesting we meet here when we go out.

I pop a cauliflower floret into my mouth, tasting the Korean flavor makes my mouth water. Opening up my Vitamin Water to cool my tongue, I ignore Luca's return, instead, fixating on the television as he rounds the coffee table in front of me. The couch dips with the weight of his body which is now closer than before.

I've never been alone with Luca, much less this close. I feel a shift in our volatile relationship like the stillness before a storm. It's too quiet. It's too calm. Too...enjoyable.

"Here." My gaze shifts from the television, although I couldn't tell you the score of the game and I see he's holding half his burger out to me.

"What's this?" I ask, loading my mouth with another califloret.

Man, it's hot.

"I think you had a little bit of drool dripping from your mouth when I opened the container. How about we share?"

He smiles. A smile I've only ever seen on his face with his friends, or his brothers, and especially his mom. He doesn't even wear this smile when he's with girls. At least not that

I've ever seen. That fact runs around my stomach stirring up the butterflies to max flight.

I don't like this.

It's too damn calm.

Where are the eighty mile per hour winds?

"Luca, if you don't tell me what you want, I'm going to kick you out of my house." I take half the burger and slide my cauliflower and fries closer to him as an offering.

"You can't just wait?" he asks, seeming disappointed.

"HA!" I point to him with a greasy finger. "You *do* want something from me. Tell me what it is."

"You're ridiculous you know that, right? A normal person would wait."

I shake my head. "No, they wouldn't."

See, this feels good. This feels right.

"LUCA!" I scream.

He blows out a breath. "Fine. I need a favor from you."

CHAPTER FIVE

Lauren

"Figures. Being nice because you need something from me." I nod and lean back into the couch. My appetite disappearing with my disappointment.

"It's not a huge thing." He also pushes his food away and lowers the volume on the television.

"I'll be the judge of that."

I'm not sure why I'm disappointed that I was right to be suspicious of him.

"It's my ma. You know how she's sick?" His eyes cast down, his long thin fingers entwining like a nervous teenager in his lap.

"Yeah."

Luca's mom has been in and out of the hospital for the past month. Vanessa told me she's going in Monday for a surgery that they're hoping will correct her erratic, out of rhythm heartbeat, but it's not a sure fix. Not to mention it's still heart surgery no matter how you cut it.

"Well." His muscular chest fills with a huge breath and if I cared about Luca more, I'd be comforting him right now. But would he do the same for me?

I answer that question before I need another breath. He wouldn't. Luca has hated me since the day I met Cody at the park when they were playing soccer. He saw me as a wedge in their friendship. The girl who stole his best friend's attention away from him and anyone who knows Luca knows he thrives on attention.

"I doubt you're going to ask me to sign up for the meal drop off. You have Maddie or Vanessa for that, so what is it?"

His eyes reach mine, the corners of his lips tipping up.

He's like a different person in front of me right now. Someone I don't recognize. Showing vulnerability isn't something I've ever seen Luca do.

The fact he's letting me in says this is more serious than a casserole delivery.

"What is it?" I sit up straighter, leaning forward.

"Ma thinks I'm a fuck up. That she didn't raise me well. She worries about me more than my brothers. Her other sons have their shit together and I'm partying all the time. Jesus, I give their deli number to my one-night stands I don't want to contact me again."

He cringes and his fingers thread through his short dark hair, his mocha-colored eyes unable to reach mine.

Does he actually feel repentant for something? Is that possible?

"You're twenty-seven. I'm sure she understands," I say, in lieu of knowing what else to say.

If anyone would've told me I'd be boosting Luca Bianco's self-esteem tonight, I would have referred them to an insane asylum.

"Trust me, she doesn't." He shakes his head.

I bite my lip unsure what I can say to convince him otherwise. I mean, I've always razzed on Luca for being a playboy who would never settle down. A guy who never wants the party to end, so I'm sure he thinks I'm insincere in what I said. It's what we do, though. We pick on one another, but now I feel bad for every jab I took at him if he was hurting this much inside because of it.

"Talk to her," I say.

He shakes his head. "Ma's not one for words. It's actions. Why do you think Mauro and Cristian are moving so fast with Maddie and Vanessa? We've been taught that you show your love through actions, not words. Words are hollow without the conviction of change."

"I tend to agree with her. I mean saying you love someone but putting them down doesn't align. But you're her son. I'm sure she understands that you're still young."

Seeing this man appear unsure of himself is unsettling.

"I'm one year younger than Cristian. Two than Mauro. It's not like I'm the oops baby. Not to mention both my brothers were always looking for that perfect girl. They wanted the marriage and kids."

"You and your brother's didn't come from a cookie cutter, Luca. Just because they're that way doesn't mean you have to be. We're all snowflakes, unique." I sit up feeling safer to start eating since I'm guessing Luca just needed someone to talk to. That was an easy favor, which surprises but pleases me.

And truth is, I get it. I'm not sure I'd want him to know the insecurities I hold about my family.

I bite his burger and yay, it tastes as yummy as it looked.

Tonight has been an okay night. Who would've thought I could enjoy time with Luca Bianco?

"I need you to pretend to be my fiancée." His declaration comes without any warning.

I choke on the vegan burger, the ground plant or whatever it is, lodges in my throat from the gasp I made with his statement.

Luca slides closer, his hand over my chest wall and pounds my back with the heel of his hand.

The burger falls from my mouth, landing a foot in front of the coffee table.

This is a first for me.

"You okay?" He doesn't move from next to me, his breath hitting right under my earlobe. Shivers run up my spine. He smells great and I wonder what cologne he wears because I could drown myself in it.

"I'm good." I take another breath, sipping my Vitamin Water to make sure my throat is all clear.

"Sorry, my timing always sucks." He lets out a strained laugh. "I don't feel so bad asking that favor now after saving your life."

He stands, grabs his napkin and picks up the piece of burger. I sit on the couch and he comes back with a wet paper towel removing the small stain off the rug.

"I can do that," I say.

He looks up from his hands and knees, his usual smirk on display. "That's okay. I get that I kind of surprised you."

His forearms flex as he uses all his strength to get the stain out. It's not really that bad, but I appreciate him doing it for me.

"Surprised me? You just asked me to marry you."

I close the top of my container because my appetite has now completely vanished.

"Not a real marriage. Just an engagement." He stands and heads back to the kitchen.

I peek at the rug and see that it looks good. Who knew Luca knew how to clean carpet?

"You say it so flippantly." I prop my feet up on the coffee table, my vision landing on the soccer game but my mind can't follow the ball when it's still reeling from Luca's request. "You're insane."

"Just hear me out." He sits down next to me, even closer this time. His hands are shaky and reach out to me, but retract immediately. "It's only until Ma's healthy. We announce it tomorrow at our family dinner. The wedding never happens, obviously."

"Obviously." I sneer. "Luca, you can't be serious?"

He slides closer, his hands going for mine but again, thinks better of it and keeps them in his own lap. "I am. I know it's a lot to ask, so I'm fully prepared to give you something in return."

"Oh, how nice of you. Let me guess, nightly orgasms in our bed of lies?"

He chuckles, his chin falling to his chest. "Well, I wouldn't deny it if that's your wish. I have a feeling you would give me a..." He stops and shakes his head. "What do you want?"

"Nothing because I'm not doing it. You might be okay deceiving your family, but I am not." I stand because I know eventually, he'll cross that imaginary line between us and his skin will meet mine. I've never touched Luca, and I don't plan on doing it tonight.

"It's for her own well-being. It would put Ma at peace before she's sedated. You're doing a good thing here. And it's only a week at most."

I walk in circles, around the chairs, the coffee table, diverting to the dining room and around the big table with six chairs.

"Are you short on your steps today? Trying to get your 10K in?" he asks, his elbows leaning on his toned thighs.

I stop just to give him a 'fuck off' expression then continue walking.

"You don't pace like a normal person," he says.

I don't respond.

"I kind of like that Hunt. It's endearing."

"Maybe you should put that in the fake marriage proposal.

She had me when she walked in figure eights instead of a straight line when she was nervous."

"You're nervous? Why?"

"I think I need to remind you of something." I stop behind the chair, my hands gripping the top of the cushioned back.

"What?" His smirk and arrogant demeanor is back on full display now.

"That you hate me!"

"I don't hate you." His forehead crinkles and the confusion in his eyes almost makes me believe him. Almost.

I tilt my head and a deep chuckle rumbles out of his throat.

"Okay, okay. Maybe I haven't been your biggest fan a few times, but I couldn't imagine doing this with anyone else." There's a truth in his dark pupils. A truth that scares me.

"Give me one good reason why I should do this?" I round the chair and flop down, pulling my knees up to my chest.

"Don't do it for me. Do it for my ma. She needs to know that she did a great job at raising all her boys. She needs to be in a good headspace before she's put under because God forbid..."

Silence hangs thick and heavy over us. Genuine fear radiates off him and I realize how shaken he is by what's going on with his mom.

"It's a pretty easy surgery, right? I mean as far as surgery goes?" I ask.

"Yeah," he says, then clears this throat. "But she still has to go under anesthetic. That's a big risk right there. Besides, do you know how many people I've had in the back of my ambulance who should've made it and didn't? That's all I can think about—all those patients I thought for sure would be fine who I found out later didn't make it because they had complications."

I blow out a stream of air, picking at my nails. "I don't know."

"I just want Ma in the best possible frame of mind going into her surgery. She doesn't need to be stressed and wondering about what I'm going to do with my life if something happens to her."

I want to help him, I do. I like his ma and it's clear that he really does just want what's best for his mom.

"I overheard Ma talking to Cristian about how worried she is about me and where I am in my life. You have no idea how much that stung. I don't want her going into this stressed an worrying about what will happen to me. God forbid, if something did happen," he pauses and swallows hard, removing his gaze from mine. "At least she'd go in peace."

"Luca..." I whisper, a heavy feeling pressing down on my chest.

"I'll give you anything. What do you want?" he asks, a clear desperation in his tone.

"I don't know. I just don't like the whole idea of lying."

One thing I won't mention to Luca is that I never imagined my marriage proposal to be 'Can you do me a favor and pretend to marry me?' I might not be Maddie who had her Barbies marrying each other every day, but I did envision this moment to be with a man who couldn't live another moment without knowing I was his. But it's not like Luca is asking me to actually walk down the aisle with him. It's a ruse, that's all.

He stands from the couch, walks over and falls to his knees in front of me, pulling a ring out of his pocket.

"Lauren Hunt."

"Oh my God, stop." I raise my hand at him to quit before he says anything else.

Instead, he grabs my hand, the tip of my ring finger on my left hand clasped between his thumb and forefinger.

"You got a ring?" I screech.

"We're not doing this halfway. My family will never believe it if you don't have a ring. I know you think I'm a douche but—"

"Luca, just stop." I pull my hand away from him, covering my face with both my hands. "I need to think."

His phone vibrates in his pocket, but he doesn't answer it.

Why am I even considering this? I owe him nothing. And maybe that would be enough if I hadn't met his mom. She's caring and sweet and you see the love she has for Maddie and Vanessa and the fact that they've chosen her sons. How proud she is of her boys.

I do think Luca is wrong. She knows one day he'll grow out of this phase of his life, but I can't pretend that I haven't heard her lecture him about the consequences of his actions and how his good looks won't always stay intact. She wants all three of her sons to live a life with a wife and kids.

I think of my boss Peter and the fact that I told him I was seeing someone. How me arriving at the Christmas party as a singleton will tell him I purposely deceived him. But I could totally claim sickness the day of the party. Then again, he'd continue to hit on me and things would become even more uncomfortable at work. I'd have to leave all my clients. Poor Briana having to work with some therapist who doesn't talk to her during her exercises to distract her from the pain. Someone she wouldn't make bracelets for or be excited to see. My fingers twist around the thread around my wrist. I must be delusional to even be considering this, but the truth is it will solve one of my own problems.

Steeling myself with a deep breath, I say, "You come as my boyfriend to my Christmas party and I want the Hawks tickets."

"Don't want to go stag?" He raises a brow.

"No, I have a boss who won't take no for an answer. He wants to date me and isn't put off by my refusal."

Luca's face morphs into an indignant scowl. "What the fuck? He can't do that."

"It's not against policy so technically he can. Look, I just want him to think I'm happy with someone else so things won't be weird at work, okay?"

"Still, that's bullshit."

I roll my eyes. "Whatever. It's that and the tickets for three games. Take it or leave it."

He inches closer, the ring resting in his hand. "Seriously? I only get every fourth game. I share them with—"

"That's fine. But I want my ass in the seat every fourth game for the next three."

He smiles and nods. "Done."

"Really?"

"Did you think tickets would deter me away?"

"I'm still not sure about this, Luca, but I'll do it."

He smiles, the circular white band with a beautiful round diamond ready to slide onto my finger. "Then...Lauren Hunt, will you do me a favor and agree to be my fake fiancée?"

"Jeez Bianco, just the proposal every girl dreams of."

He slides the ring onto my finger, sealing our agreement of deceit.

"If this turns my finger green or if it's cubic zirconia, I will call you out on your shit." I point a finger at him.

"It's real. Just call my credit card company."

He falls back to his ankles on the floor and his fingers weave through his hair. "Thanks, Lauren. I really appreciate this."

There he goes showing that vulnerable side again. Why does it affect me so much?

"I want the Hawks tickets in my hands tomorrow when

you pick me up for Sunday dinner. And this is only in front of your family and at the Christmas party."

He stands up, grabbing my hand and pulling me up. So much for never touching him.

"And you know you can't tell Maddie and Vanessa." He cringes.

My stomach sinks. Shit, I hadn't thought about that.

He must see something in my face. "They'll tell Mauro and Cristian and this has to be completely one hundred percent believable."

I nod, hating that I'll be lying to my friends. "Okay, but you do understand that they'll all eventually know the truth, right?"

"It won't be hard pressed for them to think that I rushed you into it and we're just not meant to be together. I mean we argue more than married people."

I nod. He has a point and I'm surprised at how much thought he's put into this. Not one part has been overlooked. Besides, we can cross that bridge when we come to it. I'm sure it won't be a big deal after the fact if my friends know what was up, as long as his mom never finds out.

"Fine." I walk to the door, unlock it, and open it up. "See you tomorrow."

"I'll be here at four, future Mrs. Luca Bianco."

"That would be the never Mrs. Lauren Hunt-Bianco." I shut the door to the laughter pouring out of him.

As I hear his engine roar to life outside, my back falls to the wall and I slide down, staring down at the engagement ring on my finger. I'm really not this hard up, am I?

CHAPTER SIX

Luca

"Married?" Ma asks, her cold hands covering mine.

"Yeah," I whisper.

Does it hurt a little that I'm lying? I'm not heartless but seeing the twinkle in Ma's eye and her smile starting to form steels my resolve. The smile is small right now, only the creases of her lips move upward. She's cautious to not get her hopes up.

My dad springs up from his chair, his eyes slicing through me, telling me now isn't the time for a prank. I shake my head and he dissects the scene in front of him.

My mom's hands shift to Lauren, looking at the ring on her left hand. Her eyes move from the ring to Lauren, who's been a ball of nervous energy since I picked her up. She almost flew out the car door on Irving Park Road, but I was able to convince her this is for the best. I can put up a hell of an argument when I need to.

"It's beautiful," my mom says. "You're engaged?" she asks Lauren straight up and I should've expected this.

I had figured it all out. The ring is real because my mom would know otherwise. The fact we're doing it right before her surgery. The reason we walked in together, hand in hand. But I never thought my mom would point blank ask Lauren if it's true.

All eyes in the room shift to Lauren. Is she really going to do this for me? She either runs or stays and I hold my breath waiting for her to answer.

"Lauren?" Maddie steps away from Mauro, her unasked question clear to everyone in the room.

Lauren blinks and I wrap my arm around her small waist pulling her closer to me.

She's immune to my endorphins, but I pray something about my arm holding her will soak in, allowing her to speak the lie.

She nods and Ma's entire face lights up. That's when I know that doing this is what's best for Ma in the long run.

Lauren is out of my hold and into Ma's arms, my dad coming over, too, saying his own congratulations.

Maddie and Vanessa leave my brothers standing dormant in the dining room archway. Their eyes poised and ready to judge me—nothing new there. They're just waiting to call bullshit on this whole thing. My mom is easy to convince, she wants me to settle down so bad, she doesn't want to see this could be a lie. But my brothers, they know me the best out of anyone. Selling this to them will be nearly impossible, but I'll go down fighting. It's only a week after all.

Lauren's eyes find mine over Ma's shoulder since she's hugging her again.

"Will you marry in the Catholic Church?" my dad asks.

Lauren's eyes widen.

"Relax Dad. We're not getting married tomorrow."

Ma pulls her away, ignoring my comment. "Would you convert?" She smiles over to Maddie and Vanessa. She wasn't even this excited with Mauro and Maddie and it confirms this is what she needed the night before her surgery. The hope that we need her to plan a wedding and see her grandkids. The hope that persuades her to fight to get healthy.

"I am Catholic," Lauren whispers.

My mom could float up in the air she's so damn happy. "You're Catholic?" she asks, her small hands gripping Lauren's upper arms.

Lauren nods.

"Oh!" my mom exclaims, hugging Lauren again and smiling so bright her eyes are sparkling over Lauren's shoulder.

She's so happy even a pin to a balloon wouldn't burst her elation.

"Congratulations, I guess?" Mauro's big hand appears in front of me first.

"Thanks." I ignore his question at the end.

"Never saw this coming." Cristian too holds out his hand to me.

I shake it. "The heart wants what the heart wants." I think I heard that in a song somewhere.

They both nod, stuffing their hands in their pockets and rocking back on their heels.

It'll probably take me as long as our short engagement will last to convince them.

"Congrats, Luca!" Maddie hugs me to her body. "I'm shocked and feel like I somehow missed this between the two of you. I'm a horrible friend."

"Nah, don't sweat it. We were hiding it."

The last thing I want is people to feel bad.

"Well, now we could do a double wedding!" She smiles now that's she let me go.

"Yeah, how about we start planning?" Mauro wraps his arm around his real finance's shoulders. "How about a Christmas wedding?"

"The four of you could go down to the courthouse tomorrow." Cristian chimes in to test me further.

"I think Ma wants to plan a traditional Catholic wedding," I say.

My eyes land on Ma guiding Lauren to the couch, pulling a photo album out in front of them.

Is that their wedding album?

"Yeah let them have their day, Mad. We'll go to Italy for ours. Marry at the same church my parents did," Mauro says.

She looks up at him like he really is her hero.

Lauren glances over her shoulder at me with fear rimming her eyes. Not exactly the same look. For the first time, I'd prefer the former over the latter.

"Let's go downstairs. I have this sudden urge to show you how perfect we are for each other." Mauro doesn't wait for Maddie to answer, walking backward to the stairs in the back of the house.

"I'm starved," my dad says, taking the foil from the trays of food. "Maria, come eat."

Ma waves him off. "You boys start."

Cristian and my dad get the serving spoons and forks into the food that Maddie and Mauro brought. There's only one person who has yet to congratulate me and she's approaching me right now.

"You sly dog. I knew you had feelings for her, but engaged? I thought you two would just sleep with each other and get it out of your systems. How did you ever convince her to marry you?" Vanessa asks, punching me in the shoulder. She's been hanging out with my brother too much.

"We just understand each other."

Is it odd that I think Vanessa might be even more intuitive than Cristian when it comes to people? She has this way of looking at me that makes me feel exposed. Like all my thoughts in my head are being transmitted to her in shorthand.

"So all those rides home and checking up on her, you two were really doing the nasty?" She knocks her elbow to me, her eyes trained on Cristian.

They're not engaged yet, but I wonder how long Cris will wait before asking her.

"I'm pleading the fifth." I laugh, stepping toward my mom and Lauren.

Vanessa laughs. "I'll bother Lauren for all the gritty details on how this came to be." She smiles and I honestly can't tell if she believes us or not. I didn't even think about the questions Lauren will have to answer from her friends. How hard it will be for her. Should we have gotten down our stories of how we fell in love?

"Ma?" I ask, sitting next to Lauren and extending my arm behind her back.

"I was just showing Lauren the pictures of when your dad and I got married. I've been going through all my old pictures the last few days."

The stack of photo albums that my mom keeps hidden away sits in front of us on the coffee table. She doesn't need to keep them out because every surface of the walls in my parents' house is adorned with pictures of our family. Photos of my brothers and I in our diapers up to high school graduation line the hallway to the bedrooms. Each of our pictures when we were sworn in sit in a row on top of a piano that I never learned to play, much to Ma's disappointment when I chose the guitar.

"Beautiful. I hope one day I can go there." Lauren's fingers run along the pictures of the small Italian village my parents are from.

They wed and fled is what my Nonna used to say. The ink wasn't dry on their marriage certificate before they were on a plane to America to start a new life—that didn't include her, as she put it. Although they brought her here after they got settled, she resented them and blamed my mother for taking her boy away. The strife I witnessed between my Nonna and my Ma is probably the reason my mom is nothing but encouraging to the women in her son's life.

Maddie and Vanessa have already found a place in her heart.

"Let's eat," I suggest, trying to close the album.

"Maybe Luca will take you for your honeymoon. My aunt is there as well as her side of the family."

My mom allows me to leave the album on the coffee table and all three of us head toward the dining room table to eat. "Maybe." Lauren raises her eyebrows at me over her shoulder.

I'm glad she's not feeling too guilty and having a sense of humor about what we're doing.

"Are you the only family who came over?" Lauren asks, pulling out a chair.

"No, I have a sister in New York...well, New Jersey. She has three sons and a daughter. Anthony's family is here though. A brother and a sister, and two uncles." My mom fixes her plate as she tells Lauren about how everyone who is normally here for our Sunday dinners is related. "You'll probably see them tomorrow if you come to the hospital."

My dad holds out a chair for my mom and places a water in front of her.

Lauren shoots me a worried look.

"Lauren has to work tomorrow, Ma..."

"I'll come by after though. Maybe even during my lunch. I work in the rehab building," Lauren says.

"You do?" I ask because that building faces the ER which means I've passed her work how many times on runs. "I mean..." Fuck even I can't think of something to cover my tracks.

"You didn't know where she works?" Cristian and his damn cop skills.

"It's all been a whirlwind, half the time I'm spying him as his ambulance pulls up. He's busy and I'm busy, so..." She puts a piece of chicken in her mouth like that's the reason she can't finish the end of the sentence.

"Lay off. Should I remind you, you didn't know what Van—"

Cristian shoots me a warning glare and I'm not about to piss him off and give him ammunition to call me out, so I shut up.

"Where the hell are Maddie and Mauro?" I ask instead.

"They had to get something from downstairs." Vanessa's face says that what she really means is get their orgasms.

"You guys probably understand that though, right? Can't keep your hands off each other?" Cris again.

Did I give him such a hard time about Vanessa?

Probably.

My hand slides under the table and I let it rest on the edge of the chair, knowing it will appear that I'm touching her thigh. "We're just more discreet."

Lauren gobbles down more chicken with a half-smile at Cristian that suggests he stop asking so many questions.

My dad holds up his glass of water because he's sticking to my mom's dietary restrictions. "To family."

We each raise our glasses and clink them together, Lauren's shaking slightly.

"To family," we all say in unison.

That wasn't too bad, easier than I thought it would be.

Mission accomplished—Ma believes Lauren and I are getting married.

CHAPTER SEVEN

Lauren

*L*uca's car pulls away from the curb and my head falls into my hands.

"I don't think I can do this. I mean your mom is so invested. How do you think we're ever going to tell her that it's a sham?"

Luca turns down the radio.

Ironic that it was "What I've Done" by Linkin Park playing. Probably the reason he doesn't want me to hear.

"Look how happy my ma was." He smiles over at me but when I don't smile back his face drops. "I mean, I know it's hard, but it's short. Today was the hard day. With my mom's surgery, our news will fall to the wayside. All we have to do is keep up appearances for a week or so until we know Ma's surgery worked and we're golden."

"You're more insane than I thought you were." I shift to look out the window.

"I made the decision to do this and my reasons for doing

so are justified." His foot presses a little harder on the gas pedal.

"The smile on your mom's face was pretty spectacular." I sit up, inhale a deep breath and man up, or woman up. I've agreed to this and I can't keep doing a 'woe is me' rendition.

"Nice Catholic touch."

"I'm not laying on the charm. I *am* Catholic."

"Really?" He stops at a light and stares over at me, looking much like his mother did when I told her.

"I'm not sure why you and your mom are so surprised. I mean I did attend St. George with you. That is a Catholic school."

He presses the gas and we pass under a street light. It's dark out already with winter fast approaching. "I know, but you know as well as I do that a quarter of St. George weren't Catholic."

I shrug because that is the truth.

The car stops again and it's aggravating that we seem to be hitting every red light. "Should I give you my schedule? So you know when I'm available?" he asks.

I laugh.

He doesn't.

"You're serious? Luca this is fake, remember?"

"I know, but according to our friends, it's real. If I'm off work and out at the club you should be with me."

"I don't go to clubs very often. I'll go to a bar, but not a club."

"You don't dance? I pinned you as a girl who doesn't leave the dance floor."

Someone honks and Luca presses on the gas, but his tires spin on the patch of ice from the storm earlier today.

"This is proof of how ridiculous it is to own this car and live in Chicago."

He lays off the gas and then presses down slowly until the rubber finally catches the asphalt and propels forward.

"I have a truck in storage, but I like to drive this as long as I possibly can."

I pat the dashboard. "Sorry lady, time to be tucked in for the winter. You can't even be faithful to your cars." I chuckle.

He scowls in return. "I've never cheated."

"Really? What about Blaire Nickelson?" I cross my arms over my chest.

"You're going back to sophomore year?" He turns down my street. I call it a win that we were able to stay civil the entire ride back. With the mention of Blaire Nickelson and his pissed off expression, our time here has come to an end.

"Once a cheat..."

"Give me a break. You don't even know the whole story. We weren't even a couple." He parks along the curb, kills the engine and steps out.

I follow suit. "You don't have to walk me up to my door."

"You're my fiancée, I expect a kiss goodnight." He shoots me a smile that says he's no longer upset at me for bringing Blaire into the conversation. I'm not even sure why I did other than to remind myself of what kind of person Luca is.

"You didn't negotiate those. With the amount of time your arm was wrapped around my shoulders all night, we're about tapped out with PDA." I walk up the steps, pulling my keys out of my purse.

The house is dark and lonely without Van and Maddie here anymore. If I cared for Luca, I might invite him in, but I don't so I circle back around.

"See you tomorrow. I work, but I'll try to run over on my lunch to make an appearance."

He smiles, and I lose my breath for a second because his eyes are filled with something that looks a hell of a lot like admiration or appreciation.

"Thank you. I don't know if the Hawks tickets are enough. I mean my mom was so happy and she'll go under anesthesia knowing all three of her boys found the love of their lives. It just...means a lot that you're doing this. I know it's not easy."

"Bianco, you're going soft. Calm down, your mom will be fine. We'll do this and then break up and one day you'll find the right girl to bring home to mom."

Even I'm impressed at how business-like I sound—there's no creakiness in my voice that would hint at the lump in my throat.

"I just didn't want you to think I wasn't appreciative."

"I don't think that. See you tomorrow." I open my door to the dark foyer on the other side. I disable the alarm and Luca waves goodbye as I shut the door and flick the lock.

I hate the fact I understand Luca's reasoning for this whole plan. The love he has for his mom is pure and deep and amazing. All the Bianco brothers put their mom up on a pedestal and it's hard not to find it endearing.

I drop my purse and head to the family room. As my hand moves to the light switch, two faces appear in the dark hovering above a flashlight.

"AHHH!" I jump back.

Maddie and Vanessa start laughing.

I flick on the light and they turn off the flashlight, still in a fit of giggles.

"Alright girl, what the hell is going on?" Vanessa asks and the two of them set their gazes upon me.

CHAPTER EIGHT

Luca

Driving back to my apartment, I hate the fact that Ben will be there sitting on the couch in the dark. When I first moved in with him, it was out of convenience because I needed a place to live fast. My best friends had a lease they couldn't get out of. So, I did what any normal person would do—I responded to an ad in the Chicago Fire Facebook group page. He was a paramedic too and, in my head, I figured we'd understand one another. I figured wrong.

Ben is a homebody. He likes to sit at home, play role-playing games online, watch documentaries and put together model airplanes. We have nothing in common. I feel bad complaining because he doesn't leave the place a mess, he doesn't open my mail or eat my food. But because of him, I don't feel comfortable bringing people over. And I'm the opposite of a loner. Being the youngest of three brothers close in age in an Italian family has made me a people person. I hate being by myself. My brothers want to know why I'm always coming over uninvited. Well, Ben is the reason.

Then again, maybe I could tell Ben about the fake engagement. He doesn't know anyone I do since he works on the other side of the city, but that's a lot of trust for someone I leave notes for on the dry erase board on the fridge stating the amount he owes me for the electric bill. The secret is eating away at me, but I guess it will just have to remain between me and Lauren.

My phone rings and I press the accept button on the steering wheel.

"Come to Cris's. Now!" Mauro hangs up.

I can always count on my wonderful brothers. I had a feeling this was coming.

My phone rings again and I press the accept button once more.

"Bring beer." It's Cris now and he laughs before hanging up on me.

I shake my head but smile because at least I get a little reprieve from going home to Ben.

Twenty minutes later I open the door to my brother's apartment, finding him and Mauro already lounging on the couch watching the Sunday night football game.

"Oh look, the groom-to-be has arrived." Cris stands, rounds the couch and pulls me into a hug.

"Get off me." I try to break out of his hold.

If the guy didn't have my arms pinned down, and if I was in the mood to wrestle, I'd be able to get him off me.

"I just wanted to congratulate you again. I mean marrying your archenemy is kind of a big deal." He finally lets me go.

"Come on. What game are we playing?" Mauro snags a beer from the twelve pack and cracks it open, tossing the cap on the counter. And they complain about me being a slob.

"No game." I pull two beers out, handing one to Cris.

They both stare at me like I'm crazy.

"You do understand that when it all blows up, it's gonna

be a shit show." Cris's hand smacks me on the back of the head and he walks back over to the couch.

"Nothing's gonna blow up. I'm engaged. It doesn't mean we're getting married in a week. I don't move like rocket man over there." I point the neck of my beer to Mauro who flips me off.

"Let's make a bet that there's never a wedding?" Mauro sits up, resting his forearms on his thighs.

"You'll lose," I say, wishing it were true just to show him up.

Cris side glances at me. "Will he?"

I take three hefty gulps of my beer, my eyes focused on the screen, but at this point, I have to act casual. They'll eat me up like a bunch of piranhas if I show any weakness.

"Fine, wager up?" I put my beer on the coffee table and rub my hands together.

I learned early that outward appearance is ninety percent of pulling something off.

Cris moves forward and puts a coaster down under my beer. I roll my eyes. Neat freak.

"Ante up your Hawks tickets." Mauro grins.

Fuck, how do I say those are taken already?

"When do you think this is all going to blow up? In a week?" I scoff.

"First off, the season goes to May and I have faith that this will self-implode after Ma gets better."

Cris holds up his hand for Mauro and they high five.

Clearly, there's been a lot of talk before I arrived.

"You think I'm doing this because of Ma's surgery?" See how I just throw out the truth like they're morons for thinking it. If I deny it too hard, they'll know.

"Yes," they both deadpan simultaneously.

My phone buzzes in my pocket.

Hunt: Are you getting the third degree?

"Is that the Mrs.?" Cris asks. "Get used to it, baby brother. She'll want to know your whereabouts twenty-four seven now. Probably has that app on your phone that's like a GPS."

Me: Yeah. They're on to us. You, too?

Hunt: I think the four of them had a pow wow.

Me: Say nothing.

Hunt: ...

CHAPTER NINE

Lauren

Me: Agreed.

tuck my phone back into my pocket.

"I mean Lauren, you hate him. Help me understand this." Maddie slides onto the coffee table so she can be smack dab in front of where I sit on the couch.

I cross my legs because it will be obvious if I cross my fingers as I lie to my two best friends for a man I really don't like that much. I need to negate the negative repercussions. Even if it's what a six-year-old would do.

"You know what they say," I start. "There's a thin line between love and hate. Happens to be that we swung fast to the other side of the spectrum." I shrug.

Maddie just stares at me like I'm speaking Yiddish. She glances over her shoulder at Vanessa who's smirking.

"I felt the connection," she says.

What?

Somehow, I manage to school my reaction and not ask what the hell she's talking about. If I really were in love with Luca, I would be happy that she's on my side.

"What connection? The fact they wish physical harm on one another?" Maddie focuses her attention back on me.

My phone buzzes in my lap.

"Is that him?" She glances down.

"Yeah."

I pick it up and smile.

Asshat: Gif attached.

It's a gif of Robert DeNiro and Christian Slater from Goodfellas that says, 'You don't rat out your friends.'

"Lauren?" Maddie tilts her head in a frustrated way.

"Sorry." I tuck the phone back in my lap after I send him a gif of Patrick Kane shrugging.

It's more fun to keep him guessing.

"Please tell me that this isn't because of Mama Bianco going in for surgery," Maddie says.

"I know Luca's been beating himself up about not seeing the signs, but it wasn't his fault." Vanessa comes and joins Maddie at the table.

Do they think I'll break the closer they get?

"Thanks, guys, I'd thought he asked because, you know, he wanted me to stand by his side in life, but I guess you guys don't think I'm good enough."

Ouch, yeah, I crossed my toes on that one. Please forgive me, Lord.

"That's not what we're suggesting," Maddie argues.

"Isn't it though? You're acting like no way would he want to marry me. Like he has some sort of agenda."

My phone buzzes but I ignore it because this is the only way I see out of this situation.

Please, someone, ask me why I'm sticking up for a man I hate again?

"I think it's more of a why did you say yes?" Maddie asks.

Vanessa nods. "Lauren, you've never liked him. You're always the first to say how much you hate him. What a jerk he is..."

"I know, but while you guys were off playing house, I saw a different side to him."

That's not untrue because the night Luca asked me, I did see him in a different light. I saw a side of him I'd never seen or even thought I'd ever see. He was vulnerable and he opened up his chest and let his heart fall out between us. How could I have said no? Pressure from your family can crush you. Sometimes there's no rhythm or reason.

"Have you guys been seeing each other in secret?" Vanessa asks, the smile on her face suggesting she suspected we were.

"Well..."

"I knew it. I told Cristian that the two of you have been sneaking around. You guys put on a good act though."

Look, I didn't even have to lie that time.

Maddie's shoulders sink. "You never said anything."

I lean forward, uncrossing my ankles for the first time during this conversation. Placing my hands on her knees, I lower my voice. "I'm sorry, Maddie." She doesn't know the depth of truth in my words. This is so much harder than I anticipated.

Surely in seven days when the truth comes out, she won't hate me. She'll see why we both did it.

"I just...I'm so surprised. Mauro doesn't understand why I am."

"Whoa, what, he doesn't?" stumbles out.

"I'm with Mauro," Vanessa says. "Cris thought I was crazy when I told him I was expecting to walk in on you getting a

Bianco boinking one day." Vanessa smiles. "I think Maddie and I can both vouch for the Bianco men."

"The younger men that is." Maddie clarifies because thinking of Anthony and Maria Bianco...yeah, no thanks.

"Definitely." Vanessa's face turns flush and she shivers. "Thank goodness the guys aren't here."

Maddie nods at Vanessa, the first smile since I walked in gracing her lips. "Yeah, I suggested to Mauro that maybe he should have a talk with Anthony, you know about the bedroom stuff and Maria's heart."

"You didn't?" Vanessa stifles a laugh.

Maddie sits up straight. "What's more embarrassing? An ambulance coming for her half-naked or him talking to his dad?"

"Mauro talking to his dad," I say.

Vanessa nods in agreement. "Mad."

She shrugs. "Yeah, Mauro just said no and that it's not up for discussion."

"Well, yeah," I say.

Maddie shrugs and smiles again. "Okay, well, I was just worried."

We laugh, Maddie included.

My phone vibrates in my lap again.

Is this what it's like to have a boyfriend?

Asshat: (A gif with Keanu Reeves being interrogated with wires hanging from his forehead and chest)

Asshat: They are relentless.

Me: (A gif of a woman skipping with a smile on her face)

Asshat: That's because those women know
I'm a catch.

Me: Keep on living in that warped reality.

"See, look at her smile as she texts. They are in love." Vanessa elbows Maddie who is far from being convinced and is watching my every move.

"Okay, I'm going to believe you. Since you're engaged and all, we need to talk about something else." Maddie criss-crosses her legs and picks at the small piece of lint on her leggings.

"What?"

She inhales a deep breath in through her nose and blurts out, "I have to put the house up on the market."

It's not like I didn't think it was coming. She rehabbed this house with the intention of selling it. We were only guaranteed to live here until she sold it, which was delayed with her moving in with Mauro and the two of them building their ever-after house. Vanessa already left the house a few weeks ago. So, like I said—I expected this.

"Unless..." She lets it hang there.

"What?" I sit up, hoping what? That she'll let me live here by paying a third of the mortgage?

Her and Mauro have a wedding to pay for now. I'm sure a baby isn't too far into the future.

"If you and Luca...I know he's not happy with his room-mate...Maybe the two of you want to move in together?" She winces when she says it, but I've known Maddie majority of my life.

In a way, she'd love that so she didn't feel like she was kicking me out. Even though I fully understand why she needs to sell the house.

"No."

Both their eyes widen at me. *Shit balls*.

"I mean, we just got engaged and we'd have to split the mortgage which I'm not even sure we could afford. This is a nice place and all..."

Think Lauren.

They both continue to stare and I'm slowing losing the progress I made minutes ago.

"I'll talk to him about it."

Vanessa smiles. Maddie's grin is slow to form, but eventually, she pats my leg and stands up.

"Let me know. It's not like I'm going to kick you out or something." She giggles to herself, but I'm not the type to make her do that.

My phone vibrates again.

"Man, you might as well move in together with how often he messages you," Vanessa says, grabbing her coat from the table.

> Asshat: I heard you have half a house available for rent?

> Asshat: (A gif of the sitcom Friends with Ross saying pivot as they try to move a couch)

> Asshat: I won't bring furniture though.

> Me: (A gif from Friends from the same scene with Chandler saying shut up, shut up, shut up)

> Me: Never going to happen.

> Asshat: I think I should introduce you to Ben. I need out.

He cannot be serious.

> Me: This is a one-week operation.

> Asshat: Come on. You'll never find anything like that for the money it will cost you.

> Me: You don't know how much I pay in rent.

> Asshat: Mauro is like a Realtor. Very informative.

I'm sure he is.

> Asshat: In his defense, he thinks I screw you on the regular.

> Me: Little does he know.

> Asshat: We could change that.

> Me: That is exactly the reason we'll never share a roof.

> Asshat: Maybe Ben can give me tips on cleaning out my belly button.

> Me: (A gif from Bachelor in Paradise where one guy is blowing into a straw into another guy's belly button)

> Me: You and Ben…Aww

> Asshat: Nice fiancée you are.

> Me: My detectives are leaving. See you tomorrow.

> Asshat: One of mine has left, the other is trying to kick me out. Sure you don't want to keep my mind off my mom's surgery tomorrow?

> Me: Positive.

> Asshat: I'm not sure you're fulfilling your duties as a fiancée.

I shake my head and tuck my phone away to say goodbye to my friends.

"You guys are so freakin' cute. I'm going to tell Cris he needs to send me more text messages."

"It's gifs he's sending. Luca is a man who believes an image is worth a thousand words."

Vanessa elbows me. "See, you get him. Oh, girls, we're all dating brothers. We're going to be sisters-in-law one day." She wraps her arms around our shoulders, not even realizing what she implied.

"So you're thinking about marriage?" Maddie asks, a sly smile on her lips.

"Well...I don't know...stop looking at me like that."

We let Vanessa off the hook because we know she's slow to accept change, but she's right about one thing, she and Maddie will be sisters-in-law one day. I already feel bad for my future husband.

"We'll see you at the hospital?" Maddie asks once we break apart.

"Yeah, I'm going to try to slip over on my lunch."

"Great. I think her surgery is at one, so that's perfect for you to see her right before they take her in."

I nod not entirely comfortable lying to Mrs. Bianco right before she goes into surgery.

"Go back to your men." I lightly shove both of them toward the back door since they snuck in.

"Remember, I'm always here to talk." Maddie hesitates at the door.

"Give her some space. She's newly engaged." Vanessa coos and I'm not sure if her enthusiasm is a test or not.

They leave and I lock up the door only to be distracted from my thoughts by my buzzing phone.

> Asshat: (a gif from Chicago Med where the guy is telling the girl the ring looks good on her)

> Me: (A gif from Lord of the Rings where it says the ring is my burden)

> Me: Night FIANCÉ.

> Asshat: (A gif of a guy crowd surfing at a concert)

> Asshat: Sleep is for the weak.

Just another reason why I can only handle being Luca's would-be-wife for one week.

CHAPTER TEN

Lauren

I walk across the street to the hospital. My yoga pants and sweatshirt aren't exactly dress to impress attire, but this is my work gear.

My stomach rolls over on itself for about the thousandth time this morning.

I stretch and clench my fingers tucked into my pockets.

I inhale and exhale so much you'd think I was practicing Lamaze.

My hand trembles when the sliding doors of the hospital open and I step into my role as fiancée to Luca Bianco.

Smiling politely to the information desk personnel, I walk to the elevator and press the button to the fourth floor, the one Luca texted me this morning.

I smooth out my unruly hair and pull it back into a ponytail as the elevator ascends. The silver doors part and I step out. Luca kicks himself off the wall, meeting me halfway down the hallway.

"Hey," I say, shoving my hands into my pockets again, not sure what to do with them.

"It's this way." He nods down the hall.

He's all scruffy today and I hate to admit that even this look works for him. He wears his hat backward with a hoodie and jeans. It reminds me of when we were in high school. With the exception of the amount of scruff on his face.

"How are you doing?" I ask as the sign for the cardiovascular unit comes into view.

He shrugs.

"Hey." I tug on the sleeve of his sweatshirt, stopping us from advancing farther.

We both slide to one side of the hallway to let other people pass.

He hovers over me and my chest pricks from the heartache in those coffee-colored eyes. Worry and anxiety have taken the place of his usual humor-filled eyes.

"She's going to be fine. Don't worry."

He nods.

I'm doing a shitty job at convincing him or soothing his worry. I reach out but retract my hand. That's overstepping a boundary I don't think I should.

"Luca," I whisper.

His gaze bounces around, never landing on my face.

What has happened to the man who's so arrogant you'd think he'd believe he could go in there and save his mom? Perform the operation himself? That is not this man who is shutting down right in front of me.

"Luca." I tug again at his sweatshirt, this time using the strings that fall from his hood.

His eyes land on me, but they're hollow.

"She's going to get through this and you're going to have decades with her. You'll bring home the woman you're in love with some day and your mom will hold your baby in her arms. Will probably spoil it with presents and too many sweets. This is a blip in her life. It sucks but this isn't the end, it's only a chapter."

He reaches out and before I can blink, I'm in his arms. His chin rests on my head, his arms draped around me. His fresh shower scent lingers within the little shelter his body builds around me.

My own arms slide around either side of his torso until they're clasped behind him and I'm hugging him back.

God, who knew Luca Bianco felt so good. I always thought of his height as a strike against him because I'm way too short to be with someone so tall, but if I had to re-evaluate that logic right now, I might have to admit I was wrong. Because this feels...way too nice for a comforting hug.

Just as I'm about to back away, another big body blocks the light from my left and then another on my right. I'm surrounded by Bianco brothers and soft whispers reassuring one another that everything will be okay.

I could squeeze out from under them and they'd barely notice. Well, two of them wouldn't.

"You're squishing the little one." Vanessa's voice finally pulls the brothers back from their fear-ridden hug.

"Shit, sorry, Lauren." Cristian speaks first, backing away and wrapping his arm around Van.

"I forgot you were in there." Mauro's lips tip up a bit, but his grin doesn't come close to meeting his eyes.

The two of them have dislodged, but there's still one big guy who has yet to release me.

"Luca," I whisper and he tightens his arms for a second before letting me go.

That felt better than it should.

We follow the two other couples down the hallway to an opening that says Cardiovascular Waiting Area.

Anthony isn't anywhere to be seen but I suspect he's back with Maria, waiting for the surgery.

"We'll go birth order," Cris says, nodding his head in the direction of Mauro.

"Only a few of us are allowed in at a time." Maddie fills me in before walking forward with Mauro following him through the two big double doors.

The rest of us take a seat in the chairs. "Maybe I should just stay here, I mean she barely knows me."

There's Luca's look of death. "No." He leans closer, that fresh smell stronger. His hand wraps around mine, his thumb running the length of my ring as a reminder.

Mauro and Maddie come out a few minutes later, Maddie surprisingly strong holding the hand of a Mauro who's head stays down the entire way back to his seat. When the two sit, Maddie kisses his cheek and he pulls her into him, whispering something in her ear. She whispers something back and if I was in awe of any couple, it would be them. Anyone witnessing them together knows sometimes people truly are meant for one another and bring out the best in the other. It's sickening really. Especially to a woman like myself halfway to being a spinster.

"We'll be back," Cris tells us all, holding Vanessa's hand in his as the two of them disappear behind the doors.

The whole thing is horrible and I can't imagine if someone was actually dying how this would feel. Taking turns to say your goodbye. Luca's phone chimes in his pocket. He pulls it out, mutes it and shoves it back in.

A couple behind us are talking about a friend who's going through his second bypass surgery. One of them is being negative and insisting he needs to take better care of himself. The other one positive with words of praise about how strong the man is. Another family across the way is with small kids who are reading books, playing with toys and moving from one relative to the next. Worry is etched in each adult's features even though they smile at the small children.

We sit in tense silence as I watch people approach the reception desk asking questions and receiving instructions.

I'm not sure how long I'm out of it before Cris and Van come out.

Luca springs to his feet and holds his hand out for me.

Be the good fiancée.

I allow him to pull me from the chair and his fingers tighten in mine. Maddie and Vanessa give me soft smiles as they comfort their men.

We're through the doors and it's not what I was expecting. Nurses and doctors are busy walking from one curtained-off area to another. Drapes sliding along metal sound like shower curtains opening and closing. Beeps haphazardly going off. Murmured voices from each closed off section. The smell of antiseptic pulls the gag reflex out of me.

Luca stops. "Are you okay?"

I nod and he keeps going until he opens a curtain and waits for me to go in first.

Maria Bianco lays with Anthony at her side, holding her hand.

"Lauren," she coos, trying to slide higher on the bed.

"No. Don't." I put my hand up.

Anthony stands, kissing me on either cheek a smile on his lips. He shakes Luca's hand before hugging him and then stands to the side to allow us time with his wife.

Time *I* shouldn't have with her.

I stand next to her bed but leave Luca to take the chair and be with his mom.

Luca pulls the chair out for me, signaling with his eyes for me to take a seat.

I shake my head.

He tilts his head, taking a deep breath in and out and eyes on the chair again.

I shake my head again. "You," I mouth.

He shakes his head. "You," he mouths.

All this fighting is ridiculous, so I just sit down so that at least he'll have a few minutes with his mom before her surgery.

Luca sits on the bed and I slyly slide the chair back a little to give them room.

"You ready Ma?" he asks. "They're going to find out how big that heart of yours is." I look behind me at Luca because his tone is jovial and comical. His smile is wide as he laughs at his own joke. "They might want you for science," he continues.

Maria laughs at her son, shaking her head. "Oh, Luca."

She glances over at me and shakes her head again like 'can you believe this guy, he's the best, right? I know you agree with me because you've agreed to be with him until you're gray and old and senile. So you must find his humor endearing too?'

I move my hand to my stomach, coughing from the extra saliva coating my mouth since I feel bile rising up my throat.

"Oh, dear." Maria's eyes cast to me, zeroing in on my stomach. "Are you? Is that why?"

Anthony peers over from the other side of the bed, his eyes widening at my hand on my stomach.

I retract my hand so fast I almost take out Maria's IV attached to the hanging bag. Wouldn't that be great?

Luca leans over me, his own hand drifting down toward my stomach.

"I just felt a bit nauseous. Probably just hungry." I smile, but Luca isn't changing his course of action.

He will not lie to his mother about me having a baby. That is where I draw the line.

But he saddles up to me, sitting on the arm of the chair, presenting us as a couple again, a united front.

"Thank goodness. I never want my children to marry because of a baby." Her shoulders and head fall back down to the pillow.

I shoot Luca a death glare. He slides off the arm of the chair, but I swear for a moment he could've claimed temporary insanity.

The nurse steps in and smiles at all of us while silently giving us a look that says your time is up. "Okay, Mrs. Bianco, we're going to get you all set up."

I stand, ready to stop this lying brigade.

"We'll see you in a few hours." I grip her cold hand and squeeze.

She looks over my shoulder at Luca and then to Anthony, waving them away. They surprisingly listen and step back, then she crooks her finger for me to come closer.

"Take care of him. He acts like a lion, but he's really a lamb." She pats my cheek like she does Luca all the time. "But you already know that, don't you?"

I want to scream no. That he is a lion in lamb's wool. At least to me. Maybe not to her, but he's only showing this nice side to me because I'm doing him a favor.

But I agreed to this, so I need to pull on my big girl panties. Instead of answering, I nod.

"We'll see you when you get out." I pat her hand and step away before I'm forced to lie to a woman who thinks her son is sweeter than a Sweet Tart.

I back away to the curtain's edge, as Luca approaches next. The nurse fiddles around with some equipment, grabbing items in plastic bags and moving the tubes and wires around.

"Luca, my baby."

He leans in closer, his head held high and a grim smile forced onto his lips.

She whispers something to him and he nods, leaning down and kissing each one of her cheeks.

He says something softly back before standing and joining me, putting his arm around my waist. His fingers shake where they sit on my hip.

"See you in recovery, Ma. They'll be jealous, don't let them steal that big heart of yours." Luca smiles, laughs and steps out to the other side of the curtain.

We walk back to the waiting area, he unhooks his arm from my body, stuffs his hands in his pockets and the smile vanishes from his face.

My heart has never felt so broken from someone else's pain as it does right now.

CHAPTER ELEVEN

Lauren

"I'll walk you out," Luca mumbles as we exit the doors to the waiting room.

"That's okay. I'm going to stop and get something to eat."

"I'll come. I just need to walk."

I stop in front of our friends, my hand already raised to wave goodbye. Maddie and Vanessa both get up from their seats and hug me goodbye.

"I'm walking her back to work," Luca tells everyone, his hand finding mine.

An electric current rushes up my arm and if I wasn't in front of people who don't know this whole affection is fake, I'd stare down at our hands looking for the reason. Unfortunately, I know the reason and I'd be lying if it didn't scare me. Then again, it could be sympathy for what he has to go through today.

"We'll see you later?" Maddie asks, Mauro's arm around her nuzzling her into his side.

"Yeah. I'll stop by after work."

"We'll let you…" Her eyes find Luca. "I'm sure Luca will get you the room number."

Maddie is our group's mother hen. She's the one who informs us of what we need to do and where we need to be. I see now it's a struggle for her to take a backseat since she thinks this is Luca's territory now.

"Yeah," I say and glance at Luca.

Anthony comes out of the room and all three of the boys make their way over to him, each one offering words of encouragement and arms for support. Anthony appears fine, shooing them all away from him, finding his way to a chair in the corner, isolating himself from everyone else.

"Let's go." Luca walks by me, his head down.

"Bye guys," I say, catching up to Luca.

The pressure in my chest relieves the minute we're not in direct vision of everyone's curious eyes.

"Are you okay?" I ask while we wait for the elevator.

"I'm good. Just give me a minute." He rubs at the scruff on his face and continues to study the floor.

The elevator doors ding open and I'm happy to be one step closer to escaping this situation. I don't belong here. I like Mama Bianco, she's a great woman, but I'm not supposed to be the one to comfort her youngest son.

We step in and I realize we're alone in the elevator. Seriously, isn't this a metropolitan hospital? Where are all the damn people?

Luca leans casually in the corner, each hand on the silver handrails. My eyes focus on the numbers as we descend floor by floor. Just as three moves to two, the elevator bounces to a stop.

The doors open and an attractive woman smiles and steps in. She takes me in first and then her attention shifts to Luca and they flash with surprise.

"Luca," she says in a way too excited way. One that would

make you think she's been riding the elevator all day waiting for him to pop up.

He straightens, a smile gracing his lips. "Keri," he says her name like he's said it while he's come before.

Please let this nightmare end. How many more days do we have of this charade?

"What are you doing here? You're obviously not on shift."

He shakes his head. "My mom is having surgery."

"Oh, I'm sorry. I hope it's not serious." Her hand reaches out and touches his forearm.

Perfectly manicured nails attached to long and thin feminine fingers grip the fabric of his hoodie. Everything about this woman is stunning. Her blue dress ends right before her knees, showcasing long, toned legs. And here I am in yoga pants and a sweatshirt.

"It's an ablation. I'm sure she'll be fine." He smiles again and smacks on that arrogant outward appearance that is Luca Bianco.

"Oh good. I'll try to visit her. Is she here overnight?"

"She is."

His gaze hasn't veered to me once.

Not that I care. I don't.

"And being the good son, you're sticking around, right?"

She winks. What kind of woman winks? The kind who wants to get in her fiancé's pants.

"Of course." His smirk appears. The flirtatious one that says, 'I'm interested...in you naked under me.'

What a pig.

"I'll stop by then," she says.

"Great."

This is the exact reason he's referred to as Asshat in my phone.

The elevator doors open and I slide past the pretty sophisticated woman, beelining it out of the glass doors of the hospital, greeted by the sun on my face along with the chill of winter blistering my eyes.

Water gathers in them and I blink a million times to get rid of the tears—from the cold. Seeing the pedestrian sign lit up on the street sign, I jog across the street with the masses of people.

Luca can go to bed with that woman, what the hell do I care?

Pulling out my phone I check the time. I had Cindy reschedule my appointment for after lunch just in case I ran late, which is good because otherwise, I wouldn't be able to stop for food.

Sliding into a café, I order a sandwich, but when I'm pulling out my money a familiar forearm comes into view handing the cashier a card.

Another fucking admirer stares at Luca awestricken as she takes his card from his hand.

"I got it," I snip.

"You're a hard woman to catch up to."

The girl takes his card and once she's run the charge through, I grab the receipt and pager, heading toward the pick-up line.

"Why did you run off?" He meets me because the man is about as clueless as I was when I agreed to this shitty idea.

"Why?" I ask, unable to hold it in anymore.

"Lauren?" He looks down at me, wrinkles in his forehead and confusion on his face.

"You will not disrespect me," I bite out through my teeth.

My pager goes off in my hand.

Thank God, before I give him the riot act in a crowded restaurant right in the middle of lunchtime.

I snatch my bag off the counter, drop the pager and high-tail it out of the restaurant.

"Disrespect you? When did I do that?"

I whip around, he stops, and a guy has to weave by him, the businessman murmuring something to himself.

Luca holds up his hands in front of himself. He must notice the fire in my eyes.

"You were flirting with that woman. Are you going to fuck her in the next hospital room over from your mom's? I don't care what you do Luca, but when I'm taking my lunch break to help you out, do me a favor and don't treat me like some side piece."

The minute my spew of words are finished leaving my mouth, I freeze. Those words give the impression that I care. And I don't.

"Flirting? She's a doctor. I know her because I spend a decent amount of time at that hospital. I wasn't flirting nor am I going to sleep with her."

"Now you're going to lie?" I circle around and stomp off toward the corner, steam could literally be shooting out my ears and nostrils right now.

"I'm not lying," he says from behind me.

We stop at a light, waiting for the crosswalk along with fifteen other people.

"Then you're more clueless than I thought. Actually, pathetic because you don't even realize when you're flirting. Which in that case, I feel sorry for whoever you really marry."

A gasp sounds and my eyes find all the people around us watching. I've made a spectacle which normally I wouldn't care, but for some reason, I feel exposed in this moment.

"What was I supposed to do? Say 'sorry, this is my fiancée?'"

He obviously doesn't care about the spectators to our show.

"I wasn't asking to be introduced..."

"I had to pressure you to do this. You said no one else was

to know except the few who had to. I didn't introduce you because I thought that was what you wanted, not because I want to fuck her."

Another gasp sounds and I glance around the crowd to find a woman covering her son's ears.

"Just go back," I whisper. I tap my foot.

What the hell is taking the street light so long?

"Not until this is resolved." His hand wraps around my upper arm and he leads me over into the shelter of a parking garage. "I didn't mean to disrespect you Lauren, but this is fake between us. I wasn't flirting with her to screw her. I was being friendly."

"You were practically making a date to screw her."

"Be careful, you're sounding like a jealous girlfriend." He crosses his arms over his chest.

I narrow my eyes. "I'm done with this." I wave a finger between us and step back out onto the street.

My building is only one block away. I see the sign and once I'm there, he can go back and do whatever he wants.

"You're not done. We have an agreement." He touches my arm again.

I yank it back away from him and step closer so no passerby can overhear us. "You don't need me. Your mom will come out of the surgery fine and you can make some excuse of where I am and tell her we broke up in a week."

I walk away, my eyes glued to my building. Sweet serenity.

"You're the one who needs a date to your Christmas party. Don't forget that part of the agreement," he calls out to me.

I raise my hand in the air. "I'll hire an escort."

A woman raises her eyebrows at me as she passes.

Whatever. I'm done caring what people think today.

I reach my work, swinging the door open, happy to escape the whole fake engagement. I'm done and now I don't have to worry about lying to my friends. I'll lay low for a week, tell them it was my worst mistake ever and after one pow wow they'll let it go, giving me some space. One day when we're in the nursing home, I'll tell them the truth.

"Hey, Cindy." I greet her and her focusing on whatever is behind me isn't a red flag in my mind until I'm about to disappear through the doors and I hear another voice.

"Cindy? Pleasure to meet you. I'm Luca Bianco, Lauren's fiancé."

I whip around to find his hand extended over the receptionist desk, his sparkling smile on display.

Cindy doesn't even turn to me in bewilderment, she's solely focused on the hot man in front of her.

I'm going to jail for murder because I'm going to strangle Luca Bianco.

CHAPTER TWELVE

Luca

The blonde receptionist smiles, her eyes skating over me in appreciation.

"Oh, I didn't know..."

"You know Lauren, she's so private, but it's a new development."

I turn my attention to a stunned and pissed off Lauren standing at the door to what I assume is the employee entrance to the physical therapy offices. There's a giant window that looks into a big room with carpeted floor and reminds me of my stint in a place like this when I tore my ACL freshman year in college.

Cindy doesn't say much else. She slides her hand out from mine and sits back down in her chair.

"Wait!" she exclaims a second later, making me turn back on my way over to Lauren. "You're the candy man?"

I smile back at her. "That I am. Let me guess, she didn't share?"

I claim the distance between us, draping my arm around her waist. I like the way she fits next to me.

"No, she didn't." Cindy's face lights up like I'm the real thing.

"Yeah, well, I have to get back to work." Lauren places her hand on my chest and steps back.

I hate that she's angry at me for some stupid shit I did out of habit. My mind was drowning in worries for my mom. I was imagining the anesthesiologist starting the drill of having her count backward and my stomach cramped, worried about the rare instances where people don't wake up or have an allergic reaction. I don't think my mom is allergic, but she's never been put to sleep before. Rare complications happen and to the people they happen to it doesn't seem all that rare. When you're the one in a thousand, it doesn't matter. I've seen those people in my job.

People fear what they can't control. If I'd gone to medical school and become a doctor and I could be doing my mom's surgery, I'd probably feel better about this whole thing.

I was running all that through my mind when Keri walked into the elevator.

She's a doctor I met through the ER for one particular patient of hers who has epilepsy. Keri meets us every time we bring him in after an episode. I know she's single because she's mentioned it before. We've flirted before, I'm not going to lie about that. I'm Italian and I talk a lot. No one is really a stranger. Did I overstep with Lauren in the elevator? Sure as shit. And I could argue with her and tell her how it was just a reflex, but Lauren isn't the type to understand that. I would have never taken it anywhere with Keri given the situation that Lauren and I are in, but again, Lauren isn't likely to believe that.

Not a lot of women would call me on my shit either and for whatever reason I kind of like it.

"Let's talk," I whisper.

"I finished our conversation." She glances toward Cindy who I'm sure is watching us like we're her favorite reality TV show.

"No, it's not over. Plus, I think that escort thing is out of the question now."

Her eyes narrow as the realization hits her. I just screwed her plan B by introducing myself to Cindy.

"I hate you," she grinds out through a smile on her lips that doesn't light up her face.

"I know." I wrap her in my arms and keep my head on the opposite side Cindy can see. "I'm sorry, okay. I just...I handle stress by trying to forget it and I just want to forget that some surgeon is playing Operation with my mom's heart right now."

A deep sigh falls into my ear and her arms tighten for a moment. "Fine."

It's clear that she's not fully accepting my apology and she's probably tolerating this because she needs me to be her date for the Christmas party this weekend. But I'll take it.

"You think you can keep your dick in your pants for one week?" she asks softly, sliding her cheek along my chest like we're saying a long goodbye.

"Maybe we should add a benefits clause to our contract?"

She lightly punches me in the stomach.

"Or not. Yeah, of course I can."

Backing up, she fake smiles and then turns to Cindy. "I'll scarf this down and be ready in five minutes." She holds up her bag of food. "Thanks for lunch babe," she says.

My smile is automatic and genuine at her pet name for me. I lean forward and kiss her cheek. Damn her skin is soft. My lips want to trail along her jaw and down to her lips until I can lose myself in her. She'd make one helluva distraction.

"I'll message you with the room number?" I ask.

"Oh, are you guys getting a hotel room? Kinky," Cindy interjects.

"No Cindy, his mom is in the hospital." She turns back to me. "Okay. I'll message you when I'm done here."

The bell over the door chimes in the small reception area and in walks a redheaded girl with braids and, with who I'm guessing is, her mom.

"LAUREN!" the little girl exclaims, wobbling over to us. Her legs are in braces, but she gets around well.

"Polybriana," Lauren immediately falls to her knees and opens her arms for her.

The two hug and I step aside to give them room.

"How was school?" Lauren cringes like she already knows the answer.

"Boring." The little girl's gaze peers up at me for a brief second. "I have to write a book report."

That sucks, I feel her. I wasn't one for school work either.

"What book are you going to do it on?" Lauren never stands.

The girl's eyes veer up to me once more and then back to Lauren.

"I don't know yet. Mom is taking me to the library after this."

Lauren pokes her in the stomach. "I'm sure you'll find something perfect."

Polybriana giggles, her gaze once again falling to me. I decide to introduce myself since Lauren isn't going to.

"Hey, I'm Luca, Lauren's—"

"Friend," Lauren whispers, shooting me a warning look.

"Hi, Luca. I'm Briana." The girl puts her hand out in between us. My large palm swallows up her smaller one.

"I thought it was Polybriana?" I ask.

She laughs like I'm making a joke. "Lauren says I look like Pollyanna."

I narrow my eyes.

"Lauren." Cindy grabs her attention away from us.

I bend down. "Is she confusing Pollyanna with Pippi Longstocking?" I ask. The only reason I know the difference is because my cousin Blanca came to visit from New York once and watched Pollyanna like a million times.

Briana puts her finger to her lips. "I don't want to hurt her feelings," she whispers.

I nod and smile then pretend to zip my lips and throw away the key. "Your secret is safe with me."

"Are you her boyfriend?" she asks point blank.

I glance up to find Lauren now shuffling through papers as the three women talk.

"Um..." I have a feeling she'll be pissed if I tell this little girl she's my fiancée. "Probably should ask her."

"She gave you a mean look. Usually that look only goes to Peter when he tries to tell her how to exercise my legs," she says.

"We have a love-hate relationship."

That's not a lie.

She nods, her braids swinging back and forth. "I can see that."

"Why?" I ask, chuckling.

She looks to Lauren and back to me. "There was tension when I walked up. Like when I go to the doctor, my mom gets all stiff and short with everyone."

"What about the love part?" I bend down to this girl's level because I feel bad watching her strain her neck to look me in the eye.

Brianna shrugs. "That's easy. She keeps glancing over here."

"And? Maybe she's worried about you?"

She shakes her head. "She's watching you. Wants to see how you are with me."

This little girl is crazy. Hunt doesn't give a rat's ass about me.

"I think you're wrong."

Her expression says I'm crazy for ever thinking she's wrong. "People either talk to me with sympathy or don't talk to me at all." She leans in closer. "It's a test."

"Why?"

"Because I'm her number one. I've been her client since she first started here." She puffs her chest out a bit.

I laugh holding up my hand.

She smacks it, her walking cane swinging next to us. "I like you."

She smiles brightly. "I don't take bribes."

"Excuse me?"

"You heard me. I'm not going to go sweet talk her about you if that's what you think."

Shaking my head with a smile, I say, "Only say it if you believe it."

She shrugs. "Too early to tell."

I laugh again, falling down to rest my weight on my knees. "Fair enough, but I might never see you again."

She glances at Lauren who seems like she's finishing up whatever she's doing.

"I'll hear about you though. If she likes you, she'll tell me."

I lean in closer, my eyes on Lauren. "Does she tell you about other guys?"

"A girl never tells."

I nod, unable to get rid of the smile on my face. This little girl is something else.

"Ready?" Lauren claps her hands stopping in front of the door, her hand already on the knob.

"See you, Pip." I put out my hand for a shake, which she gives me.

"Pip?" Lauren questions.

Briana and I exchange a secret smile.

"Bye, Luca."

I wink and turn to Lauren. "I'll message you later."

She nods, opening the door.

A guy on the other side of it is talking with another employee, but his eyes stay trained on us. Is that her boss?

Lauren and Brianna head through the door and when it clicks closed, my eyes shift to the windows. Lauren's gaze finds mine and she gives me a soft smile before putting her sole attention on Brianna.

As I head out of the building, I stuff my hands in my jacket, the reality that my mom is laying on a table in a cold surgery room hitting me once again. That's where I need to be right now.

My phone dings in my pocket as I make my way along the sidewalk.

Cristian: You good?

Me: On my way back. Any news?

Mauro: No just wanted to make sure you didn't go AWOL.

Me: Since when do I do that?

Cristian: Since Ma took your blanky away at five.

Me: (An emoji of a middle finger)

Mauro: Enzo's here.

Me: I didn't know the NYC syndicate was coming.

Cristian: None of us did.

I tuck my phone back into my pocket, shoving my hands in my jacket. I'm going to have to dig my gloves and hat out soon.

Heading back to the hospital, my mind is worried about my mom, but I'm equally concerned about how this will end with Lauren and me. I kind of want it to end differently than I originally planned and that's just as fucked up.

CHAPTER THIRTEEN

Luca

By the time I reach the cardio department, I find my brothers and the girls laughing and Enzo is the cause of their amusement.

My Zia is by my dad, a rosary between them with hushed prayers being whispered.

Cristian spots me first, nodding at me and causing Enzo to look over his shoulder.

With a smile on his face, he rises and heads in my direction.

"Luc, you've grown," he says, wrapping his arms around me, not at all awkward about affection.

Coming from New York and being the successful advertising exec he is, I figured he'd be sporting some exuberantly priced suit that none of us could fathom spending our money on. But he's in jeans, a black Henley style shirt with the top three buttons undone showing his chain where I know his St. Christopher medal lay in the center of his chest.

"Why the mysterious surprise?" I ask, slapping his back as hard as he slaps mine.

"Cris called us last week and I decided I had a few years' worth of vacation banked, might as well bring Ma out to be with Zia Maria." He slides his hands into his pockets, and the light catches his shiny watch.

Our Mancini cousins are by far the richest guys I know—that's why we razz them with the title of White Collar Cousins. They each do very well, heavy on the very. They're all close in age, like us, the only difference besides the size of our bank accounts is that they got a little oops sister. Other than that, we're all practically carbon copies of one another. Actually, scratch that. Dom, the oldest, isn't like any of us.

"Nice to see you." I swing my arm around his shoulder bringing him back to the gang.

Vanessa and Maddie are speaking in hushed whispers now with the helpful lady working at the desk. Their eyes scanning the progress screen.

"Tell me the rumor I heard..." Enzo lets it hang. You'd think that deception gets easier the more you do it, but it doesn't.

"You heard right. I just walked her back to work."

He shakes his head, sitting down in his chair propping his ankle up to rest on his knee, leaning back like he runs the entire waiting area. One quality I've always been jealous of is my cousin's way of being comfortable in his own skin. He doesn't really give a shit if you like him or not.

"Can't wait to meet the woman who nailed you down." He raises his eyebrows in question just like everyone else we've told.

I didn't think I was as much of a manwhore as everyone else apparently does. I mean, it's not like I'm a sworn bachelor like Enzo's brother, Dom. Kids and a wife were always on the horizon for me. Just, you know...far, far off in the distance.

"She's the best," Maddie's back now, sitting next to Mauro.

Enzo shoots her a smile that says your biased. He must have already gotten the lowdown on the interconnected ties in this group.

"I'm happy for you all. You seem...happy."

"There's no seem about it," Mauro wraps his arm around Maddie, kissing her temple, letting his lips fall to her neck.

"Luca?" Zia stands up, walking toward us, her arms already extended.

"Hi, Zia." I wrap my arms around her small body.

Sometimes you wonder how we all ended up so tall when our Mamas are pint-size. With that thought my mind wanders to my own kids and how big they'd be if Lauren was their mom.

What the hell?

"Your mama told me." She steps back, her fingers pinching my cheek. "I'm so happy for you and as for me," her eyes find Enzo, "at least I can dance at someone's wedding." Her scowl at Enzo makes everyone laugh.

Everyone but Enzo, who rolls his eyes. "It's not my fault they didn't clone a younger version of you."

Zia smiles and shakes her head at her son. "See, that's why you're so good at your job. Great bullshitter."

"Zia," I say, loving her ability to call it out when she hears it.

I'm actually surprised she hasn't called me out yet and the fear of when she meets Lauren weighs heavy on my shoulders because if I don't get the perfect cadence of a new relationship right in her presence, she'll know.

As if sealing my thought, her eyes linger on my brothers and their significant others. She might as well be that love emoji with the two heart eyes. Zia wants her boys to settle down and they are far from ready. As if I can talk.

Enzo runs his hand down the light scruff on his face. Pulling his phone out of his pocket, he puts it to his ear while stepping away.

"Lorenzo Mancini," he answers.

Her hand hooks through my arm and she escorts me to an area of seats away from everyone. "Tell me about this special girl."

———

We're all crammed in a hospital room.

My mom is waking up from anesthesia, so my dad is with her while we wait for her to return to her room. Enzo and my brothers are talking about hockey, but my eyes are on the nurse writing down my mom's information.

"Excuse me, do we know anything?" I ask.

The cute blonde girl, wearing braids making her appear too young to care for my mom, shoots me a nice smile.

"I'm sorry, the doctor will come in as soon as your mom wakes up."

"Thanks."

I know more than to press for information. She can't give it to me and I'm not going to be a dick about the situation.

Lauren walks in, her hair a little windblown, her cheeks flushed from the cool air. She's cute as hell.

She smiles at me.

She smiles like I'm hers.

She smiles like she's mine.

A stabbing sensation pierces my heart with the same feeling I had when I left her physical therapy office.

"Lauren." Maddie jumps up and wraps her arms around her, whispering something in her ear.

Vanessa joins the duo, and the three of them talk. Lauren peeks away to get a glimpse of Enzo, but her eyes travel back to me before returning to her friends.

Enzo and my brothers are too heated to notice Lauren, but my Zia is not. She stands from the chair nearest the bed, the rosary still tight in her hands.

"This her?" she asks, nodding toward Lauren.

Lauren drops her bag next to Maddie and Vanessa's and beelines it over to me, taking her gloves off and tucking them into her coat pocket.

"Hey, any word?" she asks like she's as worried about my ma as me.

"She's out of surgery. We're waiting on her." I mimic Mauro with my hand around her waist and I kiss her temple. Sweet and not overly claiming.

Lauren side glances me, but doesn't push me away or elbow me in the gut. "Oh good."

"Lauren this is my aunt, Anna." I hold my arm out.

Lauren places her hand out between them, but Zia grabs her by the shoulders, which is easy with the two of them being equal height and yanks her into her chest.

"Oh she's beautiful, Luca," she coos, talking to me instead of Lauren. "Perfect fit. We could share clothes."

As abruptly as she pulled her to her chest, she shoves her back, but her hands stop Lauren from stumbling with her hold on her shoulders. Zia's eyes fall over Lauren like she's inspecting her.

"Good birthing hips." She points to Enzo, who's figured out Lauren is here. "If you're going to push one of those out of you, you need hips."

Lauren glances at me and then back to Enzo. "Well..."

I think she's caught off guard and not sure what to say.

"We don't plan on having kids for a while," I say, saving her.

"How come, Luc? You don't want to be the first to give Zia a grandchild?" Enzo's hand slaps my back and his eyes turn to Lauren, sticking his hand out in her direction. "Lorenzo Mancini."

He introduces himself like I assume he does everyone he comes into contact with. To me, my cousin is still the kid who didn't grow until freshman year in high school. The dorky kid with glasses and a scrawny body. By the time sophomore year came around Enzo was no longer the kid people picked on. He became the kid you feared because he had a chip on his shoulder and he was out for revenge.

"Nice to meet you." Lauren's sweet voice says like she means her words.

She lightly shakes his hand and I catch my cousin's eyes linger on her body. Especially when Lauren decides now is the time to disrobe her coat. Enzo elbows me in the ribs when I don't help her. I take the collar and she slides her hands out, a surprised glow in her eyes.

"Thanks." She tries not to crinkle her eyebrows, but she can't help it.

"What is it you do that lets you dress so casually?" Enzo asks Lauren.

She giggles. "Tough gig, right? Yoga pants and sweatshirts are my go-to work outfit."

"Personal trainer?" he asks, his gaze again flicking over her body.

She should be wearing bigger sweatshirts. Not these thin fabric ones that are snug across her chest. Especially if her boss is already trying to get a date.

"Physical therapist. Peds." She pulls down the edge of her sweatshirt and under normal circumstances I'd be mad that I'm losing the view of her ass, but I don't mind when Enzo's in the room.

"Nice. You're both in the healthcare field. Stable field of

work thanks to insurance companies skyrocketing the costs of every medical procedure."

Lauren looks at me like the thought never occurred to her before. Does she not remember our conversation in the car?

"Yeah. What do you do?" She fiddles with her hands and she keeps shifting her weight from one foot to the other.

"I'm in advertising."

"Well, who doesn't need to be bullshitted into buying products they don't need, right?"

I think I just fell in love with her.

Enzo laughs. His head falling back, stuffing his hands in his pockets again. "I like you," he says.

So do I.

Lauren looks to me with an apologetic look.

I rest my arm around her back, my hand molding to her hip and I kiss her temple again.

This time it isn't an act, I kind of wish she was mine.

Enzo's eyes follow my arm and a genuine happy smile forms on his lips.

"She's here," my dad announces coming in while an orderly opens up the other door to make room for the big bed.

My mom smiles, her eyes still a little droopy. I doubt they'll let us stay for long.

Everyone crowds around her and she cries when she sees my Zia, the two embracing for a long time.

The doctor comes in some time later and Lauren entwines our hands, squeezing mine, letting me know that she's here for me. The older man with a receding hairline, checks on my mom a little and then situates himself so everyone is looking at him. He holds his tightly clasped hands in front of him, a somber look on his face.

I've seen enough doctors talking to families to know he

doesn't have good news. My stomach sinks and a painful lump grows in my throat.

"I'm sorry, Maria, the procedure wasn't successful."

Silent tears stream down my mom's face, my dad holding one hand, my Zia the other.

Fuck.

"We're going to let you heal and then we'll talk in the morning about where we go from here." He pats her shoulder. "I know we had high hopes, but it's not like we can't try the procedure again."

My mom nods and the doctor nods at each of us with his lips pressed together before he leaves the room.

Lauren looks up at me, sorrow filling her eyes. Her other hand grabs my bicep as though she's trying to hold me in place.

Mauro and Cristian chase the doctor out the door and I do what I do best...I flee.

CHAPTER FOURTEEN

Lauren

I'm going to kill him. Here I am for him and he just runs away.

Maddie and Vanessa chased after their boyfriends, so here I stand in the middle of a room with people I've met only a handful of times.

Enzo notices Luca's gone and saddles up next to me.

"Did you not know this is how Luca is?" He laughs, rocking back on his heels. "This one time when he was five, my Zia decided he was too old to keep carrying around his blankie everywhere, so she threw it out. He ran away. Everyone was out looking for him well after dark."

"I'm guessing they found him," I add in since I don't really care what he did when he was five. I care about him leaving me, right now, when I'm here as a favor.

Just when I was starting to think he was an okay guy.

"Yeah, he was in the neighbor's shed. Luca can't handle feelings. I figured you would have discovered that already. You know since you're wearing his ring and all." He stares at me. This set of sparkling blue eyes questioning me. Does he not believe us?

"Well, as I'm sure you've heard it's been kind of a whirlwind with us."

"I did."

The more judgemental tones this guy throws at me, the more I want to dig my feet into the sand and scream from a pedestal that I am Luca Bianco's fiancée.

"So this is really the first time I've had to see him really affected by something. You know since we're madly in love and all." I throw his phrase back at him.

The corners of his lips lift until he can't stop the smile from emerging. "Okay, now I *really* like you."

"Too bad, your cousin saw me first." The words come out before I can think better of them. He may construe them a whole different way.

"How am I supposed to interpret that? Is that a give me your hotel key and I'll meet you later, or you don't hold a candle to Luca?" Humor lights in his eyes.

"The latter. I'm with your cousin." I hold up my left hand and the light catches the diamond.

He holds his hands up in the air. "Do I look desperate? I don't touch my brothers' or my cousins' girls. Actually, I stay away from any woman who would bring drama to my life."

"At least for more than a night, right?"

He laughs. "Jeez, do you have a sister?"

"No. Three brothers."

"Ah," he nods. "That's where this spunky attitude comes from. That's why I like you. You remind me of my sister Blanca."

So I was wrong about him being attracted to me. That's kind of ego bruising even though I didn't really care for him, other then he's fun to banter with.

"Maybe I'll meet her one day."

"You will. At the wedding."

My eyebrows furrow. Maddie and Mauro haven't started planning theirs and unless it's Blanca's...

"Your wedding," he clarifies and there goes his damn eyebrows again.

I wish I had some duct tape to keep them in place.

The coupledoms walk back in, all whispering until they see all eyes are on them and they plaster a fake smile on their faces.

Vanessa's gaze deters to me, a questioning look on her face.

"Exactly," I mouth.

She elbows Cristian and nods in my direction.

He shoots me a look of apology.

Great, so I'm the pity party.

I need to leave.

I step forward to the hospital bed and place my hand on Maria's cold forearm.

"I'm going to find Luca. Rest and I'll stop by tomorrow." I smile and step back.

Zia Anna steps behind me, blocking my departure.

"You kiss on the cheek," she whispers like all the eyes in the room aren't on us and I can just slyly go back in and kiss Maria's cheek without anyone being the wiser.

But I do. Her cheek just as cold as her forearm.

"Hug him," Maria says softly and when I pull back, I see the pained expression on her face. Like she expected him to do this all along, but she's passing the torch to me.

I smile then say my goodbyes and by the time I'm in the hall, I exhale a big breath, thankful to be done.

Where would Luca go?

I will find him, but then I'm going to kick his ass for leaving me alone in there.

Pulling out my phone, I dial him up.

No answer.

Shit. Where would he go?

The only place I can think to try is his apartment. He drove me home one night when we were all together and then to make a stop there. I waited in the car, but I'm sure I can probably figure out what apartment it is once I'm there.

Well, I guess I get to meet Ben after all.

———

I step off the elevator surprised by the building where Luca lives. Part of me assumed it'd be like a frat house with trash outside before I even made it to the door.

But the carpet in the hall is nice and the foyer was spacious and clean. Luckily, I snuck in after someone else because I'm not even sure if Luca would let me up. I mean I didn't do anything to him, but he might be worried about my wrath after leaving me—which would be wise on his part.

I knock on the door with numbers 2354. Thankfully the mail slot downstairs had his last name on it and yes, I slipped in behind someone who lived in the building. You'd be surprised what people will let you get away with if you look like you know what you're doing.

No sound from the other side.

Great and I'll be sitting here waiting for him to answer all night.

I knock again.

"Coming." I hear a deep voice on the other side, but it's not Luca's. "I'll call you right back honey."

The door springs open and there stands who I assume is Ben.

He's normal looking. His pants are a little tight and his shirt a little faded with a stain or two, but I'm not judging. He's in his home.

He's clean shaven and his hair is an unkept mess.

"I was looking for Luca?"

His gaze runs up and down my body.

I've had about enough of men looking my body up and down today.

"He's in his room." He points down a hall.

I take that as a welcome and step into the apartment.

Luca wasn't lying. I don't see a lot to complain about. The place is modern and clean with a couch in the living room and a coffee table in front of it that has a bunch of controllers and a headset sitting on top.

"I was playing with my fiancée. She's moving to Chicago." Ben's tone is one of excitement.

"That's nice." I smile.

"Oh take off your shoes please." He points to my sneakers.

I untie them and slide out of them thankful I don't have holes in my socks.

"I've never met her. Isn't that crazy? I mean she's moving out here from Russia... for me."

I wish I could be more happy for Ben, and his excitement is a little intoxicating, but unfortunately, I've known the guy for less than a minute. Not to mention, I'm skeptical about the whole 'girl from abroad' scenario. I'm sure there are legit relationships where someone isn't using the other for a green card. Maybe I've just watched too many episodes of *90 Day Fiancé*.

Then again who am I to cast stones? I have my own fake fiancé.

"That is great. Well, good luck with all that." I take a few steps toward the hall.

"Thanks. I mean I feel bad for Luca, but I gotta give this a shot."

I stop in my tracks, my eyes leaving the closed door at end of the hall and turn back to Ben.

"Why would you feel bad?"

He runs his hands through his hair. I understand the hairstyle now. "I own this lease and since Daria is moving here, I just don't think she'd be comfortable with another guy living with us. Especially with our schedules..."

I hold my hand up in the air. "So you've kicked Luca out?"

He shrugs. "Yeah but..."

"Good luck with Daria, Ben, and I really mean that."

I turn back around and walk toward the door at the end of the hall. Not bothering to knock, I close my eyes on the off chance he's naked and open the door.

"Jesus, Hunt."

"Are you beating off? Because if you are, we really need to talk priorities." I cover my eyes with my hand just in case I can't be trusted not to peek. It wouldn't be intentional, but the way Vanessa and Maddie brag about the Bianco men and how they aren't lacking makes me kind of curious.

"Open your eyes."

I shake my head. "Nope. You're not going to trick me."

"You're the one who just barged in." I hear him scrambling, a rush of air hitting my face every few seconds.

"Because you left me in a hospital room with my fake family-to-be."

"You're being childish. Take your hand away."

"Childish? You're the one being childish. You ran away like a baby."

"Luca, I'm really sorry," Ben says from behind me.

"It's all good, Ben." The door slams shut and a lock slides into place.

I should open my eyes.

"You locked me in here?"

"Don't be ridiculous. I don't want Ben barging in again.

The guy thinks he's ruined my life or something because his mail-order bride is coming to Chicago."

"Is she a mail order bride? I kind of suspected but I didn't want to assume. I mean he's an okay looking guy."

"Hunt." His voice is so close, I swear I just smelled his minty breath.

Then his fingers touch mine, lifting each one with ease.

"Open your eyes." His voice is so seductive this close. I squeeze my thighs together to clench the unwanted desire.

"Are you sure? Because you're very close and my knee is right there," I say in a low voice.

He chuckles and I peek one eye open to find him front and center.

God, he really is good looking. When I'm away from him, I think I forget the effect he can have on a woman.

All of his features are sharp and defined. His dark hair tousled in a way that Ben could never pull off in the sexy way Luca can. His eyes are so dark it's hard sometimes to distinguish the dark brown from his pupils. And his body...

"Hi," I say in a soft voice.

His lips lift and I swear it's like the sun shining through a line of dark clouds. I'm speechless.

"As you can see, I'm fully clothed."

That comment makes my eyes head south down his body. Bad idea. Very bad idea. If I was speechless from his face alone, I'm worse off now.

"Yep, you sure are," I croak out.

I scan the room, one box sits in the middle of a made bed while a duffle bag sits half-filled beside it along with an empty suitcase.

"When exactly do you have to leave?" I kind of want to sit, but I'm afraid he may never wash his sheets. This *is* Luca we're talking about.

"Daria gets in tomorrow night."

"What?" I look down at the comforter. It appears stain free but I'm still skeptical so I continue to stand.

"Ben said he's been wanting to tell me but our paths didn't cross. He wrote it on the board today and then, bonus, I surprised him tonight." He sits down on the bed.

"And your plan is what?"

The bed looks kind of inviting. I shift my weight from leg to leg.

"Hunt?"

"What?" My tone is a little exasperated.

"Sit down." He pulls on the sleeve of my coat until my ass is on his bed. Right next to him. "Promise I wash my sheets every week."

I raise an eyebrow.

"Well, my ma does." He chuckles.

"And there's been no girls?"

"I don't bring them here. Could you imagine with Ben?"

I laugh because the guy seems so lonely, he'd probably talk to them through the door.

"Not exactly an aphrodisiac. But I have a feeling Ben isn't the reason you don't bring girls here."

He shrugs.

I need to get back on track and not think about the size of Luca's dick or how many girls he's slept with. "So where are you packing up to go?"

"Funny you should ask…"

"Nope." I shake my head and stand like I'm going to flee.

"Hear my argument out." His arms wrap around my body from behind to stop me from leaving.

"Luca get your arms off me!" I'm surrounded by his scent and I'm reminded again of how good it feels to be in his arms. And I *hate* that for some reason I like it.

He lifts me and I kick my legs. Somehow, he slides me around until I'm over his shoulder firefighter style.

I don't stand a chance.

He drops me on the bed, holding my arms down. I'm laughing at how ridiculous this is, but I have to stop and show him that I'm just as strong as he is. My legs flail, and I push my body off the bed.

"Are you going to listen if I let you go?"

He's right on top of me, his leg so close to my center I could grind against him and probably have an outstanding orgasm.

No, no, no. I do not *want Luca Bianco to give me an orgasm.*

Bad body.

"Maddie's putting the house up," he continues, still holding my arms down. "You can't afford to live there on your own. If I move in and we split the rent, you can stay."

I hate it when people I like to prove wrong make sense.

"I'm not living with you."

"Why?" He releases me now and I sit up pretending to rub my wrists.

Damn it, he is stronger than me.

"It's a big house. Separate bedrooms."

"Uh-huh," I say with zero enthusiasm.

"I'm never home. I'm gone all night every third day. Ask Ben, I'm clean and I only leave a mess at my brother's place and that's just to drive them crazy."

He cannot be serious.

"Luca," I sigh.

We haven't even talked about his mom and the fact that the surgery didn't go well or our fake engagement.

"People are going to ask us why we're engaged and you won't let me live with you."

"That's not my problem."

"Let's remember you needed something out of this arrangement, too."

"I needed one date to a Christmas party. You're asking for

people to believe we're living together. And not just as roommates."

I drop my head into my hands because the truth is, I don't want to move.

I did some looking last week and everything in my budget sucks ass. I'm living with a roommate no matter what. And the only two people I'd actually want to live with have left me to be with their significant others. If Luca moved in, we'd probably be able to hold Maddie off until spring on selling the house. She'd have the mortgage covered and be able to sell higher in the spring market, so, all in all, it would be better for her. Luca and I would have two bathrooms. No reason to have any embarrassing half naked run-ins.

Disappointment flares over that last point which should *not* be a con. Damn lady parts always chiming in with their own opinions.

"Please, Hunt." He falls to his knees in front of the bed, his hands clasped in prayer. "You won't even know I'm there. Promise."

I run my hands down my face. Bad idea. This is a very bad idea.

"No girls. No friends. And you must be fully clothed at all times."

He holds out his hand between us.

"No guys. No eating my junk food and feel free to walk around naked."

I shake my head while simultaneously shaking his hand.

I know I'm going to regret this.

"I'm an awesome roommate, Hunt. And this is perfect since we need to stay engaged until my mom and her doctors figure out what's going on."

Wait...what?

CHAPTER FIFTEEN

Lauren

"I can't believe you convinced me to do this." I open the door to a smiling Luca holding a box in his hands.

"Oh come on. Think of it this way, we can compete all hours of the day." He winks and walks in with the box.

"You're in Maddie's old room since she and Mauro took her bed."

He walks right up the stairs.

"Once you're moved in, shoes are off in the house!" I holler up to him.

"Got it, boss."

That humorous lilt is back in his voice after yesterday. Hopefully last night wasn't just a ploy to get me to agree to let him move in.

He walks back down the stairs like a teenager, two stairs at a time. Might as well just slide down the railing.

"We need to talk," I say as he passes me with his winning championship smile.

"I gotta get the truck back in an hour. Can we talk then?"

Two guys come in through the door with a mattress in their hands.

"Hey," a redhead as big as Luca says.

"You must be the wife," the second redhead says as he passes by.

Whoa, am I seeing double?

"No, you're not delusional. We're twins." The second one must notice my look of confusion.

"Up the stairs, first door on the left." I point them in the right direction.

"Thanks." They head upstairs while Luca follows right behind with another box.

"How much stuff do you have?" I ask.

He winks. "Not much. Don't worry."

For the next half hour, the three men are either used to moving or do it professionally because it's like a well-oiled machine. As I watch the parade of boxes, a dresser, mattress and box spring go upstairs, I never hear anyone bang anything against the wall. I'm impressed.

That is until the twins bring in a chair and drop it in the family room.

"All his stuff goes to his room." I pop a carrot into my mouth.

"Luca said to put it here." They stand on either side of the chair, obviously waiting for Luca to return.

"That monstrosity is not staying in here."

I'm not an interior designer, but that chair is gross and I'm afraid the foul smell in the room now isn't from these guys.

Luca walks in with a matching ottoman. "Thanks, guys." He drops it in front of the chair, placing his hands on his hips catching his breath, then smiles over at me.

"The lady of the house says the chair goes upstairs," one of the twins, whose name I haven't gotten says.

"She's wrong." Luca picks up the chair, walks through the opening of Maddie's two matching yellow chairs and drops it next to the couch.

Tweedle Dee follows with the ottoman.

"You said you had no furniture." I stare down at the ugliest piece of furniture I've ever seen.

"I forgot about the chair. Ben had already furnished his place before I moved in so I was letting a buddy borrow it." He plops down, practically sinking down to the floor because I have a feeling the springs aren't able to hold his weight properly. Both of his arms rest on the arms of the chair and he looks like a child in a big chair. He runs his hands up and down what looks to have been velvet fabric at one point. "I missed you old girl."

"Great. You talk to a chair. Maddie is going to have a conniption. Do you have any idea how long she stressed about the color scheme in here?"

"She doesn't live here anymore, what does she care." Luca continues to massage the chair like it's the legs of one of his one-night stands.

"I care when I agreed to this thing between us."

Luca's hands stop moving and he glances up to the two men smirking at our argument.

Fuck. They think he's moving in with his fiancée, too?

"I don't know Bianco, first you're sleeping in a different room and now she won't let you bring in one little chair." Tweedle Dee looks over at his brother. "We're definitely staying single for life."

Luca jumps from his seat. "I told you, the second room is a front for my ma. She doesn't want us living together before marriage."

He cuts me a look as he crosses the room to his friends. Is

that true? Is his mom not happy about us moving in together? I shake my head because why do I care? I'm not really engaged to him.

"Thanks a lot, guys. I gotta return the truck."

The twins wave and say it's nice to meet the woman who can tame Luca Bianco, referring to him by his full name like he's some rock star or something.

Whatever, I'm skeptical that there's a woman on this earth who could pull off that feat.

"I'll be right back and then we can have that chat. I was going to stop at the grocery store. Do you want to join me?"

I sit down on the couch, already thinking of plans for his chair and ottoman. "Nah, I'm good." I crunch down on another carrot.

He shrugs. "I take it this is mine." He swipes a key from the entryway table.

"Unfortunately, yes."

He smiles, looping it onto his keyring. Somehow that solidifies this deal to me. The key of a house I live in is now a fixture on his keyring. The same silver ring that holds Luca Bianco's car key, motorcycle key, and his locker key from the station.

Shivers run up my back. What have I done?

"Aw, we're gonna have fun, Hunt. You'll be begging me to stay."

Stay where? We'll probably both be escorted out by Cristian or one of his fellow officers because this place is about to become a war zone.

CHAPTER SIXTEEN

Luca

The truck is back at the rental place and I've done the grocery shopping to stock up on food at my new place. When I glanced in the fridge, it was all health food garbage.

I'm as excited as I was when I was ten and finally had enough money from my allowance and mowing my neighbor's lawn to buy Grand Theft Auto.

The thought of not going home to Ben lifts a weight off my shoulders I didn't realize was holding me down.

My phone rings and I click on the accept button thinking it's Hunt and she wants me to pick her up something. With my newfound happiness, I'd buy her a pound of carrots and a huge-ass tub of hummus to thank her and I wouldn't even comment about how she's missing out by eating bunny food.

"You're all moved?" Cristian asks me, the background noise telling me he's off shift and getting into his own car.

"Yeah."

"Good. I wanted to see if you needed help. Seems my timing was perfect."

I chuckle. "Nah, I got Timmy and Jimmy to help." I turn the corner to head down my new street. Oh crap, I meant to ask about the garage space, I hate parking my baby on the street.

"That must've been interesting. Timmy never shuts up and Jimmy doesn't say a word."

"Good thing they still have their twin language still going on at twenty-five."

Cristian chuckles and his engine starts. I wait for the sync to hook us up again.

"Zia's doing the dinner on Sunday. Are you off?"

I tap my fingers on the steering wheel. "I am. We have Lauren's Christmas party on Saturday so I took the day off."

"Great. Mauro is working so can you swing by and get Maddie? Mauro will meet us over there later."

"Sure."

"You know Zia does things differently than Ma, right?"

How could I forget? Zia is not your typical Italian woman. She might coddle her sons, but she expects them in the kitchen. To her credit, the Mancini boys all know how to cook whereas none of us do. I glance back to my boxes of mac and cheese and Hormel Chili cans. I'm one step above a Ramen-eating college student.

"Yeah, I know."

"Enzo said he'll handle the seafood. I figure I'll make the pasta. Do you think you can handle the sauce? I'm sure Zia will help you."

I hate how my brothers treat me like I'm ten years younger than them, like I can't tie my shoes or dress myself.

"I got it."

"Since when do you know how to make sauce?" He laughs, his blinker clicking in the background.

I park along the curb, idling until I can get in the house and make myself something to eat. All this newfound happiness is making me hungry.

"Since I used to help Mama."

Which is true but only so she could watch me. She'd act like she was letting me in on the secret family recipe but we both know it was so she could keep me out of trouble.

"Okay then. Don't act all offended."

I am, but I'm going to keep it to myself since we have enough going on. A tiff between me and my brother should be the least of Ma's worries right now.

"I got another piece of news." Cris's voice lowers.

We all have our responsibilities in this family. Cristian's is to give the bad news. I'm not sure when he drew that short straw, but times like this when I hear the strain in his voice, I know that Mauro and I put too much on his plate when it comes to family obligations. With Vanessa in the picture now he'll have to put her before us, which means the only one left to step up would be me. Which means I'm gonna have to buck up and stop running away from the hard moments like I did at the hospital.

"Okay." I turn off my car and hold my keys in my lap.

Better chance I won't run.

"They're waiting four months until they do the ablation on Ma again. They think she'll be okay and she'll continue to be monitored. Medication will be prescribed..."

I knew it wouldn't be immediate. Which is information I withheld from Lauren because if she knew this fake engagement was going to carry through until early spring, she might actually take a butcher knife and Lorena Bobbit me. But four months? Man. I didn't expect that.

"I'm sure the doctors know what they're doing. How is Ma with the news?"

"She's okay. She feels good right now. Said she has more energy."

"As long as she's okay then I am, too. I can't believe we have to wait so long." I tap my finger on the bottom of the steering wheel.

"Yeah I know but safety first. The doctors know more than us."

I really should've gone to get my doctorate and specialized in the heart.

"Thanks, Cris, for handling all that."

"Sure. Okay, I gotta go. I'm taking Van to some Broadway show she wanted to see."

"Whipped," I cough out.

"I think you need to look in the mirror. I just saw a picture on Lauren's Instagram with a big sign that says free on your ugly as fuck chair."

"No way!"

"Yep."

Click.

CHAPTER SEVENTEEN

Lauren

"*I* feel like I'm betraying bro code." Reed shuts the door to their garage.

The ugly chair is wedged between Victoria's car and Jade's bike.

"Nah. I'll give it back to him...eventually." I laugh. "Sorry to disturb your party though."

Reed glances through the windows of his back door to the table full of guests.

"Oh, believe me, I think the two other couples in there understand. They all had their share of enemies-to-lovers."

I narrow my eyes at my next door neighbor who also happens to be the city's assistant district attorney.

"It's not like that," I say.

"It's not? You're hiding a chair from the man."

In the distance, I hear Luca's car because his damn engine is so frickin' loud. My stomach flutters—not from butterflies —but from the exhilaration of pissing him off. It really is a sick addiction I have to pushing his limits.

"Sounds like he's back. You couldn't find a guy who drives a nice Honda?"

I laugh. "Sorry. It wasn't part of the interview process. You should meet him though."

"Why don't you two come over for dessert? We have a cake from that bakery down on the corner. Jade would love it. She's very bored with all the adults."

I mock offense. "I'm an adult, Reed."

He rolls back on his heels, his eyes shining with humor. "You're hiding a chair in my garage."

Reed has a point. I guess I am a tad immature when it comes to Luca. This constant strive to be one step ahead of him always wins out over maturity.

"You got me there. But Luca isn't Victoria."

Just then Luca yanks open the back door of our house and steps out onto the small wooden deck that leads to the stairs.

His eyes slice at me, but I don't care.

"HUNT!" He runs down the stairs.

"He's a firefighter?" Reed asks.

"Paramedic," I correct.

Luca does fill out his CFD jacket nicely though.

"Now I feel like I'm betraying the city and the Y chromosome. Fix this, Lauren."

"Victoria can soothe your ego later. Ready to meet your new neighbor?"

I step forward to the fence line, Reed's footsteps follow behind mine, though a little slower.

"Hey, Luca, meet your new neighbor."

Luca glances past me to Reed and then focuses back on me. Thinking better of going at me right away, or maybe he recognizes Reed, he puts his hand out over the waist-high fence. "Luca Bianco."

Reed steps up to my side, extending his hand. "Reed Warner."

Luca nods. "I thought so. I've seen you on the news. Nice to meet you."

"You as well." Reed's eyes veer to mine. "I was just telling Lauren that you two should come over for dessert."

Luca peers into the window seeing the table full of guests.

"Oh." He looks at me like we're a couple and it's my decision.

"We'll be there in a little bit, we just have to handle something first."

"Yeah, we do." Luca's eyes bore into the side of my head.

"Sounds good. Stop by whenever. Nice to meet you, Luca." Reed holds his hand out again and Luca shakes it. "If I was a shitty neighbor I'd tell you to get a quieter muffler."

Luca laughs understanding the point. "Sorry, but I will be storing her for the winter and my truck is quieter."

"Come spring?"

"I have a bike."

"How come I don't think you're talking about a bicycle?"

Luca laughs again. I've never witnessed him so willing to appease authority. Not that Reed is his boss or anything.

"You assume correctly."

"Shit, I'm old." Reed walks away, his fingers threading through his hair. Climbing the stairs up to his house, their dog Snowball follows him. The laughter from inside pours outside as he slides through the back door.

"Truck back?" I ask, walking down the side of Reed's fence to get into my yard.

"Where is it, Hunt?" Luca follows me down the other side of the fence line.

"Where's what?" I ask, opening the Warner gate, sliding around and through our gate.

"My chair. Don't act coy."

I walk by him, biting hard on the inside of my cheek so I don't smile. "I assume where you left it."

We stop outside the door and I turn the knob. It's locked.

"You locked us out?" I try the knob again but to no avail.

"No. You were out here first."

"I unlocked it."

He breezes by me, his hand moving to the knob.

"Do I not know how to open a door? Could you be any more condescending?"

"Well, Chandler I'm just checking." He barrels down the wooden stairs.

"Chandler?"

I follow because we have to find a way inside. Especially since I'm in a long sleeve tee and sweatpants.

"Could you be..." He does the imitation of the *Friends* character and if I wasn't so mad at him, I'd compliment his imitation.

I'm right on his heels as we walk along the side of the house to the front door.

"Let's hope you didn't lock the front door," I mutter.

I run my hands over my arms because now I know which way the wind is whipping today.

"Since I live in the city, I'm usually pretty conscious about the locking of my doors. We don't live in Pleasantville." He runs up the stairs two at a time because he has the longest legs ever and I do not. His way of telling me he's faster.

He tries the knob and his forehead falls to the door.

"Tell me you have a spare key somewhere?" he mumbles into the door.

"Yes. Cristian had us install an alarm system but said, 'hey be sure to put a key under the welcome mat.'" My hands do not warm up the shirt. What was supposed to be a quick trip to the Warner's garage has turned into hunker down and wait for... "Do you have your phone?"

"No. Everything is on the counter."

"Why would you not put it in your pocket?" I roll my eyes.

"Why did you go outside without unlocking the back door?" He shakes his head standing on the opposite side of the porch as me.

"It was you." I stick my neck out at him.

"Keep telling yourself that." He unzips his jacket, removes it, and holds it out to me.

"I'm fine."

"Just put the damn coat on."

When I refuse to take it, he tosses it at me and the heavy fabric lands on my head.

Either I freeze or he does. Better him than me since this is his fault. So, I put on the coat that makes me look like I'm five and wearing my dad's suit jacket. How embarrassing.

Now he's rubbing his hands on his strong biceps. His shirt that says, 'Sticks and Stones May Break my Bones but Lights and Sirens Excite Me.' It's gray and tight fitting along his more than defined torso.

His eyes land on mine, focusing on my lips.

"I'm sure there are no windows unlocked. I could break a window or try to get through the basement, but..." He leans over to look down below the stairway.

God, his ass. Give me a quarter.

I suck in the drool from my mouth when he turns back around.

"I'd have to break that, too."

"Maddie might kill us," I say through chattering teeth.

His coat offers shelter, but the wind is still whipping up from the bottom.

His teeth bite down on his bottom lip, looking me over. His hands slide into the pockets of his jeans but then back out and his contrite expression suggests he's going to offer up a solution he's fearful of verbalizing.

"Just say it." I roll my eyes.

"I was gonna suggest body heat exchange because you're already shivering…"

"Jeez, so nice of you."

"I am nice Hunt, you just fail to recognize it."

"Nice like when you called me a boy for three years in high school. Made comments about my non-existent chest and told Cody he should break up with me every Friday."

He blows out a breath. "That's high school shit. Every guy is a dick in high school because we're immature and can't handle our feelings."

I laugh. "Oh but you can handle them now?"

He sits on the ledge of the porch, holding his arms open to me. "I promise I won't cop a feel."

I stare blankly at him. Very bad idea. I drooled over his body not even a minute ago.

"This is only for the sake of survival," I mutter as I take a tentative step toward him.

With each step closer, my body hums. Right as his arms wrap around me, my mind loses the war to my body because I sink into him.

He's so warm. So strong. I might just stay here forever.

"Now my whole plan is out the window," I mumble.

"You have a plan?" he asks, resting his chin on top of my head.

"Your chair. I was going to make you play me for it to stay."

His chest vibrates under my cheek. "Hunt, you're not like any chick I know."

My fist punches in him the stomach, but it only spurs his laughter to deepen.

"I didn't mean it in a bad way. Thanks for not giving it away on Instagram."

I tilt my chin up. "You follow me?"

"Cris," he corrects.

I nod.

Of course he doesn't.

We're not friends.

"Expect that to change though. I don't want to find my boxers on there."

I shake my head. "You are so arrogant. As if someone would buy your boxers."

"I'm a hot commodity if you didn't know."

All I know is that it's too bad we ever started in on this hate/hate relationship before I figured out that Luca Bianco isn't all that bad of a guy.

"And I'm just a tomboy."

He doesn't say anything and I'd wish I could hear his thoughts. Does he feel this between us? This shift over the past week? Can he explain it because I can't.

"Where is my chair anyway?" he whispers, his arms holding me tighter.

I tilt my head up and there's his chin—a day's worth of stubble and his strong jaw, begging me to place my lips there. Just once to see if this zing coursing through my body has room to grow.

"Reed!" I exclaim, breaking apart from his arms. "We'll use Reed's phone to call Maddie. Shit. I don't think I know her number. I usually just hit the button on my phone."

He jumps down from the porch and takes my hand in his. "I know Cris's. Let's go."

As happy as I am that the Warners have heat and a phone while we wait to get us back into the house, I kind of liked being with Luca just then.

I'm losing it because even if I did like Luca, I'm far from his type. He didn't argue when I called myself tomboy. It's obviously how he still sees me.

CHAPTER EIGHTEEN

Luca

I'm in the kitchen eating some chips when I hear heels click along the stairs. I fold up the bag, wash my hands and dry them, moving to grab my coat off the chair.

After tonight, half my obligation to this agreement is over. Of course, I haven't broken the news to Lauren yet about my mom. Since she hasn't mentioned it, I'm guessing the girls haven't talked about it either.

Then again, I was on shift and since another fucking arson fire hit a warehouse, I ended up working late. We missed each other for two days in a row due to our schedules. I started following her on Instagram because I missed her snarkiness. What is this world coming to?

"Luca?" she calls out from the foyer.

"I'm here." I walk out of the kitchen and my coat falls from my fingertips when I cast my eyes on my fake fiancée.

Lauren's in a green dress that molds to every curve. The neck is high, giving no glimpse at her cleavage, but her curves are still visible. The length is short enough that her legs look longer than they do in her usual yoga pants. She's gorgeous, stunning really, and I bite my tongue because I'm pretty sure it's about to flop out of my mouth like a damn Bulldog in front of a steak.

"Nice dress," I mumble, picking up my coat and placing it on the chair.

"Thank you. You look nice. I know you don't usually dress up so...thank you."

I take her coat from her arm and hold it out for her.

"I'm not a caveman."

Her arms slide into the sleeves and in this moment I wish she was mine to kiss or to hold. The usual scent of her perfume is stronger and more intense when I'm this close to her.

"Thank you," she says softly.

Step back, Luca.

You're making this weird.

For the life of me though, I can't move back. If anything I want to wrap my arms around her and pull her toward me so she can feel my response to her.

Tomboy my ass. I've kicked myself for not correcting her earlier this week. I should've said there's nothing tomboy about her, but my damn fears kept me quiet.

"Sorry." I back up and she circles around, a smile on her lips.

Can she hear my inner thoughts?

"Can we call a truce for tonight?" she asks.

The girl who hid my chair wants a truce. Interesting.

"Did you think I was going to call you out on the dance floor?"

Lauren would do it. She'd be the one to call me up for a dance-off.

"No. I just...work has been difficult this week and Peter is going to be watching everything between us. We have to be believable, you know?" She tucks her purse under her arm.

"Hey, you've been a great fiancée when it comes to my mom. I promise to be the same."

She looks up through her long, thick eyelashes. "Thank you."

I quickly get into my own coat and find my keys because we need to get out of this quiet house where no one would be the wiser if we ripped each other's clothes off.

"You're welcome. After you, Ms. Hunt." I hold out my arm and she walks toward the front door.

Damn, I thought this would be some boring Christmas party with crappy buffet food and cheap booze. That Lauren would want to leave early and I'd happily agree, then head to the club, but I'm kind of hoping she wants to stay until the waitstaff is watching us dance to the last song.

What the hell has happened to me?

———

For a small company, they sure know how to put a party together. There's a photo booth, a DJ plus a live orchestra during dinner. It's held in what used to be an old theater down on State, so, we're essentially having dinner among thousands of open seats all around us, colosseum style, like we're on the fifty-yard line of a football field. There are trees with white lights and the chandeliers are dimmed to a warm yellow glow.

Lauren's gasp when we walked in suggests they don't usually do things this elaborate.

"It's a great place." I take her coat off, handing it to the coat check attendant.

My eyes fall to the back of her dress. Primarily the

amount of skin revealed. One dip of my hand and I'd be squeezing her ass.

Is she doing this to me on purpose? Could she tell the other day outside the house, how fast my heart was beating while I held her?

The coat check attendant hands me a number and I stuff it into my pocket, my hand moving to Lauren's lower back and almost touching her skin to let her know we're ready. Thankfully, my mind is still working, but pretty soon my dick is going to steal the wheel away.

"Want a drink?"

She smiles. "Sure. Just a white wine."

"I'll be right back."

Again my hand moves toward her and I'd normally lean in and kiss her on the cheek. If she was mine, which she's not. But she wants people to believe she is. I should clarify with her what her expectations are for tonight.

The bar area is surrounded by small clusters of people who obviously know each other. A few faces do a double take, probably to try and figure out who I belong to. Most significant others would know small tidbits about the people their girlfriend, or in my case fiancée, work with. I've got the receptionist I met last week as well as a guy I saw in the doorway. That's about it.

The bartender puts out a napkin in front of me.

"White wine and a soda and lime."

He fills my order and since it's open bar, I tip him a generous amount. I'm sure I'll be back and this will ensure I get prompt service every time.

No one approaches me on the way back to Lauren. Thank God. When I find her, she's laughing with another couple. She looks good happy and it's rare to see her like this when I'm in the room.

"Here you go." I hand her the drink and stay close to her

but not on top of her like I want to make sure everyone within a fifty-foot radius knows she's mine.

Since she doesn't step away, I figure she's happy with where I am.

"Luca, this is Katie and her husband, Craig."

I shake each of their hands.

"And you're the fiancé we've heard so little about." Katie glances to Lauren with a raised brow.

"That I am."

"Lauren has been keeping us in the dark," Katie says.

Craig shoots me a small smile.

"You know Hun...Lauren."

The fact is I don't know Lauren that well so I leave it open-ended with the hopes that Katie will fill me in. Does Lauren talk about the guys she dates? Does she share if she slept with him or not with her co-workers?

"Yeah, we know. She's a bore come Monday morning." Katie pretends to yawn with her hand over her mouth.

"Are you suggesting that Lauren knows too much about me?" Craig asks his wife with his eyebrows raised.

"No." She swats him, but even though I just met her a minute ago, I would say yes. Lauren probably knows Craig's dick size.

"How about those Blackhawks?" Craig ignores his wife and concentrates on me.

Obviously, he doesn't know Lauren too well.

"Luca's got season tickets. We went recently," Lauren says. "Kane is so impressive."

I smile down at Lauren and wrap my arm around her waist because she's fucking fantastic. Who wouldn't want a knock-out who can talk sports?

"Damn and it was a close one." Craig sips his beer. "Do you ever sell?"

I shrug. "Sometimes. My buddies and I work weird shifts so if none of us can go, we sell."

He digs into the inside of his suit jacket, handing me a card. "Call me." He looks at his wife. "Wouldn't you love to go?"

She shrugs and tries to talk to Lauren about her shopping trip to find a dress for tonight.

Using my awesome male multitasking skills, I nod while Craig goes on and on about his paper business while eaves-dropping on Lauren and Katie's conversation. Does Lauren like to talk about girl things like clothes and makeup? I would've said no back in high school.

"Mine is from Nordstrom Rack. My friends and I do a Cheapster Challenge and I found it for forty dollars at the end of last year. I've eaten more carrots than Bugs Bunny to fit into it, but I really like it."

"Me, too," I lean in and whisper, but I must be too loud.

"You're a keeper." Katie points her long manicured nail at me.

Lauren's conflicted gaze takes me in. I'm pretty sure there's a whole world peace problem behind those eyes that I'd never solve. I can read body language and the flush quickly rising up her chest and face means she liked the compliment. Though knowing her, she hates that she liked it.

"I wouldn't win that challenge because I paid too much for this thing." Katie raises her hand to block her mouth and moves into Lauren, whispering the price I assume.

However much it cost, Lauren's eyes widen and she shakes her head. "The benefit of being married to a CEO," Lauren smiles. "That's my housing budget."

Since I pay the same rent Lauren does, I figure out the cost of the dress and I can't believe women spend that much on something they might only wear once.

"Are you guys hiding out?" The guy I saw behind the door at Lauren's office walks up. Alone.

"Peter," Katie says, giving him a quick wave.

So, this is that shit stain Peter who doesn't know that you shouldn't hit on your employee.

He and Craig ask how the other has been and shake hands.

"Hey, Peter," Lauren says in the quietest voice I've ever heard come out of her mouth.

"You both look spectacular." His words are for both women, but his gaze remains on Lauren.

Both women mumble their thanks.

"Hi. I'm Luca. Lauren's fiancé." I put my hand out in between us and then tighten my hand on Lauren's hip, making sure there's no distance between us.

If we're going to play the part, we're not going to act like we're ashamed because Peter has a crush. Something he shouldn't have made known to Lauren given the fact that he's her boss.

Lauren's body kind of stumbles into me which is good because it enables me to show my strength by steading her with one hand.

"Nice to meet you. I'd say I knew something about you, but Lauren never mentioned you until that delivery last week."

"Are you ashamed of me?" I look down at Lauren with a smile on my face. Like it's a joke.

She might very well be embarrassed if we were a thing.

"No." She shakes her head but keeps it down.

"The candy is a running joke. We went to high school together and every day after school, Lauren would put a few quarters in the Brach mix thing. Remember those?"

"I do! I was a Neapolitan girl." Katie high fives Lauren.

"Lauren loved the Royals and she'd always buy them, put

them in her pocket and eat them the entire time we all hung out. I think she used to sweat them out because I can't smell vanilla and caramel without thinking of her."

I look down like a loving fiancé would, but I'm caught off guard by the emotion in Lauren's eyes. They question if I'm telling the truth or not, but she can't ask in front of everyone right now.

I lean down and kiss her cheek, but my lips linger. "Yes," I whisper in her ear.

Her body dips, but I keep her up using my arm as leverage.

Maybe I should've kept that to myself.

"So you've been dating since high school?" Katie asks.

"No. Lauren never gave me the time of day in high school. She was in love with my best friend."

"No, I wasn't." She bumps me with her hip.

As an outsider, it seemed that he was her first love. "We kind of ran into each other more recently and she finally agreed to go on a date with me."

"Aw. So you've liked her since high school?"

I shrug. Lauren glances up at me, more question marks popping out of her eyes.

I didn't intend on her ever finding out. I figured it'd be good to convince people if I stuck close to the truth. Now I'm starting to regret heading down this path. But there's no U-turn to be had so I speak the truth again.

"Yeah. Ever since the first time I saw her."

I feel Lauren tense under my arm.

"And when was that?" Katie leans in thinking this is *The Notebook* and I'm about to tell her some epic love story. If she only knew the truth. That I made sure Lauren Hunt hated my guts because it was the only way to be sure I wouldn't betray my best friend.

"On a soccer field. She had just scored a goal and all of the guys looked over to see what the commotion was. Lauren was jumping around into her teammates' arms."

"Wasn't she sweaty and..."

"Katie!" Lauren sighs.

"That's what I loved about her. She didn't care to be prissy and look put together like most of the other high school girls. She was herself, screw anyone who didn't like it. We've been competing with one another ever since." I smile down at her and Lauren's lips turn soft, tipping just a little bit at the corners.

I don't blame her, I'd be just as confused if she just laid her hand out in front of me.

I'm not even sure what made me do it.

Peter clears his throat. "What do you do for a living?" he asks, interrupting my appreciation of an embarrassed Lauren. Her flushed cheeks make my insides thump with a reason to go all dragon slayer on her.

"Paramedic," I answer, but my attention stays on Lauren.

"Excuse us." She takes my hand in hers, dragging us away.

"Oh someone is getting some coatroom head," Craig says as we depart.

Man, I should have gone into acting.

CHAPTER NINETEEN

Lauren

 I drag Luca into a back room, tucked away from any spying eyes, needing answers to my questions.

"Is Craig right?" Luca holds out his arms, like I'm about to drop to my knees and suck him off.

"Forget it." I spin on my heel to head back to the door.

What was I thinking? That he was making some deep confession out there in front of my colleagues? It was all a fucking act. Of course it was. I should've known he'd lay it on thick tonight.

"Hey." His hand cups my elbow and without the added barrier of fabric my pulse surges.

Slowly, turning around, I try to avoid eye contact.

"Isn't this what you wanted?" He dips his head while lifting mine with his thumb and forefinger. "They all think we're fucking in here. Your boss will never ask you out again."

"Yeah. Sure. It's just...those things you said?" I form as a question because I'm a chicken shit and I want him to take the ball I'm passing him and run with it.

"It's not exactly confidential information about you and the Royal candy." He shrugs.

My chest squeezes painfully, but I nod and smile, though he doesn't. Which means I'm doing a shitty job of convincing him that was the answer I was hoping for.

"Yeah. I mean you always got a Red Bull and Mike and Ike's." I do my best to keep my voice light.

"The question is, which flavor?" He winks and the fact that I know the answer proves Luca's point. We know each other and we can use that to our advantage for this stupid fake relationship.

"Red. All red," I say with little enthusiasm.

He smiles and nods. "See?"

"Yeah. Sorry for freaking out there."

"No way, you made it seem like you couldn't wait to rip off my clothes." He chuckles, finally letting go of my elbow and stepping away from me.

Why is my body left with a cold chill running down my spine?

"True."

"Want to mess up your hair and makeup a little bit to give the full effect?"

I push him and he pretends to lose his balance.

"Come on, soon-to-be Mrs. Bianco, let's go back out there and finish this so no one questions our undying devotion to one another."

He holds his arm out and I slide mine through the opening. As we exit the small room, the pit of my stomach sours because the small hope I had that I wasn't alone in this attraction has been stomped on.

I've tried to deny it, but ever since we were locked out, it's been Luca on my mind when I'm lying in bed alone.

What was I thinking? We may not hate each other

anymore, but we'd never work out. Especially when only one of us feels like a dog in heat.

———

The waiters clear our dishes and I sit back, letting Luca win everyone over at our table. Surprisingly it's not with stories of his running beer pong championships and little black book starring system.

"Tell us your craziest case." Cindy leans forward, her chin in both her palms.

Luca leans back, his hand finding my thigh.

That's the third time he's done that move.

It's the third time I've noticed Peter's eyes focus on the movement.

It's the third time a wave of heat pooled between my legs.

"You know I can't. HIPPA." Luca shrugs.

Cindy laughs, tilting her head in a flirtatious way like she'd go home with him.

"But I can tell you about crap that goes on in the station."

Cindy perks up again.

Peter stands from the table. "I'm getting a refill. Anyone?"

He smiles, but everyone declines, way more interested in the real-life drama Luca is about to fill them in with.

With Peter's departure, Luca's hand leaves my thigh and that little puddle of heat chills colder than a milkshake.

"Just kidding. Can't tell you that either." He chuckles and everyone else does, too.

"Now if you want stories about my brothers, I'm more than willing to throw those out."

"Your brother is a firefighter?" Katie asks. I've mentioned Maddie and Mauro to her in the past.

"Yeah, and my other brother is a police officer."

"And they're with your best friends, right Lauren?" Katie points to me.

I pick up my glass and sip my wine, mostly to disguise any hint my expression might give away.

"How perfect, right?" Luca glances over at me. "We're having a charade tournament in a few weeks."

"What?" I ask.

"Christmas. Couples against couples." In my mind, this little charade would be up by then, but I say nothing.

"That has to be fun. Lauren can get a little serious with competition. We had this company picnic last year and you'd think she had military training by the way she played paintball." Craig is the one to chime in with his little all-about-Lauren factoid.

Luca chuckles, his dark, sparkling eyes landing on mine once again. To others, it probably looks like we're having our own special conversation without words. The table probably believes Luca's saying, 'you're the love of my life' when in reality he's saying, 'you couldn't even taper down your competitiveness for the company picnic.'

"Our son came screaming out saying she wouldn't stop," Craig says.

"That's an exaggeration," I sigh, sipping my wine again.

Luca smirks over at me and we share the same thought. "She's competitive, but so am I, so you should all hope I'm on shift for next year's company picnic."

Peter returns with another beer just as the table breaks out into a fit of laughter. He sits down with a sour look on his face.

"That's why we were so surprised she didn't sign up," Cindy says.

"Sign up for what?" Luca's hand lands on my leg again. Convenient just as Peter returns. It's scary how good of an actor Luca is.

"The talent show," Cindy says with a tone that screams, 'duh.'

Just as the words come out of Katie's mouth, the lights dim and the owners, Ollie and Reba, hold hands as they shuffle across the floor to the microphone.

Luca leans back, turning to me. "Talent show?" he whispers.

I nod, more intrigued with my drink than anything else. The bubbly feeling taking over my blood is nice.

"And you didn't sign up?" he asks.

I shrug. "It's a couple thing."

He waves his finger between the two of us. "Which we are."

Ollie clears his throat but Reba whispers something to him and they laugh which spurs more chuckles and giggles from the audience. They are the cutest couple. Rumor has it that Reba comes from old-school money and Ollie was the son of her family's landscaper. They fell in love and the rest is history.

Luca nudges me with his thigh, disturbing me from my thoughts.

"What?" I mouth.

"Why didn't you sign up?" He leans closer, moving his hand off my thigh and around my shoulders for the sole intent on whispering in my ear.

"I told you. It's a couple thing."

Katie glances over at us but thankfully shifts her attention back to Ollie and Reba.

His hand reaches over and fiddles with my ring, then he shoots me a look to say once more we are a couple.

"You had a lot on your plate and..."

"What? You're crazy. I feel like I don't even know you right now."

While everyone's eyes are poised and attentive on Ollie and Reba, Luca's are on me.

I shift in my seat, circling my neck. What does he want from me? This whole thing between us has been a whirlwind and I wouldn't have thought he'd be interested in a stupid talent show for my work.

"Let's begin with Jenny from accounting and her husband, Rich," Ollie says before he and Reba return to their table.

The lights dim further and spotlights shine where Ollie and Reba just stood.

"Come on." Luca stands and holds out his hand.

"No," I whisper-shout.

He holds his hand out again.

"I'll cover for you." Katie elbows me and winks like we're about to go screw in the coatroom again. Little does she know.

Then I spot Peter's eyes on us so I take Luca's offered hand and he leads me out of the room.

Once we're out, he turns around, digging into his pocket. "So, what are we going to do?"

I crinkle my eyes. "Nothing. I told you it was voluntary and I didn't sign up. Why am I repeating myself?"

My attention moves to the bar that's now closed because everyone is getting their drinks inside. Great.

"Since when don't you want to win? Come on. Let's see. Can you sing? Dance? Juggle?"

"Yes, I juggle flamethrowers on the weekends," I deadpan, not in the mood for any of this. I should've come by myself.

"Oh, I have a soccer ball in my trunk."

I raise my eyebrows. Is he not listening to me at all?

"What on earth are we going to do with a soccer ball?"

He winks and makes this clicking sound with his mouth. "What we do best...compete."

Before I can stop him, he's out the front of the complex, heading to his car in the parking garage.

Great. I'm thinking Cher wouldn't have been that bad now.

"Oh, sorry." Peter steps out of the room, a new beer in his hand.

"It's okay. How are you doing?" I keep my voice light, trying not to make this any more awkward than it feels.

"Fine. Luca seems to be winning everyone over." He sips his beer, or chugs it would be a more apt description.

"He has that personality, you know?" I shift my weight from one high heel to another, resulting in crossing my legs and holding my clutch in both hands in front of me.

"Obviously that's what made you fall in love with him."

I shrug, not wanting to lie any more than I have to. "He's like one of those people you either love or hate."

He chuckles. "Sounds about right."

A cool breeze hits my face and my attention shifts off Peter to Luca standing in the doorway. The soccer ball is tucked under his arm and his eyes shift between me and Peter like an overprotective boyfriend.

"Pete," he says, breaking the distance between us, switching the soccer ball into his other arm as he secures himself next to me.

"Peter," Peter clarifies.

"You don't like Pete?" Luca asks.

"No. I prefer Peter."

"Peter it is."

"I was just telling Lauren how much everyone seems to love you."

Luca huffs a little but does smile. "I have that effect on people."

The two men stand there, eyes set on the other and I wonder if this was the old West would we be in some gunslinging standoff. As much as I hate to admit, I know who would win. The wild man Luca Bianco and then he'd leave me for some new girl with big breasts who was breezing through town.

"What's with the ball?" Peter asks, pointing to it with the tip of his beer.

Luca removes his arm from around me, spinning the ball on his finger. "Our talent."

"Spinning a ball?" Peter laughs and although the outside door is closed, that chill reappears in the small area.

Luca takes two hands and pretends to throw it at Peter, but catches it. Peter flinches. "Wanna try it?"

"Luca." I sigh because that was some macho high school asshole bullshit.

"Well, Cindy and I have a pretty good number," Peter says and I look to him through the side of my eyes.

Maybe Peter wasn't blind to Cindy's flirtatious touches after all.

"Care to wager who wins?"

I pull on Luca's arm. "This isn't for anything other than a gift card to Chili's." I look to Peter. "Good luck."

Peter nods, his eyes on Luca.

Seriously?

Thankfully Peter heads back into the main room which allows me to openly glare at Luca.

"What the hell was that about?"

CHAPTER TWENTY

Luca

I'm used to getting a reaction out of Lauren similar to the glare she's shooting me right now. One that suggests she'd like to jump on top of me and rip my tongue out.

"What? I hate guys who try to act like they're not attempting to steal another guy's woman away."

She circles her finger up in the air. "There are so many things wrong with that sentence."

"Don't even deny it. He's been scowling at me all night. He's got it bad for you."

She rolls her eyes. Something else I'm used to.

"Do I have to remind you that the reason we agreed to this..." her voice lowers her gaze shooting around the room, "is so he knows I'm taken. You don't have to go all caveman and high school jock on him. I want to keep my job."

I laugh. Does she not know me at all? We went to the same school, right? I was friends with everyone no matter if they were into sports or the marching band.

"I thought you'd like if I acted protective. It comes off as real."

My sentence is half bullshit. I'm not really a guy who acts overly protective of the girl he's with. Actually, that might be because I've never had a serious relationship before. Or I never cared enough? Damn, that's way too heavy of a subject to dig into tonight. The only thing I know for certain is when I walked into the venue and I saw Peter out here with Lauren I was pissed.

I should apologize, but I'm not going to.

"Whatever. Just don't do it again and another thing. I'm not your woman."

I chuckle, swinging my arm around her shoulders. I really need to stop the touchy-feely shit, but I can't seem to. My hands just reach out for her all on their own. Before I even realize it, I'm touching her soft skin again. I wanted to kick Peter in the shin when he left the table earlier because with him gone there was no excuse for me to touch her.

I'm actually surprised I still have my hand, and that Lauren didn't stab it with a fork.

"Let's go win this thing," I say and squeeze her into my side.

"Again, it's a Chili's gift card," she deadpans.

I let go of her and walk backward toward the door, messing around with the soccer ball. "What happened to the girl who does it just for the win? Why are you so resistant?" I stop and wait for her to respond.

"This is where I work and you know competition makes me a tad crazy. You see the way they're all talking about the company picnic."

Damn, this is a first.

"Hunt." I step forward, my hand moving up to her face but I clench it in a fist and bring it to my side before I tuck that strand of hair behind her ear and nudge her chin to look me in the eyes. Every word is on the tip of my tongue, ready to reassure her that she's perfect the way she is—hyper-competitiveness and all. But this is all an act and when the curtain falls, I don't want things to be awkward between us.

She shakes her head. "Forget it. Let's just do this." She barrels past me and her hand is on the door when it springs open from the other side and she flies backward.

The soccer ball drops and I'm rewarded with her small frame falling into my chest.

A couple comes out the doors, laughing with each other. They're both drunk and their hands can't stop touching one another. They don't seem to have noticed that without me here, Lauren would've fallen flat on the floor.

Lauren sighs and I urge her to her feet, my hands resting on her hips. "You okay?"

She squiggles out of my arms. "I'm good. Thanks."

Then she's opening the door and stepping through while I'm still processing how good she felt pressed up against me. If she was mine, I would be doing exactly what those two people are doing down the hall.

"A soccer ball?" Cindy asks when we reach the table. "Kinky."

I take off my jacket and roll my shirt up to my elbows. Lauren's gaze is on my movements the entire time.

"You think everything is kinky," Katie says in a snarky way.

Just as the current act of Danny and Sandy from *Grease* singing the song from the end of the movie finishes up, the owner comes by. He nods his head in a hello to everyone at the table.

I stand up to introduce myself. "Hi, Mr. Garfield, I'm Luca Bianco, Lauren's fiancé."

The man stares down at my hand.

"Luca." Lauren's hand is on my arm, and she's standing

next to me now. "Hello, Mr. Garfield." She lowers her head to him.

What is this? Some bowing thing?

"Now Lauren, you know it's Ollie." He pats me on the arm. "Nice to meet you. You got one of the good ones with Lauren. She's a real pistol. Did she tell you about the company picnic last year?"

A low grumble falls from Lauren's lips.

Since the guy isn't going to shake my hand, I use it to once again to touch Lauren.

"I heard a little about it. What can I say? She's got drive. No competition, no progress, am I right?"

He smiles and nods his head. "True enough. I'd say you got lucky too, Lauren."

She saddles up to me a little tighter. "I did."

Our eyes lock and I lose sight for a moment that this is all an act. Her love-drunk eyes aren't for me, they're for the benefit of everyone at the table. I blink and we both see that Ollie has moved on to the other people at the table.

"Oh and before I leave you all, you should know that there's an extra bonus if you win the talent show," Ollie says.

I want to rub my hands together and say give it to me because although I'm a huge fan of Chili's chips and salsa, a little more might put me into overdrive.

"What is it, Ollie?" Cindy asks, her hand moving forward to the man but she retracts it fast.

What the hell is up here?

"We're giving away a weekend trip to a cabin in Wisconsin."

"Your cabin?" Cindy's eyes gleam with amazement.

He nods. "Yes. Hummingbird Cove."

Cindy smacks her hand on the table. "You're kidding me, Ollie. Why wasn't this mentioned earlier? I would have prac-ticed more."

The whole table laughs.

"You should've done your best either way." He eyes her like a stern father.

She looks into her almost empty drink like a disciplined child.

"Good luck to you all. I must say Reba and I were disappointed to see your name missing from the list, Lauren."

"Well—"

"We want to sign up. It's not too late right?" I interject earning a glare from Lauren.

A big smile appears on Ollie's face, the wrinkles around his eyes creasing farther.

"Not at all. There are some props by the stage just in case anyone changed their mind. I can't wait to tell Reba."

"When did Lauren turn into Beyoncé?" Cindy asks. "And how come she doesn't get the stern father act about not putting herself out there and facing her fears."

"Fears?" Lauren asks.

"Stage fright," Cindy says like she's sure that's the reason for Lauren not signing.

I might not know inside out, but there's no way she has stage fright. She thrives on anything that puts her in the spotlight.

She tugs on my arm. "Let's go figure out what we're going to do. Thanks for letting us jump in on the fun, Mr. ...Ollie I mean."

"I can't wait to see what the two of you cook up." His eyes zero in on the spinning soccer ball on my finger.

"Me, too." Lauren leans to touch his arm but retracts quickly, ushering me forward with her head.

By the time we reach the side of the stage, one couple is getting ready to tap dance. Their shoes clicking on the floor in preparation.

"What's with the not touching your boss thing?"

"Germaphobe." Lauren digs through a bin of costumes. "I can't believe you have me doing this."

"We're not going out there as clowns."

"Then what are we doing?" She throws her arms up in the air and I've never seen her so unnerved. Makes me wish I could take her into a back room and unwind her a little.

"We're doing what we do best." I take the soccer ball, sliding it up my arm, behind my neck and back down my other arm. It falls off. Fuck I'm out of practice.

"We're going to go out there and fight?" She crosses her arms over her chest and cocks a hip.

I laugh, trying the trick again. "No, we're going to do some awesome trick shots." After finally getting the motion right with the ball, I bounce it on my knee like in the movie Karate Kid.

"No one is going to be impressed with that unless Ralph Macchio is up on stage."

"Ye of little faith." I kick it up and to her. She immediately reacts like I knew she would. "I doubt any of those people could do what we do."

Since Lauren has the ball, I scour another bin. Another twosome of women are head deep in the costume bin while Lauren chats with them. I don't know what this Hummingbird Cove place is, but it seems to have gotten a fire under everyone's ass.

I pull out a hula hoop and a kid's basketball net then dump out all the contents from the box. "I'll be back." I venture around the hallway and other rooms, scrounging up everything I can find to make sure we win this.

When I return to the side of the stage, Lauren's dress is inched up her legs, her heels are kicked off and she's practicing her tricks. It's scary how well I know her when I actually don't.

"What's all that?" She kicks the ball up and if she wasn't

so fast, I might have caught a glimpse. As much as I love seeing her toned olive skinned legs, I can't in good faith allow her to go to the stage. Especially with Peter there.

"You're going to have to put on some pants."

She looks down, the ball dribbles away and she pulls the hem of her dress down again.

"Yeah, maybe this wasn't the brightest idea."

"No, we just need to find you some pants."

I dig through the costume bin, finding a pair of pink spandex that might be from the Jane Fonda era.

"Seriously?" she asks, holding them up in the air.

"Either that or everyone sees your bearded taco."

Her eyes narrow. "What did you just call it?"

"Sorry, are you shaved bare? Just a taco then?" I laugh, but she doesn't see the humor because she continues to scowl at me. "Fine. Your flower." I roll my eyes a little.

She puts on the pink spandex, and maybe I should've picked the overalls because it's like a second skin. Her dress is wrapped around her waist now and please Jesus. No. She circles around to pick up the ball, bending over. My meat is all about sliding into that taco shell all of a sudden.

"Lauren," I bite out, my eyes refusing to look away.

"What?" she says, picking the ball up. "You know I've decided that if you're not going to change up that saying for my vagina than I'm going to refer to yours as small fry."

"There's nothing small about me." I want to jut out my hips, so she can see exactly how big my Beefeater fry is growing right now.

"Please," she drones. "Never heard that one before." Her eyes roll into the back of her head.

"Oh good, you guys are here." A woman approaches with a clipboard. "You're next."

"Next? We just signed up." Lauren's face pales.

"Sorry, we did a random draw." The young blonde shrugs.

"We're good. Thanks."

The girl smiles at me before turning to leave.

"How can we be good?" Lauren whispers, trying not to disturb the couple who are out there doing a comedy act.

"I just have to set up. This is nothing you haven't done before. We're going to kick the soccer ball off obstacles and into a box. A net would've been better, but we can make do. Between both of us, we can totally impress everyone. I figure you bounce the ball off your head and I'll pick it up with my feet. We'll try to never use our hands. I'm telling you no two people would be more perfect to pull this off."

I approach her, taking her hands in mine. She needs to trust me and that's not easy for Lauren to do. I get it because it's not easy for me to trust someone else either. We're both way too used to being the dominant person. Both of us were captains of our teams in high school. We both like the attention on us. We're so similar it's probably another reason we'd be horrible together if we were a real couple.

"Well, other than Mia Hamm and Lionel Messi. Yeah, I guess we're second best." She shakes her head like I've been smoking crack and am currently hallucinating.

"Just trust me."

"Trust you?" she asks, her hands limp in mine.

"I promise I won't fail you." The words come out with so much conviction that it feels like I'm talking about more than just the talent show.

The comedy couple comes off stage and wish us luck. Lauren's gaze shoots to the stage and back to me.

Eventually, she nods. "Let's do this."

CHAPTER TWENTY-ONE

Lauren

*L*uca is insane.

He rushes out to the stage setting all the obstacles up while I stand to the side, biting the inside of my cheek. I stare down at my crazy outfit of pink eighties workout spandex and my green dress around my waist. How did I allow him to convince me to do this?

"And now our very own Lauren Hunt with her fiancé Luca Bianco." Sam introduces us, her sweet voice almost putting me at ease.

I meet Luca in the middle of the stage and like everything in his life he takes our talent by the horns thinking he's brilliant. His hand on the microphone, he waits for me, which is a tad surprising. Everything I know about Luca says the spotlight is where he loves to be.

"Before we begin I'm going to give you a little backstory about me and my gorgeous fiancé."

A few laughs echo through the crowd when they see my outfit. Katie and Cindy's cackles float up to the stage. I can't blame them I'd be doing the same if I was down there and one of them were up here in some ridiculous outfit.

"I've known this woman since she was just a girl. From the first moment I saw Lauren, it was clear that she was the female version of me. We thrive on competition and winning. Yeah, yeah, I know what people say, but I think in both our minds, there's no such thing as second place. You either win or lose." He looks over to me with an 'am I right expression?'

I nod.

He smiles, holding out his hand for me to come a little closer.

I do, and a million pulses of electricity skitter over my skin when we come into contact.

"I know in this day and age there are participation medals and everyone's a winner, but we don't play by those rules. We both played soccer in high school. Each of us was the captain of our teams. We were enemies in every sense of the word. If I wasn't raised by a great Italian Mama, I would've tripped her going down the hall."

I balk, he can't be serious, but he nods in confirmation to me right after saying it's true. Just further clarification that what he said in the lobby was all part of the act of playing my fiancé.

"We met at the corner of love and hate. Luckily our paths crossed there again, but the second time we took the right path...love."

I swallow down the lump in my throat. I'm staring at him like everyone else in this room. He really should have gone into acting because everything about what he just said felt...believable.

"Anyway." He clears his throat. "We're going to do what we do best and that's compete with one another. This time doing soccer tricks. Enjoy!" Luca squeezes my hand to begin and walks to the side of the stage. But I'm blinking back the wetness coating my eyes for some stupid reason. "Ladies first," he says, gesturing to me.

The spotlights unnerve me, but I bounce the ball off my knee and then the other knee, warming up.

"Bring it, Hunt!" Luca yells from the other side of the stage.

The crowd claps and the DJ starts playing some techno music. Luca hops off the stage, striding over to the DJ, and then the music stops.

Ludacris's "Stand Up" starts playing as he hops back up on the stage.

I wonder what Ollie and Reba are thinking right now, but the audience begins clapping as I start to find my rhythm. Quickly, the ball and I are one. I kick it behind me, and forward, using my knees, my feet and every part of my body except my hands. Kicking it to Luca, he catches it flawlessly behind his head and the guests cheer. Some of them leave their seats and make their way closer to the stage, still clapping to the beat.

What I thought was the stupidest idea ever has everyone admiring what we can do with a ball. Luca makes the ball slide down his arm, bounce on the floor and then he starts his own routine, getting a lot of oohs and aahs.

Sam comes out with a hula hoop in her hands, holding it up between me and Luca. When did she become our assistant?

Luca eyes me across the room, non-verbally asking if I'm ready. He kicks the ball through the hoop and I catch it on my back, popping it off, starting off with another twist and turn of my body keeping the ball going. Kicking it high in the air, I hit it off my head through the small hula hoop right to Luca.

Everyone cheers and I see Ollie smiling with everyone else over at Luca who is on his back, his feet pedaling the ball in the air. He kicks it in the air and I'm even floored when it falls into the basketball hoop Sam is now holding up.

Claps roar and Luca springs to his feet, rolling the ball over to me. I stop it with my toe and then roll it up. I'm sure Luca has practiced that move a million times with his friends, but I've never tried to get a soccer ball through a basketball hoop.

Luca claps getting the crowd to follow his rhythm while nerves weigh like boulders in my stomach. Delaying the inevitable, I kick the ball, closing my eyes so as not to see when the ball ricochets off the edge of the hula hoop.

At the yells and roars hit my ears, I open one eye to see Luca running toward me with a huge smile. He picks me up and swings me around.

"I knew you could do it!"

My arms tighten around his neck and for a moment he really feels like my fiancé. A man who loves my crazy competitive side and believes I can do whatever I set my mind to. He brings our spinning to a stop and I slide down his hard body until my feet reach the floor.

"Still think it was a stupid idea?" he asks, quirking one eyebrow my way.

"I'll never admit different," I say with a smile.

He chuckles, his head falling back, and I stare at his Adam's apple and five o'clock shadow that starts under his chin. I have the urge to kiss him there, run my tongue over the coarse hairs there until I reach his lips.

Every part of me wants to call a truce for one night only. Get him out of my system because surely that's all I need. It's been too long since I've had sex and my sudden attraction to him has to be because my hormones are going crazy.

His chin dips back down, his eyes on me. Our vision locks and for a moment I almost rise up to my tiptoes. His slide gaze slides to my hips and I swear he leans forward.

"Great job!" Sam's voice through the microphone has me jumping back. "Let's hear it for Lauren and Luca."

Everyone else claps and we do a bow before leaving the stage where I pull my dress down then strip off the pink lycra, pushing my heels back onto my feet.

We leave the stage to find our seats and all that's running through my mind is not whether we'll win or not, but whether he felt the shift between us, too.

Fuck, I should've come stag to the Christmas party.

I have to bite down my smile over how happy I am that I didn't.

<hr>

CHAPTER TWENTY-TWO

Lauren

I'm in the middle of a pretty great dream when someone jumps into bed with me.

At least I feel really, really happy until I realize there's a man pressed to my back and his arm is dangerously close to my breasts.

"What the?" I whip up only to find a bare-chested Luca next to me.

"Shh." He presses his finger to my lips and he slides forward.

So close that I can feel his small fry pressing against my hip now.

"Luca!" I scold inching away.

He glances down like he doesn't understand what I'm referring to, then laughs. "It's the morning. What do you expect?"

I hear a door close downstairs.

My eyes widen and I push him on the chest. "Get out of my bed. What will they think?"

He pulls the blankets up and tries to manhandle me to lay back in bed. I'm not even sure what I got dressed in after the Christmas party, so I lift the covers. A pair of boxer shorts and a cami. Nothing too revealing.

There's a lot of commotion in the kitchen now.

I throw the covers off me and get out of bed.

"What are you doing?" Luca asks, who I now realize is wearing a pair of boxer briefs with a very large fry bulging out the front.

The throbbing between my thighs is immediate and I quickly avert my gaze.

"I'm going downstairs. We could be getting robbed."

I peek out my window onto the street and let the curtain fall back when I spot Maddie's car.

"It's Maddie and Mauro."

Luca's shaking his head. "Not Mauro. He's working."

"Which means?

He nods, inviting me back into the bed with him.

"Keep that thing away from me." I point.

He looks down, impressed with himself he smiles up at me. "You sure about that?"

"UGH," I say just as I hear footsteps on the stairs.

I hop back into the bed and we flip flop around trying to find a position without his junk touching me.

The doorknob turns and I roll onto my side. Luca panics and rolls in behind me, his hard dick sitting right between my ass cheeks. His hand rests right below my breasts and he brushes my hair from my neck and rests his lips on the skin at the bottom of my neck.

My body ignites like a roaring fire with no extinguisher in sight. I call upon the strong willpower I've developed through sports to get through this.

The bedroom door opens and almost immediately all I

hear is, "Oh, I'm so sorry!" Maddie rushes out, putting her hand over her eyes and slamming the door.

Luca chuckles into my neck and I swear he circles his hips.

"Stop it," I say.

"What? I'm literally just lying here," he whispers.

"Maddie?" I call out.

"I'm so sorry. I forgot...I'll be downstairs."

The descending footsteps on the wooden floors and stairs tells us she's nowhere near us anymore, but still I find myself staying in place. Being pressed against this man feels nice.

Luca doesn't move either.

I'm not sure what game of Russian roulette we're playing this morning.

"Lauren," he whispers and I inhale a deep breath.

His finger runs down the length of my torso until his long fingers wrap around my hip and this time I'm not imagining the circling of his hips and the hard length of his cock pressing against me.

"What?" I ask, breathless and intoxicated from his scent, his touch, his everything.

"Last night," he says softly, not stopping the rhythm of his hips. His breath tickles me right under my earlobe. "I had a good time."

"Me, too." I sound like I'm panting. Maybe I am.

I allow my eyes to drift closed and push my ass back into him. My clit throbs, begging for some attention of its own.

"I have a confession."

This is it. He's going to tell me what he said at the party about us as teenagers was true. That he did have a crush on me. We can address it and maybe figure out this thing between us.

"Yeah."

He shifts forward, leaving no space between us.

"No!" a scream sounds from downstairs.

Luca throws the covers off us and flies out of bed. I follow, running down the stairs.

Each of us find Maddie with the phone clutched in her hand, her teary eyes on the television.

"Another one." She points.

Luca and I follow her finger to read the breaking news that there's another fire at an abandoned warehouse and at least one firefighter is being transferred to the hospital.

"I keep getting Mauro's voicemail." She pulls the phone from her ear with a shaky hand only to immediately hit redial.

"Sit down for a second. I'm sure it's not Mauro," I say.

Maddie allows me to guide her to the couch. When I turn to find Luca for some guidance on how to handle this, he isn't there.

I take the phone out of Maddie's hands. "You know he can't call you. He won't have his phone on him on a call anyway." I place it on the other side of my hips.

She rocks back and forth, her body trembling as her eyes stay laser-focused on the television.

The cameraman zooms out and three firetrucks with their ladders extended and water shooting down show on the screen. The ground is a mess of yellow, blue and red flashing lights. I have no idea how Maddie's been handling this with everything that's happened in the past months.

"I'll be back." Luca runs down the stairs, dressed now and out of the house.

"I'm coming!" Maddie runs out, forgetting her jacket and phone.

"Maddie!" I screech.

Luckily, Luca stops her at the bottom of the stairs outside. "It's fine. I'll message you as soon as I have word. Just do me a favor, someone go over to Ma's." His gaze rests on me.

I nod.

"I'm sure he's fine. Mauro is the best firefighter I know and..." He lowers his eyes to hers. "I know a lot."

Figures, Luca can pull a laugh out of someone at a time like this.

His phone rings in his pocket, he stares at it for a second and then answers. "Cris. Yeah, I'm at the house. Maddie's here." He listens and walks away for a moment. I shiver, clinging to Maddie for comfort.

Luca walks back over to us, where he shrugs off his jacket and hands it to me. "Cris is on it. He was already on his way for a run so he'll stop by the fire station." Luca doesn't look very convinced at this new plan, but he nods for us to get back in the house.

We all head back into the house, Maddie taking her place on the couch, her eyes searching for Mauro with every firefighter they show on screen. Luca nods for me to follow him.

When we reach the kitchen, we discover bags of groceries sitting on the counter.

Luca sneaks a peek in them, shaking his head. "Sauce ingredients. When will they ever fucking trust me?" He slams the bag of tomatoes back down on the counter, the insides leaking from under his palm.

"What's going on?"

"Well, the fact we were in the middle of something and now." He gestures to the tomatoes dripping down the cabinet.

"Yeah, let's talk," I urge. The topic is long overdue.

"I think we both got carried away which is probably normal since we're pretending to be engaged and all." His voice is whisper soft.

I tense for a moment before I'm able to get a response out. "Yeah, of course."

"I mean unless..." He almost seems like he's waiting for me.

"No, you're right and last night was just so..."

"It was." His confirmation pulls a smile from me. "Except for the part where we came in second."

Who would have thought that yodeling could outdo our soccer skills?

"True. But still..."

"Yeah." He sighs.

"I'll run up and take a shower." I need something to shed this skin of bitter disappointment.

He glances down at the tomatoes. "I'll clean this up. And Lauren?"

I turn back to him from the archway of the room. "Thanks for...understanding."

I nod not sure if he means the fact that he was allowing his dick to rule him upstairs and now he's made it clear where he stands or if he means for today, going to his mom's.

I shrug like it's nothing. "Sure. I kind of owe you after last night."

He glances down to the ground one more time and back to me, his honest and genuine coffee-colored hues burning through me. "You owe me nothing."

I nod. "Yeah, but last night..."

"What happened last night?" Maddie comes breezing into the kitchen like the last ten minutes never happened. "Oh, your Christmas party. How was it?"

She sits down on the stool at the breakfast bar and notices the smashed tomatoes. "You ruined the tomatoes, how are we going to make sauce?"

"Maddie?" I ask.

"I saw him on the television getting back on the truck so I'm sure he'll call me soon. I'm so sorry for worrying you. You guys looked so comfy in bed." She starts unpacking the bags.

"I already called your mom and Cristian to apologize for ruining their morning." She crunches the plastic bags in her hands. "So, the plan is that we're going to make the sauce here and take it over because Zia says she's got a lot going on over there today and there's no room for our mess."

"Mess? When did this turn into a we? It was supposed to be me?" Luca asks.

"Well, they said you know the recipe and I really want to learn it." She sheepishly looks to Luca who smiles over at me and shakes his head.

"I'll be in the shower." I escape the room and Luca's eyes that feel like they can see my every thought.

Once I'm secure in my bedroom with the door locked, I lean against the door and bang the back of my head against it a few times. Another day of acting ahead of me.

"This is a good thing, Lauren. Nothing good could come of you and Luca."

I get in the shower and rinse off last night's makeup and hopefully all the feelings I'm starting to have for Luca.

CHAPTER TWENTY-THREE

Luca

I come in through the back door because I finally got Lauren to give me a garage door opener for my car. I step out of my shoes, head out of the kitchen, through the dining room to the family room where I find Lauren with a spoonful of cookie dough in her mouth. She's in a pair of sweatpants with a tight cami and an unzipped sweatshirt. I know she's sans bra since her nipples greet me first. Her hair is in a high bun revealing her slender neck that I've wanted to bite and nibble my way up and down.

She spots me from the corner of her eye and scrambles for the remote. The spoon falling into the bowl of cookie dough in her lap. I wait patiently because it's a funny scene.

She flicks the channel and an announcer talking stats turns my attention to the television. I'm fairly sure that's not what was on when I walked in.

It's been a whole week since I almost confessed my feelings to her. We've been able to co-exist in this house because I've had a million things on the go this week and she has, too.

Other than Sunday dinner, I've seen her once on the way out of the shower and another time in the garage. Having nothing else to do today, I wouldn't mind falling down next to her and sharing that spoon to indulge in a little cookie dough.

"Good morning," I say, sitting next to her.

"You want the TV?" she asks, already collecting all her things. I notice that one of those things is the crumpled tissues next to her.

"What were you watching?" I reach for the remote, but she grabs it off the cushion before I can. "You're hiding something," I slide closer, reaching over her body for the remote.

She tries to hold it up higher. "No, I'm not. I'm watching the highlights from last night. Speaking of which, when do I get to go to the next Blackhawks game?" She raises those perfect eyebrows at me while moving the remote under her leg since she knows I have her beat in height.

"I've had to work most of their play days and then Saturday..." I leave it hanging because Saturday were my tickets but I swapped so I could go to her party.

"You gave up your Blackhawks tickets for my party?"

"Of course. That was a stipulation for you to act like my fiancée, remember?

"Yeah but... I'm sorry." She puts the bowl of cookie dough on the table.

"Don't be. I had a lot of fun."

Just as I have her feeling bad about me missing the Blackhawks game I move my hand over her and under her thigh to grab the remote.

"You sneak!" she yells, her hand gripping mine, nails digging into my skin.

"Ouch!" I retract my hand and she stands up, hiding the remote behind her back. "You're kidding me, right?"

"No." She shakes her head.

I'm sure she's gripping it pretty hard behind her, but I

stand, towering over her and putting our bodies flush so I can wrap my arms around her.

"You play unfair," she says, wiggling around in my arms.

I could tighten my grip, but this is way too much fun, so I let her flail in my arms like a fish out of water.

"Come on." My hands feel the metal and plastic but she pushes her breasts right into me, and her nipples poke me through my thin shirt. My dick stirs to life in my pants.

"Why do you care?" she asks, escaping my hold.

I knew I should've tightened my arms. She jumps up on the couch, barely getting the height advantage now. I could step up on the couch, but her tits are in my face now and what heterosexual man wouldn't want that?

Her arms are held up straight in the air and she's shimmying back and forth giving me a tease I'm quite enjoying, but I need to keep playing this game of keep away, otherwise, she'll be on to me.

I pick her up by the waist and this time I do tighten my arms.

Her fists nail my shoulder blades and I figured this would go no other way. Laying her down on the couch, I lean over her, searching for the remote. Her one leg winds around mine, her body like a python. How do I continue to underestimate her strength?

"Luca!" she yells when I try to tickle her and she dodges my fingers.

"You're ticklish?" I go after her again, but she shifts her weight farther into the couch.

I have no idea where the remote is now.

Her hips shoot off the couch, her leg gripping mine. "Oh my God."

She's got a smile on her face, laughing. And it's beautiful.

Her hands grab mine, jarring me from my thoughts and I lose my balance, falling on top of her. We both hold still.

Our eyes meet and everything disappears except her lips. They're all I see. Her tongue slides out of her mouth and she licks her fuller lower lip and it feels like an invitation. Does she mean it as one? All the reasons this won't work evaporates from my thoughts, leaving me with one subject on my mind—how good would it feel to kiss Lauren Hunt? Are her lips as soft as I've imagined? Will she try to take the reins or let me control the pace?

I can't pull my vision from her lips. The shine from where she licked them teases me and I can practically taste the cookie dough she was eating when I walked in. Shifting, she opens her legs and I fall between them. My athletic pants and her sweatpants leave only the thinnest layer between us and I can feel the heat between her legs calling to me. It has to be a sign that she's into this.

My neck strains and I lower down, my resolve vanishing into thin air.

"Luca," she sighs, the tone of her voice stalling me a millimeter before our lips meet.

"Yeah," I say, not moving.

"Is this a mistake?" she asks and I look back up to her eyes. The lust from moments before has been replaced by wariness.

Sliding off her, I sit up, running a hand through my still sweaty hair. "Do you think it is?"

She gets up and tucks her legs against her chest. "Are we doing it because we're here and we've been shoved together for the past few weeks?"

I hate that I can't answer her question with certainty. I have no clue. Usually it's 'do I like you enough to sleep with you? Okay, let's go back to your place.' After the night, I leave and it's over. I've never seen anyone more than a few times and even then it's usually just a mutual let's have some fun, screw around with each other for a bit, then move on. Feelings were never involved unless you count horniness.

But being with Lauren is bringing up all those old feelings from way back in the day, and that's some serious shit. What if she's right and it is just because we've been together so much and neither of us has slept with anyone else since we started this.

"I don't know," I admit, albeit with reluctance.

"Then I'd say this is a bad idea. We should keep this platonic. No matter what, we're going to be at a lot of events going forward with your brothers dating my best friends. We don't need to end up hating each other more than we already do." She stands and reaches for her cookie bowl.

My gaze falls to the remote on the cushion.

"Lauren," I say to draw her attention back to me. "I don't hate you. That I can answer with absolute truth."

She smiles. "Same. You have a way of making people warm up to you."

"Is that a compliment?" I ask with mock astonishment.

"I guess it is."

I smile and snatch the remote off the couch. In a last-ditch effort, she jumps me, but I click the last channel and I find out Lauren's little secret.

"Hallmark Christmas movies?" I chuckle.

Her body lays limp in my lap.

"You tell anyone and you're dead." She pokes my chest and I grab her finger.

"Another secret in the L & L vault, huh?"

"Yes." She pushes up off of me and I miss her body immediately. Grabbing the cookie dough bowl again, she grabs the remote that's now limp in my hand. "Now that you know, move on with your day because my Saturday is going to be this." She props her feet up on the table and spoons a heaping mound of cookie dough onto the spoon.

I reach for her wrist and direct the spoon into my mouth. Lauren's eyes widen.

"Me, too, then. Roommate bonding day it is." I smile and wink.

She points the spoon at me. "No talking. Do not ruin my vice."

I laugh, grabbing the blanket from my chair—which has once again found a place in the house—and bringing her feet over my legs. "Let's see what the hype is all about." I turn my attention to the television.

Maybe it'd be easier for me to just admit the truth to her, but that's just another area where I differ from my brothers.

CHAPTER TWENTY-FOUR

Luca

I pay for the pizza, thank the delivery guy and head back into the family room where Lauren hasn't moved off the couch. We've watched two Hallmark Christmas movies. Parts of it are cheesy as hell and other parts make you question why you would wait so damn long to tell the person you love that you can't live without them.

"What'd you get?" Lauren asks, lifting the box.

"Gino's thin—it's the best ever." I head to the kitchen and grab some sodas and napkins. Lauren's going to learn how I do things and we're eating right out of the pizza box.

"I've never had it."

I stop outside the kitchen, grabbing my sweatshirt out of my bag. "You're joking." I sit down and position our stuff. Bringing the table closer to us.

"You seem like a pro at this whole vegging all day," she says.

"Honestly." I hand her a piece of pizza and crack open our sodas. "I haven't had a place to veg in so long, I'm loving this

—even if I have to watch romantic movies where miracles happen and Santa is real."

She kicks me with her foot and sits up. "Santa *is* real." She waggles her eyebrows at me.

"Sure. Hope you get that Barbie house you asked for under the tree." I tap her nose and reach for my own piece of pizza.

"I'm well past toys nowadays." She bites into the pizza and a slow moan falls from her lips. "Man." She inspects the pizza. "I never would've guessed."

I take a bite of my own pepperoni goodness. "Told you. The best."

We each devour our pizza and drink our sodas while the television is on pause.

"Ready to start?" I ask and she nods.

We watch on as singing carolers ring the doorbell of an inn. Snow falls outside and the fireplace roars inside, decorated with stockings hung for every guest at the bed and breakfast. I can practically smell the gingerbread. Hallmark sure knows how to make you fall in love with the holidays.

"Don't you think it's a little cheesy to propose on Christmas?" I ask when it becomes clear where this storyline is going.

"No," Lauren scoffs, attention still fixed on the TV.

"Valentine's Day?"

She shrugs. "Maybe, but all that really matters is that the couple is happy. I don't think you need a grand proposal. Like why make a huge spectacle?"

Mauro did it low key, just him and Maddie, but I always imagined myself pulling out all the stops.

"I'm sure to you bigger means better, but who are you doing it for? For your hopeful fiancée? If she wants to marry you, she shouldn't care how many people are witness."

She pauses the movie as I go for one more slice of pizza. Even cooled down, Gino's is still a piece of heaven on earth.

"I don't think that's true. I think to some people, the size of the proposal says how much they love that person. It's great that you don't need that, but some do."

She shrugs. "I guess everyone is different. I'm sure you'll ask your girlfriend with a plane in the sky or on a jumbotron at some sporting event."

"What's that mean?"

She shrugs again. "That you're a 'go big or go home' kind of guy."

"Is that a bad thing?" I set the half-eaten piece of pizza down in the box.

"No. It's just you."

"Then why do I feel like you just insulted me?"

She laughs, tossing her crust into the pizza box.

I pick it up. "What's this? Are you five?"

"I don't eat the crust."

I bite into it and she laughs.

"I kind of thought you'd want a big scene," I say when I'm done swallowing.

"Nope." She wipes her mouth.

"Are you embarrassed in front of crowds?" I ask the question that's been bugging me since her Christmas party.

"Not really. Why?"

"The Christmas party..."

Her face turns as red as Snow White's apple, and she draws her legs up to her chest.

"No hiding." I toss her crust into the box and pull her arms loose from around her legs. "What am I missing?"

"I don't want to talk about it. Let's just get back to the movie." She presses play on the television.

I grab the remote and press pause again. "Come on. You should tell your fiancé everything."

She looks up at me through her eyelashes and shakes her head. "Fact, you're not my fiancé."

"Minor detail."

After a minute of silence and my gaze boring into her, she finally appears to be ready to talk.

"It's just…" She starts, then stops. "I…competitive women aren't exactly attractive to an employer or a man."

I have to snap my jaw shut. She's shittin' me, right?

"What the hell are you talking about?"

"See!" She points at me. "I don't want to have this conversation. It's like admitting some fear to your enemy so they can use it against you down the road."

I slide closer to her on the couch and wrap my arm around her shoulders. Her body is stiff in my arms.

"Lauren, relax."

"I'm so stupid, how did we get on this topic?"

I move her so her legs are draped over mine and run my hands along them over the blanket, trying to ignore how nice this feels.

"First off, I'm not your enemy and second, I'll never use anything against you. We've come a long way since this whole thing began. And if it helps, I'll tell you something about me."

"What? That you haven't actually fucked all the Lovables?"

I laugh, but it comes out a bit caustic. "What? You don't really think I've screwed my way through the Bulls cheerleaders, do you?"

She shrugs, and I have to work to tamp down the anger that's brewing inside over the fact that she believes I'd really do that.

"Come on. You obviously need to talk about it. Trust me."

She stares at me for so long, I start to doubt if I can be trusted.

With a resigned sigh and a look down at her hands in her

lap, she starts to speak. "You heard how everyone was talking about how competitive I was at the picnic. I didn't want to do the talent show because I can't control that part of me. I *want* to win. Always."

"And good for you." I squeeze her thigh.

"You don't get it. You're a guy."

"So?" I shrug.

"Guys can be competitive assholes and women will want to screw you and men will want to *be* you. Especially if you're a winner, but women? What kind of guy wants to have a girlfriend who won't let him win?"

"No man should want his girlfriend to let him win. He should be letting her win."

She rolls her eyes. "You say that. But take us for example. Could you imagine if we were a couple? You'd grow tired of me." I furrow my brow. "Maybe not you, but men don't like to lose, Luca. You said it yourself when I was in high school, I act like a guy. Name one heterosexual man who wants to screw a woman who beats him at everything."

"Whoa, let's back up a sec. If you met a *real* man, he won't expect you to give anything other than maximum effort. A guy like Peter? That's not the guy for you. You'd eat him alive."

"And he's the one guy to show me any interest lately."

"Bullshit."

Her eyes flare and she knocks her head back like I've slapped her.

"You had that date. I saw you on the porch."

"That one you honked the horn on." The corners of her lips tip down a bit.

"I told you, my hand slipped."

She sinks into the cushions of the couch. "So, that's my big fear. I didn't want to compete in the talent show because people like to make fun of me for my competitive nature."

I rub my hand down her leg again. It hurts to see her this down on herself. Especially when it's a part of her that I admire the most.

"Lauren, your competitive nature is sexy as hell and you shouldn't be with someone who doesn't see it that way. Your lucky guy should be your biggest competitor *and* your biggest cheerleader. Don't settle for less."

A small smile graces her lips and though I'd rather convince her of how desirable she is by placing my lips to hers, I hope she can feel the conviction of my words.

"Your turn." She nudges her knee into my chest.

I run my fingers through my hair and pull at my neck. Never in my life did I think I'd share this with anyone, but Lauren's secret wasn't something she wanted to share with me and in the interest of being fair I should do the same.

"Come on. Are you scared of spiders?" She laughs.

"I'm afraid I'll be a shitty boyfriend." The words spill from my mouth before I can talk myself out of it.

Her laugh comes to an abrupt stop and her eyes widen, telling me I should've gone with the spider thing.

"Oh." Her shoulders fall.

"I mean, what if I get into a serious relationship and things go south. I'm not exactly the type of guy who talks about his feelings. I'm not like my brothers that way...at all."

Insecurity eats away at me and I look away from her, regretting saying anything.

Her hand touches my shoulder and I close my eyes briefly, enjoying the sensation. "I think everyone feels that way."

I shake my head. "What if I disappoint her? Or I only selfishly think of myself? Or can't live up to her expectations?"

She smiles at me.

"What? Why are you looking at me like that?"

"You're blind." She shakes her head like I just don't get it.

I don't say anything but screw my face up in a 'what the hell are you talking about' expression.

She laughs. "Look at you with me."

"What do you mean?"

"You're sitting here watching Hallmark Christmas movies with me and talking about our fears of being in a relationship."

"That doesn't prove anything."

"Luca." She leans forward and forces my chin in her direction so I'm looking at her. "You know how I know you'll be a good boyfriend? And believe me, I'm as surprised as you that I'm going to say this to you."

I chuckle. She seems to realize that her hand is still on my chin and she lets it fall. I miss the feel of her skin on mine, even if it is as innocent as her fingers on my chin.

"I know because you care. You care enough to want to be a good boyfriend and you care enough to even think about it in the first place."

I give her a small smile, still not entirely convinced.

"And like I said before, you've sat here for hours watching Hallmark movies with me. That goes a long way toward scoring good boyfriend points."

"Yeah, but this is different."

"Because it's me?" she asks.

"Yeah. I've known you a long time and—you better never repeat this—I enjoy things when you're around."

I think my words affect her based on the way her breath seems to come out shaky before she speaks.

"And you will when it comes to your real girlfriend, too. You should change your type though." She knees me in the chest and then swings her legs to the side and stands.

I miss the feel of her immediately.

"What does that mean?"

I stand and follow her into the kitchen.

"You tend to go for women who don't challenge you, you know?"

"No, I don't."

She opens the fridge, grabs a water and takes a sip out of it. Her head is tipped back giving me a glimpse of her long neck and I check the impulse that has me wanting to run my tongue along the skin there.

"You do." She walks past me, back into the family room and flicks on a light since the sun has already started to descend in the sky. I hate how early it gets dark this time of year.

"I do not."

"Oh, Luca." She saunters over to me, her finger running down my chest as she leans her cheek against my chest. "You're so hot and you're a paramedic, too. Do you know mouth-to-mouth? I think I might need to be resuscitated." Her voice is all sultry and sweet like syrup pouring out of a bottle.

Damn her, I've heard those lines more than once.

"That doesn't mean I'm purposely picking them. Maybe that's the kind of woman who's attracted to me."

She gives me a blank stare, walks away and sits down on the couch, grabbing the remote. "Yeah, that's it."

I'm rankled at her impression of me, no matter how much I might deserve it.

"Okay, if you're so right, let's take you as an example. How come you picked Cody over me?"

The mood shifts in the room and the air suddenly feels dense and electric. Her eyes narrow at me and turn cold. "We're gonna go there?"

"I think it's about time we did." I sit down but not as close to her as I was moments ago.

"Cody asked me out," she says like that's all there was to it.

"That's bullshit."

Her phone dings on the table, but she ignores it. Looks like she wants to have this conversation as much as I do. I feel like we've been building up for it more than a decade.

"Blaire seemed like a suitable replacement for me. I mean she is your type after all."

My fists clench in irritation.

"Come on. At least be truthful. You're preaching about how I pick the wrong type of girls, but you had your chance and chose my best friend."

She sits up straighter on the couch. "I was fifteen, Luca."

"You still haven't answered my question." I pin her with a stare, not willing to let it go until I get an answer from her.

She stares me dead in the eye not backing down an inch. "You would've hurt me. Dating you would have been like signing up to get my heart broken."

Just like that she pierces me in the heart with a jagged arrow because she's right. She chose my best friend over me because I would have hurt her, as ashamed as I am to admit that fact.

Before I can respond, her phone rings and she grabs it, putting her finger to her lips for me to be silent.

"Hey, Ashton." She pauses for a second to listen to whatever her brother has to say and a panicked looked washes across her face, her eyes widen. "What? It is? Well...yeah...it was fast. She did? When?...Oh crap. Yeah, okay. Thanks."

She hangs up on the call, but her thumbs move a mile a minute over the phone while she ignores my questions about what the problem is.

Eventually, she shoves the small screen in my face. I steal the phone away from her, standing and pacing when I make sense of what she's showing me. My Zia put a post on Instagram with a picture of Lauren and I congratulating us on our engagement by tagging each of us in the photo.

With St. George's high school having been like a small town where gossip ran rampant, I know before I even ask.

"Guess where we're going tonight? Time for you to meet your in-laws." She smacks me on the back, takes the phone and heads upstairs. A minute later her door slams and I hear her argue with her mom.

Fuck. This engagement is like a snowball rolling down a hill and now that it has momentum, we can't seem to stop it.

CHAPTER TWENTY-FIVE

Lauren

"Mom, I'm sorry," I say over the phone, pacing my room. I hear the water start in the bathroom which means Luca's getting ready. He better after everything I've done for him. *Shit.* I can't believe this got back to my family.

I have to roll with it though because the only thing worse than my family thinking I'm marrying Luca Bianco would be admitting to them that I agreed to a *fake* engagement with Luca.

"Not to mention, it's Luca Bianco. He comes from a good family, but he's the black sheep. Why couldn't you be marrying Cristian?" my mom goes on.

St. George is way too small.

"Mom, we were going to come over to announce it. We were just keeping it quiet for now."

"Quiet? He never even asked your dad for your hand. His aunt from New York posted a picture where the two of you look pretty cozy. Lauren, this is unacceptable behavior."

I haven't heard her this mad since my brother knocked up his high school girlfriend and surprise, instant daughter-in-law and grandchild. Although only the grandchild stuck.

"I said I was sorry, okay, but I was feeling it out to make sure it'd stick."

Damn it. Even I know that was the wrong thing to say.

"Stick? What the hell does that mean? You have his ring on your finger. You've agreed to spend life together until death do you part. You kids today are so ridiculous. Marriage is serious business, Lauren." I hear pots and pans clattering in the background.

"Mom, don't cook for us."

"Oh, I'm supposed to have my future son-in-law over and not cook a proper meal for him? I'm sure Maria Bianco has already cooked for you."

"You don't have to keep up with her." I grip my hair in my hands.

"So she has. You know, Lauren." I hear her voice crack and right now I'd prefer to be swallowed up into a hole. "I'm your mom. You're my daughter. We're supposed to go dress shopping and plan your wedding. I've always dreamed of that."

And that is the exact reason I never told her.

"I'm sorry, Mom. Listen, I'm going to shower and then I'll be over, okay?"

"Okay. Oh, and Ashton and Davis will be here, too."

"Great," I deadpan, thinking of my brothers.

"I'm sorry if we're so embarrassing, but we are your family," she huffs.

"That's not it, it's just the boys will be protective."

"It's Luca Bianco, give me a break. He can hold his own. I'll see you in half an hour."

The phone dies and I sit on my bed. My head falls to my

hands and tears leak down my face as I weep for everything I've done in the last few weeks.

Who am I? This isn't me. I'm not the girl who lies to everyone around her.

A knock sounds on my door and I really want to ignore it, but I can't. So, I stand and swipe my eyes.

"Come in," I say, heading to my closet to pretend I'm searching for something to wear.

"Hey. I just want to say I'm sorry," Luca says.

I turn in his direction. "Luca! Put a shirt on."

He crosses his arms, his biceps on display and smirks. Classic Luca. Using his good looks to get me to forgive him for what I'm doing to everyone I love.

I can't lie. If I wasn't so down, it would be working. The man has the body of an Adonis.

"Lauren," he sighs, approaching me. "I'm sorry. I never meant for your family to find out." His hands land on my shoulders and the fresh scent of his soap wraps us in a blanket.

Everything we discussed today runs through my mind and I can't even find it within myself to make him feel better. I have to keep reminding myself that I agreed to this.

"Just do me a favor, okay? Act like the doting fiancé tonight. So, when I break the news about our break up, they can't say I told you so."

His arms wrap around me and his chin rests on my head. It feels good—too good, too comforting, too everything.

"I'll make sure I'm the one they hate when this over and they never question that this wasn't real."

I swallow the elephant-sized lump in my throat.

"Thanks."

I pull away from him and stand waiting for him to leave. As I flip from one garment to the other, he pauses at the door.

"I know it's not much, but I would've done everything in my power not to hurt you. Though you're probably right—back then it was probably inevitable." He looks uncomfortable for a second, like there's something more he has to say. He pushes a hand through his damp hair before he continues. "The reason I hated you in high school was because you picked him over me. And for the record, I never saw you as a boy. Ever." He pauses and clears his throat. "I'll meet you downstairs."

With the click of my bedroom door, another tear runs down my cheek. I close my eyes and draw in a ragged breath.

I did not need his admission right now. What is happening to us?

This whole thing has gone too far. I need to stop the madness, but first I need to put on a happy face for my family.

CHAPTER TWENTY-SIX

Luca

I'm cleaning up the family room from our day of vegging when Lauren comes down the stairs. Her long hair is braided to the side, she's in a pair of jeans and a long sleeve t-shirt. There's not a ton of make-up on her which is my favorite look on her.

"Ready?" she asks, grabbing her purse from the front hook and sliding into her boots.

"Yeah." I carry the pizza box and cans to the kitchen. Grabbing our jackets, I hold hers out to her and shrug mine on.

"I can drive," I suggest.

"Thanks. My dad would think less of you if I drive," she mumbles, but I catch it.

"Really?"

She puts her hand on my arm. "Don't worry, they'll love you. You'll have to make amends for not asking permission but other than that my family already loves you. Well, my mom did back in school anyway." She cringes.

I'm still reeling from admitting to her why I hated her less than twenty minutes ago. I didn't really expect any rushing into my arms or anything, but she's ignoring it and I'm kind of pissed. It took a lot for me to admit that.

Opening the door, she walks out, and I throw the pizza box and cans into the recycling bin before we climb into my truck.

"Sorry," I apologize for the older truck that's my winter vehicle.

"It's okay. I feel safer in this anyway."

I stare at the rust bucket with only a cassette player wondering how that could be.

"You're definitely not the go-big girl."

I start the truck, the engine rumbles and I back out of the garage.

"I told you I wasn't."

We drive for a few minutes. Lauren doesn't need to give me directions because I've dropped her off myself or was in the car when Cody did enough times when we were in high school. I had to witness them kissing goodbye on numerous occasions on the front porch. Not the highlight of my high school experience for sure.

"My mom is super mad and disappointed with me. My dad doesn't know yet and my mom said it's our job to tell him."

I place my hand on her knee, happy to be driving an automatic at the moment. "We'll get through this. I'm sorry."

I feel like I'm apologizing non-stop and it's still not enough.

"You already said that. When we get in there, you can't be all sad puppy dog eyes okay? Otherwise, they'll know something is up."

"I'm not all sad puppy dog eyes."

"You are. Stop it. I knew the risks when I agreed to this."

She's a fucking rock star, I swear.

"Okay, I'll get rid of the puppy dog eyes and put on my love goggles."

She laughs, and it might be my favorite sound in the world.

I pull up to her parents' bungalow and kill the engine. Her brother Ashton is on the porch smoking a cigarette which means there's no pep talk in the cab of the truck for us. I know her brothers a bit from school and parties and stuff, but we're not buddies.

"Wait for me?" I ask.

She nods, unbuckling and putting her purse over her head and onto her shoulder.

I get out of the truck and walk around the front, opening her door.

"Luca Bianco, I should kick your ass," Ashton yells just as I open Lauren's door.

"We both know he can kick yours," Lauren calls out to him and steps out of my truck like she isn't the least bit fazed or worried when I know she is. Just like the girl I knew in high school—her walk is confident, her shoulders strong, her tongue sharp.

Ashton disposes of his cigarette into an ashtray. Last I heard he was working in the city with troubled youth. "I feel like I have to at least try for the sake of the family name." He puts his hand out in front of me. "A Bianco. Never would have thought you'd taint our bloodline like that, Lauren."

I shake his hand. "I'll only be improving it."

Ashton tilts his head back and forth. "I think your babies might be powerhouses." All three of us laugh and as we enter their parents' house, my mind wanders to what having kid with Lauren would be like. Would our kid take on our competitiveness or would we have a kid who hates competition? Would we raise him or her by always letting them win or teach them to work hard for their wins?

I'm so busy thinking about Lauren and me as parents that I don't even realize that Nora Hunt is standing in front of me with her hands on her hips and anger-filled eyes.

"Mrs. Hunt," I say, putting my hand out.

She crooks her finger to have me bend down. I do and a second later...

Smack.

I place my hand on the back of my head, used to the treatment.

"You're trying to steal my daughter," she accuses.

"Mom," Lauren sighs. "I'm sorry, Luca."

"Mrs. Hunt, it was wrong of me not to ask for your permission. And we should've come sooner. I apologize for you finding out the way you did."

I see where Lauren's vicious looks come from. Her mom appears to want to slice me open.

"You're going to make it up to me by allowing me to plan a huge and elaborate wedding. That's what's going to happen Luca."

"Done." I put my hand out again, the lie eating away at me. Mrs. Hunt will never see a wedding with her daughter walking down the aisle toward me. That'll be some other lucky bastard's blessing.

"Aw." She waves off my hand and opens her arms. "Luca Bianco, I can't believe it." She hugs me to her and although I'm taller, she somehow feels like the one controlling the hug. Stepping away, both her hands land on my cheeks. "You are just as handsome as you were as a kid."

Her hands fall and she elbows Lauren. "Lucky girl."

Lauren gives her a half smile.

"So, Fred is downstairs. Good luck, Luca." She smacks me

on the back and winds her arm through Lauren's leading her to the kitchen.

"I was going to go with Luca." Lauren tries to stop, looking over her shoulder at me.

"Nope. You know the way, Luca."

Lauren sends me an apologetic look and I run my sweaty palms down my jeans. "I totally have this," I mumble and head toward the basement stairs.

The creaky stairs announce my arrival before I hit the bottom.

Fred Hunt stares right at me, while both his sons sit on either side of him.

"Luca Bianco?" His forehead is scrunched up in confusion.

Ashton laughs.

Davis, Lauren's other brother, raises his eyebrows.

Both of them take after their father with his six-foot stature and broad shoulders.

"Hi, Mr. Hunt." I break the distance, hearing the Illini's playing on the television.

I shake his hand and Ashton slides over on the couch, a shit-eating grin on his face, giving me room to be front and center to his dad.

Bastard.

We shake hands and then I put my hand in front of Davis. "Hey, Bianco."

Sitting down, I run my hands down my jeans again.

"What brings you here?" Fred asks.

"Well..."

"Yeah, Bianco, what brings you to the Hunt household? Just visiting?" Davis razzes me. He obviously knows, too.

Fred glances at his son giving him a 'shut the fuck up' look, which Davis listens to.

"I brought Lauren," I say.

Fred straightens his back. "My Lauren?"

Ashton laughs. Davis throws a pillow at him.

"Yes, Sir. We've been seeing one another."

"Seeing? Like running into one another?"

Now Davis laughs and Ashton throws the pillow back.

"Seeing as in dating."

"My Lauren?" he clarifies again, confusion still laced in all his features.

"Yes."

"Didn't she date that Cody fellow. Your friend?" he asks.

Why the fuck does everyone have to bring up Cody?

"Back in high school, yeah, but lately..." I swallow to try and coat the dryness in my throat. I could really use a water right about now.

"She was the love of his life, right?" Davis tries to throw the pillow to Ashton, but Fred intercepts it.

"You two. Upstairs." He points to the stairs with a look I've seen on his daughter's face a few times.

They must know better than to not listen since they fly up the stairs at record pace. I didn't mind them being here. Witnesses might've been good.

"Sorry, they've yet to mature." He leans back in his recliner. "So, you and Lauren have been dating?" There's a small smile on his face.

"Yes. And the thing is...I proposed to her."

The smile falls from his face.

"I'm sorry, Sir. I should have asked your permission. That was wrong on my end. We just got so caught up in the moment that I blurted it out."

If he only knew how I deliberated for days on how to convince her.

"You're still a paramedic?"

Not the response I was expecting. "Yes, Sir."

"Pay good. Enough so she can stay home?"

"Well, I do side jobs so yes, I can take care of her financially."

Maybe. Hopefully. I cringe inwardly. I hadn't really thought about that.

"She'd want to stay home like Nora did with the kids. You have to plan that sort of thing. Nora can teach her how to shop for a family and coupon clipping always stretched a dollar."

I have to be staring at him in shock.

"Lauren loves her job. She went to school for it," is all I can come up with in response.

"And she's got loans to prove it. So, make sure you factor that in the budget, too. Maybe once the kids are in school, she can work part-time. You come from an Italian family...I'm sure you want a lot of little ones running around."

My head spins. Did I just warp back about five decades?

Lauren picks this as the time to bounce downstairs. When I say bounce, I mean it's like she's Princess Belle happy and skipping over to me.

"Did you hear Dad? I'm getting married?" She kisses him on the cheek hello and then sits next to me.

"Luca just told me. I think it's wonderful. You can finally stay home and your mom's been wanting to show you how to be a good wife."

Lauren's face falters.

"I told him you love your job."

"I do. We're not going to have kids for a long time." She laughs, staring up at me.

"Well, you're only getting older, sweetheart," Fred says.

"Mom sent me down here because dinner is ready." Her tone is frosty now and she stands up to leave.

"Lauren, you just always want to be like your brothers. Women were meant to stay home."

Fred follows after his daughter and I follow him. How did

I not know this about her family? And why am I so pissed that he wants to take away her independence when this whole thing between us isn't real. It's like what she wants doesn't matter.

I can't help but wonder if I know my fake fiancée better than the people who raised her.

CHAPTER TWENTY-SEVEN

Lauren

My dad sits at the end of the table, my mom passing him the food first. He shovels what he wants onto his plate and passes the dishes around.

"I would've made a cake if I had time. To celebrate," my mom says, handing my dad the potatoes.

"We don't want you to go to any trouble." Luca's hand slides under the table to my leg, squeezing it a few times.

"It's no trouble, is it Nora?" my dad asks my mom.

I hate this and I hate that Luca is witnessing my family dynamic. Where his mom seems to run his household, my dad runs mine and though I know he loves me, it's always been clear where my and my mom's place is in the family.

Pictures adorn the walls of this house of my brothers in their football uniforms, track and field. My pictures are only ones of prom and homecoming. None of my soccer pictures are hung because that'd be like admitting I'm an equal to my brothers.

Some families have daddy's princess.

Not the Hunts.

My brothers have always gotten all the glory and I've gotten questions like why would I want to play a sport when I could cheer on the players? I've fought for everything I've done. You'd think my dad would be proud of me becoming captain when Davis didn't even make the cut for football senior year, but nope. That night I got lectured about over-shadowing my brothers in my achievements.

"Where do you think you'll live?" my dad asks as we all eat our chicken and potatoes.

"We don't know yet," Luca says. "We're living together over where Lauren's been living for the moment."

Complete silence blankets the table.

Damn it. I should've warned him.

"You're what?" My mom's fork hits her plate. "You are just engaged not married, correct?"

"Mom," I plead for her not to make a big deal of it.

Ashton and Davis snicker and I glare at them both.

My mom stands and disappears into the kitchen.

"You've got to be kidding me." I throw my head back and slide the chair out.

"Luca, we don't believe in living together until marriage. I'm sure I don't have to tell you this, but our Lauren is a virgin," my dad says.

My feet stop right before the archway to the kitchen.

No. No. No.

Ashton full-on laughs out loud and coughs out the word delusional. My dad throws a roll at his head.

Luca's fearful eyes meet mine and my head falls forward in defeat. I should've known this was never going to turn out the way I'd hoped.

"Mom," I say and enter the kitchen, where she's seated at the table.

"You're living together?" Her shoulders are slumped and she's shaking a bit from crying.

"Yes. Luca needed a place and I needed someone to help me pay the rent after Vanessa and Maddie moved in with their boyfriends."

Her hand goes to her chest. "All of you are living in sin?"

You'd think I told her World War three has started from the look in her eyes.

"Yes. Mom. It's the twenty-first century."

"Lauren." Tears stream down her face. "You're not a vir…"

She can't even finish the word. Even worse is the fact that I have to have this conversation with Luca in the room. A man I haven't actually even had sex with.

"No, Mom, I'm not."

Her forehead falls to the table with a big thud and she cries so hysterically you'd think her dog, Parker, died.

"Why wouldn't you wait? This is the problem with today's youth. I married your father at eighteen. You girls all want a career and your own money before you settle down."

"Yes Mom, we do and we deserve it. Did you enjoy always being Dad's servant? Didn't you ever want something for yourself?"

She raises her head to look at me. "I was happy with you and your brothers. I wanted to be a mom."

"Well, I'm sorry, but I'm not. I want a career and a family."

"I know." She pats my hand. "I just…it's different now."

I came to grips a long time ago that my family dynamic would never change. The boys would always be superior in my dad's eyes and my mom would never understand me wanting to have a career after I got married and had kids. This is why I wanted to keep this fake engagement to myself because I knew they'd be so happy. They've been waiting ever since

Cody for me to announce that I'm getting married so I can fulfill my destiny.

"I can't do this!" Luca's voice pulls my mom and I's attention away from each other.

We rush back into the dining room to find Luca standing up, his napkin on his chair.

"Mr. Hunt, I'm sorry." He's looking at me now. "I can't sit here and listen to it anymore. I come from a family without a sister so maybe I don't understand." He pauses for a second, trying to collect himself I think.

"Nope. You know what? I'm not even going to use that as an excuse. Lauren is an amazing woman. She's strong and independent. She loves her job and have you ever seen her with a client? 'Cause I have and she's so good with them. There's this little girl Briana, and she adores your daughter.

Yes, Lauren is gorgeous, but there's so much more to her. She's faithful and loyal to her friends and her family. After we marry, she will continue to work. She will make her own money and we will build a house together. Our kids will probably go to daycare so she can continue working. Maybe I'll balance the checkbook, maybe she will. Maybe I'll clean the toilet, maybe she will. Maybe I'll take the trash out, maybe she will.

"I'm sorry Mr. Hunt, but I can't sit here anymore and listen to you degrade your daughter just because she's female. She could probably kick both Ashton and Davis's asses at the same time and you should be proud of that fact." He points to the wall that is like a shrine of my brothers' athletic accomplishments. "She should be on that wall. She worked her ass off to be captain of her soccer team and she deserves to be up there more than Davis who was third string."

Tears well up in my eyes and my mom threads her arm through mine. We stare at one another in amazement.

I thought my mom might fear my dad's wrath after Luca's speech, but she seems almost proud.

"I do not degrade my daughter," my dad says, throwing his own napkin down.

"Then you're blind to your own ignorance."

Luca's eyes find mine and he shoots me the apologetic look he has most of today. I shake my head, he shouldn't apologize for sticking up for me.

My dad looks at me. "You think this? That I love your brothers more?"

I nod.

"Oh. Well." He stands up and without another word he walks downstairs, leaving even Ashton and Davis' jaws hanging open.

"I'm sorry, Mom," I say.

"Give him time. You know your dad." She pats my shoulder. "You two go and give him some space."

"I'm sorry, Mrs. Hunt," Luca says as we both walk toward the front door.

"Too many sorries tonight." My mom opens the door and shoos us out. Luca hesitantly steps out of the house while my mom embraces me in a hug.

"Everything will work out how it's supposed to." She pats my back.

Her words do nothing to help me feel better.

The door shuts before we make it to the truck and I stare at the windows where the basement light shines out into the night. I should go down there and hash it out, but my mom is right, that's not how my dad works. He needs to stew for a bit.

When I turn around, Luca's leaning against the truck, his hands stuffed in his pockets. "I'm sorry, Lauren. I'm fucking this all up. I never meant to cause more problems with your family."

I approach him, rising to my tiptoes to do the one thing I've been dying to do. Luca's speech empowered me to love the person I am. And I'm the kind of person who takes what they want when they want it. Without thinking of the future or what it means, I press my lips to Luca's.

CHAPTER TWENTY-EIGHT

Luca

*L*auren's lips are softer than I imagined. She presses them to mine and I swing my arm around her waist pulling her into me.

A current of warmth rushes down from my lips to my toes. I want to unleash her hair from that braid and bury my hands in her long dark strands. She opens her mouth to me and I slide my tongue in between the seam of her lips. I groan when we make contact and she sinks farther into my body.

Our kiss continues like we're saying a long goodbye and parting for a long time rather than heading back to the same house, but I'm more than okay with that. We delve deeper and then lighter, and my cock strains against the zipper of my jeans. The hunger for one another that we've been denying each other unleashes. My hands slide down her body until I cup her ass. She hops up and straddles me, so I turn us around and she's pressed against the truck.

I'm grinding and she's bucking, neither of us able to get

enough of one another. Needing more, I close the kiss, letting her legs go.

She slides down my body and rests her forehead against my chest, both of us gasping for breath. "I just told my mom I'm not a virgin, let's not scare her too much."

"Home?"

"Definitely."

I open the truck door, Lauren slides in and I round the front of the truck, sliding the key into the ignition immediately.

On the way home, my mind works overtime questioning why she decided to kiss me *now*. I tell myself that it doesn't matter, who cares? I'm finally doing something I've wanted to do with her since I was fifteen. Only an idiot wouldn't take what she's giving you and ask questions instead.

But I am an idiot because instead, I say, "Why?"

"What?" Her voice pierces the darkness of the truck's cab.

"Why did you kiss me?"

"Because I've wanted to for a long time and your speech made me realize that I've been a coward. I've been so worried about you not feeling the same that I've shied away."

I let her words sit with me for a moment because I almost can't believe them.

"You wanted to kiss me?" I know we had that moment on the couch, but I considered it a one time heat of the moment thing for her.

I stop at a traffic light and lean over to kiss her on the neck. Let her get a glimpse of what's going to happen in fifteen minutes when we pull up to the house. If we make it to a bed, it'll be a miracle.

But her lips find mine and my hand lands on her cheek as our tongues try to perfect a rhythm.

Horns honk behind us and I strip myself away from her.

"I have," she answers the question I asked before we lost each other again.

"For how long?" I ask.

She leans over the console, her head resting on my shoulder for a second. "I don't know, but from that kiss, I'm thinking you might have wanted to kiss me, too?"

We're stopped at another light. Seriously we can't catch a break. "Lauren, I've wanted to kiss you again since we were fifteen."

I catch her smile right before I land a kiss on her lips, but we're cut short when the green light illuminates the cab of the truck.

"What? We haven't kissed before." I haven't seen her this easy going and happy in so long. It shouldn't elate me as much as it does seeing her like this.

"We kissed during spin the bottle, remember?"

She laughs. "I do remember, I'm kidding."

Thank God for a second I thought I was the only one.

"I've wanted to kiss you since then."

"Luca, you can't be serious." She's shaking her head and her body is buzzing with energy. Energy I need to make good use of.

Finally, I get us into the garage, but I have to see her face when I confess. So we file out of the truck into the house and I toss my keys on the kitchen island.

"Lauren, since you've decided to throw balls to the wall tonight—"

"Well, not really balls," she says.

"Tits to the wall?" I ask, and she laughs, falling into me.

"I guess so."

"Regardless, since you're taking a chance, I need to as well. Just don't freak out."

"Okay." She slides up on the counter, opening her legs for

me to nestle between them. With my hands on her outer thighs I rub back and forth.

God, it's so good to be able to touch her how I want. Now that the invisible wall has dropped away from between us, I'm not going to stop touching her.

"I've had a thing for you for a long time. I meant everything I said at the Christmas party and earlier today. Caramel and vanilla do remind me of you. I used to watch you with Cody, wishing it were me. This entire engagement was for my mom, but being this close to you again, made all those feelings resurface. You're the girl I've compared all others to since high school and the prospect that I might hurt you scares the hell outta me."

Her hands land on my cheeks and our eyes lock. I have no idea what she's thinking so I stand there on edge until she speaks.

"You won't hurt me. I won't let you." She smashes her lips to mine and I don't shy away from where this is going.

Somehow, I manage to undo her braid, unwinding her hair with my fingers and once the silky strands are freely moving through my fingers, I groan and dig deeper, never having enough of her.

"Upstairs," she mumbles against my lips.

She'll get no argument from me. Picking her up, we make our way to my bedroom.

I place her on the bed, toeing out of my shoes and she flings hers off. Then my lips are attached to hers again as she slides up the bed to the pillows. My leg wedges between her thighs and she grinds along my hard thigh.

I can't remember the last time I wanted someone this bad. Every taste makes me hungrier for more. My hands are a frenzy of wishing I could touch every inch at the same time. Like I'll never have enough time to explore her. Like she'll cut me loose, leaving me a mess of a man who never quenched his thirst for the only woman he's ever really cared for.

"Luca," she pants, her head falling to the pillow and I nibble along her jaw and down her neck. My knuckles trace a path between her breasts until I reach under the hem of her shirt. She's so responsive to my touch. Her torso arches as my hand runs up her bare skin and cups her breast.

She rocks against my thigh and I pull the cup of her bra down, needing to spur another response out of her.

Every moan and whimper are a high I chase with my hands and mouth.

Pushing her shirt up, she groans when my thigh leaves her center. My fingers unhook her bra and she helps me remove her shirt and bra.

Fuck. I gaze down at her, bared to me and my balls pull up tight.

"Pure perfection." I cup each breast, my thumbs running over the pebbled nipples.

Needing to taste her, I devour one breast while squeezing the other.

Her hands fall to the back of my head and her legs widen for me to fit between them. Please God, let me stay here for infinity.

I unbuckle her jeans and I slide my hand down under her panties. She's hot and wet and my cock strains against my pants. "I'm not sure how slow I can go," I admit. I've imagined this with Lauren for longer than I care to admit and the fact that we're here, about to do this, has me on the edge.

She pulls at my shirt. "Me either."

Clothes make their way off our bodies, landing in a heap on the floor. Before I know it, we're skin to skin and nothing —nothing—has ever felt so right.

"Condom?" she asks.

I reach across her, grab a condom and get to my knees in front of her.

"Let me." She takes the wrapper from my hands and rips the foil packet open, sliding it down my length.

My cock in her hands? Beat off material for a month.

"And that's enough playing before I embarrass myself." She lies back on the mattress and I follow her down. I entwine our fingers, locking them at her side until I guide the head of my cock into her wet opening.

A groan leaves my throat. She's tighter than a fist. I pull back and push in a little more, looking down to watch my length disappear inside her.

Taking her other hand, our fingers stay locked together as I fully push inside of her.

"Fuck, Lauren, you feel better than I imagined." I pause for a second before I lose my load in the first two seconds.

I start rocking my hips, thrusting in small bursts, her hips meeting mine with every push. Soon I have no choice but to unlock my hands, to sit up with my heels to my ass so I can go deeper. I want to claim every part of this woman until it's only my name to leave her lips.

Her shoulders still press to the mattress as I thrust into her and grind my hips. I have the best fucking view in his position and I glide all the way back and then slide all the way back in, watching while her body accepts me.

Her hands clench the sheets beside her and moans fall from each of our lips at the same time. We find a rhythm that drives us both half-crazed. I should've known this is where we'd be perfect. We're both intent on getting the other off. Making sure it's the best fuck we've ever had because that's the way we are. Winners in all aspects of our life.

I need to feel her lips, so I adjust back to where we were —her underneath me with her legs like a vise grip around my hips and I search her mouth out.

Pleasure infused words leave our lips as our hands explore every curve and crevice of each other's bodies. Bringing her leg up to her chest, her fingernails almost break my skin from how deep I claim her.

"This is the best," she pants.

I kiss her neck, my tongue sliding across her sweat soaked skin. "It's never been better."

She's exactly as I envisioned all those times I've beat off. In my mind, I've had her bent over my desk, up against a wall, in the shower—and I fully intend on doing all of that with her.

Her hips rise off the bed, and I don't need her to say the words, I know she's close. I thrust harder, faster. My kisses grow hungrier. Our caresses turn into grabbing and pulling.

"Luca," my name falls from her lips like she's being punished and needs me to save her.

"You're so beautiful," I whisper, and I feel her clench around my cock before she gives up her fight and enjoys the spiral back down from euphoria.

I fall to my elbows, my lips at her ear, my jagged breathing unable to even out as my own orgasm builds inside of me. She brings her legs up and squeezes my cock as my hips work double speed, riding out my own pleasure until I come.

I let some of my weight fall and I kiss the skin under her ear, never wanting to leave, praying nothing is awkward with us as I push up on my elbows.

"Luca," she says, breathless. "That was..."

I tentatively open my eyes. "You're really fucking good at that."

She laughs, rising up on her own elbows to kiss me. "So are you."

I kiss her relieved she wanted this as much as me. It wasn't just her desire that spurred this, but maybe, if I'm lucky, her feelings for me.

CHAPTER TWENTY-NINE

Lauren

You know the worst thing to happen after you sleep with the guy who's been occupying your mind for weeks? You can't tell your friends. You can't share your excitement that he really is as good in bed as you predicted. You can't send a quick text and say 'got him' because according to your best friends, you're already engaged to that guy.

His fingers run down my center until they rest between my thighs. I think he believes he's stirring me awake. But I've been up since he took me again in the kitchen when we went down for a snack. His light breathing in my ear is a constant reminder that we've crossed the line. The one I thought was permanently in place, but I guess even the Berlin Wall crumbled. Why did I think we had better odds than that?

"Good morning," he whispers and rocks his hard dick into the crack of my ass.

Déjà vu hits me from only a week ago, but this time

there's no reason to stop us from enjoying a lazy Sunday morning of sex.

"Good morning," I say and arch my back off his chest as his fingers run the length of my folds.

He sprinkles kisses along my neck and down my shoulder, pushing his finger into my heat.

A groan escapes him as he adds a second and my body reacts to his touch. He rolls me over, his hand never leaving me, using his thigh to open my legs. I buck into his palm and his mouth fuses to mine.

The benefit of falling asleep naked is that there's no time lost on disrobing. He pulls away from our kiss, biting my lower lip while our eyes lock. He studies my reaction as he pushes in and out of me until he dips down and trails a line of kisses along my jaw. My head falls back to the pillows and his tongue slides down the curve of my neck.

"I've wanted to do that for so long," he murmurs into my skin, his fingers slowly moving in and out of me with a lazy rhythm that's igniting the spark inside of me.

My legs widen to give him as much room as he needs, my body buzzing with the expectation of his tongue on my clit.

"Luca," I pant, begging for him to reach his destination but he's intent on teasing me. His tongue circles along my nipple before he latches on and my back arches up off the mattress. He shifts to my other tit and I lose all control, clenching around his fingers inside of me.

"I love turning you on." His mouth pops off my tit and his stubble scratches my stomach as he stares up at me.

"You do a good job of it."

He smiles, that arrogant smirk that I used to hate, but he should wear it proudly because the man knows how to make a woman morph into Jell-O.

I whimper as his fingers leave me and shift under my legs,

clutching my hips as he positions himself between my thighs. My fingers, needing something to grip, fall to the sheet.

"My head, baby," he says. "I want you to tug the closer you get."

I do what he says, still surprised at how soft the strands of his dark hair through my fingers are.

The tip of his tongue teases me as he licks long strides up and down my center. He pushes a finger back inside of me and I grip his hair, eliciting a groan from him I can feel in my center. I buck, and he grasps my hips harder to keep me down.

A breathy sigh falls from my lips when he sucks my clit into his hot mouth. My fingers grip his hair harder and I fear I'll rip a patch right out from the follicles.

Luca groans again, his mouth ravishing me. His fingers and mouth work in tandem at the same pace. He cranks the chain inch by inch and just when I think I can't hold on anymore, he switches the game, adding a second finger, arching them inside of me.

His moans are muffled between my legs and I yank at the strands of his hair, my thighs closing in on his face from the sheer unrelenting demand he has over my body.

Just when I don't think I can get any higher before I come, he fucks me with his fingers, adding a third while simultaneously feasting on my clit, twirling his tongue around and around.

"Luca." His name falls from my lips as I clench so hard that I can't stop my orgasm from shattering. My back is off the mattress and my hands have his hair fisted through my fingers. Falling back down to the sheets, I gasp for a breath. "So good. So, so good," I repeat over and over again.

He withdraws his fingers, sitting up and licking them. And isn't that the filthiest and somehow hottest thing I've ever seen.

He grabs a condom from the nightstand.

"How is that skull of yours?" I ask, a flush of embarrassment heating my skin.

"Hurts like fuck." He bends down, pressing his lips to mine. "Just the way I like it. Means I rocked your world." He chuckles.

Somewhere between our kisses and praise of his tongue and fingers, I miss him putting the condom on because the tip of his dick is poised at my opening.

"Ride me?" he asks, rolling us over.

I position myself over him, and guiding his dick into my opening, I sink down on him. The feeling of his length and how glorious he completely fills me will never get old. I don't know how I know that, but I do. Even less than twelve hours since the first time I had him, I know that I'll never experience this with anyone else.

Luca plays my body like an instrument he's perfected since he was three. A prodigy of everything Lauren Hunt enjoys most.

"Fuck, your pussy is the best." He pumps his hips up while my hands splay across his chest. I try to find a rhythm that will prolong the end.

I could fuck him every minute of every day and never tire.

His hands slide up the sides of my torso and he covers my tits, his thumbs rolling over my nipples in a sweet gesture of possession. And they are his, for he's ruined me for any hands that may come after.

I fall forward, needing the connection of our lips and he slides his tongue into my mouth. His hands having no choice but to leave my tits, grab my ass, and he dictates the pace as my mind hazes over, consumed with sensation.

Moans and whimpers and groans bounce around the quiet room as the overcast sky of a snowy December day casts a grey pallor over the room. He rolls us over and our mouths continue to explore one another's skin. Our necks, our shoulders, no inch left untouched by our lips.

"Luca, this feels so good." I can't help but try to put words to everything I'm feeling right now.

He brings my leg up to my chest, enabling him to get deeper but he doesn't change his pace. It's still slow and languid, like his kisses. I'm addicted to the way he cherishes me. His lips skate across my collarbone as I push my hands into his hair.

"You're amazing. So fucking perfect, Lauren. I never want to leave this bed." His lips capture mine and he rocks a little harder.

It always feels like a gift when Luca uses my real name instead of calling me Hunt and I can't stop the warmth from spreading through my chest with his declaration now.

I thought that if Luca and I ever fell into bed with each other, it would always be a raucous frenzy of fucking. But as he pushes into me now, the only way I can think to describe it as is love. Luca Bianco isn't fucking me, he's making love to me and I'm doing the same.

Unable to process that thought completely, I buck up into him and he presses into me, undulating his hips against me when he's fully seated.

"Lauren," he murmurs. The way he looks down at me, almost mystified, is my undoing.

"I know."

"I never..." He shakes his head almost unbelieving himself.

"I know," I whisper.

We share a space that feels sacred. And though neither of us can get the words out, we're both here, in this moment, feeling and living and breathing the same experience.

"I'm so close." He takes my earlobe into his hot mouth. "Come with me," he says, grinding into me.

Pushing my leg as high as he can get it, he occupies my

entire center of my being, his pelvis digging into my clit as his hard length slides in and out of me.

It doesn't take long for the feeling to build up to a level I can't control.

"I think..." He's breathless. "You're everything," falls from his lips and with his confession, my body tumbles over the edge, into the abyss that is Luca Bianco.

He pumps inside of me a few times and stills. His hands smooth down my hair and his lips don't leave my skin. "God, Lauren, I fucking..." His words trail off into a groan as I feel him jerk inside of me. I have no idea if he was going to say what I think he might have.

His lips make their way back to my mouth, and he slides his tongue past the seam of my lips, letting my leg fall. I wrap it around his thigh, locking him to me, wishing we could be locked together forever because outside the safety of this room, things will be real.

Slowing the kiss, he presses one last chaste kiss to my lips. "I'll be back."

I unhook my leg and let him leave. He kneels to get up but then falls back down, kissing me one more time. "I need one more hit."

With the cold still air from the hallway floating in with his departure to the bathroom, I realize that I've fallen in love with Luca.

How in the hell did I let this happen?

<hr>

CHAPTER THIRTY

Lauren

Family dinner is a little easier to swallow when we're not completely faking our relationship.

"Lauren," Mama Bianco calls me over to the table. Her and Zia are looking through a book.

"Yes?" I slide down into a chair to get closer to her.

"This is you?" she asks, pointing to a picture from one of St. George's high school yearbooks.

My hair is cut chin length, I have a big black headband on and I'm front and center as the team captain of the soccer team.

"Oh my God," I say, covering my mouth and trying not to laugh over how dorky I looked.

"You played?" Zia asks, unlike my own parents her expression says she's impressed.

"I did."

Luca stands from the couch, making his way over to me, wondering what the commotion is. His protectiveness over me is a nice change.

"She was better than me, Zia." His hands land on my shoulders, massaging them.

I don't miss Vanessa and Maddie admiring me leaning back and allowing him to do so. Somehow, I've been appointed pasta maker, so I rolled so much dough that Zia and Mama decided to freeze some for all of us.

"Really?" Zia's raised penciled-in eyebrows ask.

"No." I shake my head.

"She's modest." Luca's hands fall off my shoulders and he takes the seat next to me.

"That explains the two of you fitting so well together." Mama's hand lands on mine, staring up at me like I'm her savior. It's been less than a day since I've figured out that I'm in love with her son and she thinks I'm ready to get married. I send a small prayer up that this whole thing doesn't blow up in our faces.

"You told me Van and I fit because we were opposites." Cristian nudges Vanessa with his arm. He sits down, and she plops onto his lap and places a quick kiss on his neck.

"Yes. Opposites love." Mama smiles at the two of them.

"Opposites attract," the two of them correct her and she waves them off.

"Afraid we're beating you out for couple of the year?" Luca winks at his brother.

Seriously, the competition. I love it.

"You both know you've already lost. Maddie and I were first, therefore we're number one." Mauro joins the party, taking the seat between Maddie and Zia.

Is the game on commercial or something?

Zia's hand squeezes Mauro's forearm. "You seem the happiest."

Mauro places his hand on hers and then arrogantly looks at the rest of us with an 'I told you so' wink.

"Zia!" Cristian argues.

"Relax. Ma's got something for firstborns." Enzo enters the room, looking over his mom's shoulder. "Dom can do no wrong in her book." He rolls his eyes what with him being the middle son.

"Not true. It's just I haven't seen you two much." She points to Cristian and Vanessa. "You never show affection. When Saul and I were younger, we couldn't stop touching each other."

"So, if I lay a big sloppy kiss on her you'll say we're the most in love?" Luca asks, and I can't help but laugh silently. In it to win it—always.

"Hello...Zia?" Cristian points to Vanessa sitting on his lap while the rest of us are sitting in our chairs.

"Just because you were too lazy to find your own seat doesn't mean that's affection." Mauro laughs and Enzo and Luca join in.

"Come here, babe." He places his hand behind Vanessa's head to guide her to him, but she shakes her head and then whispers something to him. No one misses his hand sliding up her thigh and grabbing her ass.

Luca puts his arm around my shoulders, pulling me in to lean against his chest. Which I do effortlessly. I'm like a needy, clingy girl unable to get enough and it scares the crap out of me.

"You played soccer, huh?" Enzo asks, staring at my God-awful high school picture. No wonder Luca called me a boy, I dressed like one.

"Yeah. You?"

"I don't play that pussy sport. Football." He winks and high fives Mauro.

"Enzo." Zia turns her head to look behind him and gives him a scowl.

"Sorry, Ma." He massages her shoulders like Luca was doing to me moments ago.

"Let's play." Luca stands and heads out of the room.

"I'm not playing anything. It's like thirty degrees out there." Cristian doesn't move.

"What do you say, baby? I'll let you tackle me." Mauro kisses Maddie on the cheek.

"I say I'm warm." She smiles sweetly while saying it and Mauro grabs his coat off the hook at the front door.

"Oh, this is going to be fun. I wish I had my brothers here." Enzo joins Mauro at the door.

Mama shuts the yearbook, thank God, and leaves the room, touching my shoulder as she goes. Always affectionate Mama.

"Dom plays dirty." Cris nudges Vanessa to get up to retrieve his own coat. "Want to play?" he whispers to her, kissing her briefly as he shrugs his coat on.

I don't really see what Zia is talking about. I get it with Luca and I because we were pretending until right now, but Cris and Van never stop kissing while Maddie and Mauro never stop touching. Maybe that means Luca and I will never stop fucking. That's a pleasant thought I can live with.

"Come on, babe," Luca screams from the doorway.

"I'm not going to play." I fold and refold a napkin on the table.

Silence blankets the room. Mama drops a bag full of hats, scarves, and gloves on the table.

"Everyone wears one." She points to her boys.

"I can't throw with a glove," Mauro whines.

As the other guys dig through the bag for winter gear that I think might've been theirs when they were teens, Luca's arms wrap around my body from behind the chair. His mouth comes to my ear on the side no one can see except for Zia. She smiles at us.

"Why aren't you playing?" he whispers.

I shrug. "It's a guy thing."

He stops my hands from folding the napkin. "Not in this household it's not. And definitely not when you're my ace in the hole." His lips attack my neck. "Come on and roll around on the cold, hard ground with me?"

I laugh, bringing everyone's attention to us.

"What if?" I turn into his lips, his teeth latch on to my earlobe.

"You know you want to play. Come on."

"I'll be your cheerleader."

"Fuck that. I don't want a damn cheerleader, I want a running back."

I laugh and shake my head because he doesn't really understand what he wants from me. Wait until his mom sees me in action with outbursts of swear words and unsportsman-like behavior.

"Don't make me beg," he says softly.

"Come on, Luca. Stop kissing on your girlfriend," Enzo calls out.

He straightens up, coming to my side and taking my hand until I stand up.

"Fiancée *and* my running back."

"Really?" Enzo nods, impressed I think that Luca believes I can hold my own with them. "Let's go then."

"Give them hell, Lauren." Maddie pumps her fist.

"You know what?" Vanessa stands. "I'll play."

"Really?" I ask and I want to smack my mouth shut for questioning her. "Let's go then."

"Perfect. I'll take the girls." Luca holds my coat open for me and Mama throws a hat over my head and a scarf around my neck. Zia does the same with Vanessa.

"Come on Mad," Mauro begs his girlfriend.

"I'll totally embarrass myself and you."

Van and I walk over to her dressed up like snowmen. Each of us takes a hand and yanks her up.

Mauro puts on her coat and Mama and Zia dress her with a Spiderman hat and Ninja Turtle scarf.

"So you four against us?" Mauro asks, opening the door.

"Shut the door," Anthony says, not even knowing what's going on right now, his eyes glued to the game.

"We'll watch from the window. Go get them, girls." Zia fist pumps in the air.

We all smile and once we're on the porch, Luca crouches down. "Your chariot awaits."

I jump on his back and he effortlessly stands up. I kiss his earlobe whispering bedroom promises about what I'll do to him if we win while he carries me across the street to the park.

"I will hold you to those," he says, his hand on my cheek after I climb off him. His body presses my back to the light pole, his lips on mine.

Needing more of him, I open my mouth and his tongue finds mine. Gliding and sliding, suddenly it doesn't feel so cold anymore.

I'm lost in Luca until a football hits him with a thud.

He rips his lips from mine. "Fucker!" He jumps on Enzo's back, tackling him to the ground.

"Okay, boys." Mauro grabs the football off the ground. "Luca already decided teams, so I say let the girls go first. They'll need it." He mumbles the last sentence.

"Mauro!" Maddie scolds him.

He and Cris are laughing until they look at their girl-friends. Oh, how quickly their smiles vanish.

"Okay. We'll go first then," Mauro says.

"I'd have it no other way." Luca's now off his cousin and comes over to me, his arms finding my waist and his lips my neck.

"You can't play with Lauren attached to you," Enzo deadpans.

"Jealousy doesn't befit you, dear cousin," Luca bites back but does finally let me loose only to wrap his arm around me and Vanessa pulling us into a huddle. Maddie joins us. "Okay girls. We're at a disadvantage size wise, but I have no doubt you know your man's weaknesses. Use them."

Maddie and Vanessa exchange a look that says, 'we got this.'

"Lauren, you've got Enzo. He's heavy right side, so you know what to do."

The faith Luca has in me shocks me.

"All hands in. Bianco," he screams.

"Why are we called Bianco? I'm not a Bianco," Vanessa says.

I point to her spot. "It doesn't matter. You stand there and remember you've got Cristian."

She blows a bubble out of her gum and nods her head. "I've got you, baby."

"Yeah you do," Cristian coos and his gaze falls down her body.

"Van, eye on the prize. No flirting with the enemy," I say.

Her lips dip.

"She can flirt with me anytime," Cris says while Mauro is counting down to Enzo to shoot him the ball between his legs.

Once the ball is hiked, Mauro shoots out to Maddie who's pretending to block her massive boyfriend. I run to Enzo. Maddie jumps on Mauro's back as he passes her. Good girl. Vanessa stands there blowing bubbles, making Luca have to get Cris. Right before Enzo throws the ball, I jump to block, falling on top of him and we both tumble to the ground. Him somehow rolling over me. Man, he's as big as Luca.

"Damn you are feisty," he says, standing up and brushing off his legs.

I look to see what happened and Luca has the ball which means he intercepted the pass.

Getting up, I run toward him. "HA! You doubted us." I point to Mauro and Cris, jumping into the right man's arms this time.

Luca drops the ball, catching me. He laughs into the crook of my neck. "God I love..."

I hold my breath.

"Your spirit," he finishes.

"Thanks." I fall down.

Maddie and Van give us high fives and this time Luca will be the quarterback.

"You can't be center again," he says as I stare at him through my legs.

"Well, you're not staring at Maddie or Van's ass, so I'm center until there's a guy to take my spot."

He grins and pushes his hands out, sliding his thumbs along my center as I pass him the ball. A rush of need zips through my core and it takes me a second to straighten up and get my head back in the game.

I run out, but Enzo is on me, following me all the way to the end zone. Vanessa escapes Cris, and he's on the ground, too bad there aren't replays in touch football. Luca looks to me and there's no way I'm catching this ball, my height a pure disadvantage compared to Enzo. Maddie and Mauro are busy flirting with one another, pretending like they're covering one another. Vanessa is jumping up and down and Cris is getting up, prepared to go after her.

"Throw it!" I yell.

Luca lets the ball go and it's like a movie where the ball is suspended in the air forever until it lands in Vanessa's cradled arms.

I jump and flail my arms, running over to her. "Way to go."

That ended up being the only touchdown that day because it's fair to say we all kind of played dirty. Two of us jumped on Mauro's back, Luca included to stop a touchdown.

By the end of the game, we all laid on the cold ground catching our breath, realizing we're not as in shape as we were when we were younger.

"I have no doubt that you were captain now," Enzo says next to me. "You're a fighter for sure."

"My fighter," Luca crawls toward me, climbing on top of me, finding his spot between my legs.

"Ew, stop trying to get Zia to say you're the happiest," Maddie complains.

As the group of them head back to the house, Luca and I lay in the grass, staring up at a dark dreary sky that, funny enough, will forever remind me of one of my happiest times. The time when I found the place I fit the best. The Bianco's don't care about how crazy I can get. They like me for me, and I have Luca to thank for that.

CHAPTER THIRTY-ONE

Luca

On the drive home from work, all I want to do is crash after an endless night of calls that never stopped. As I turn down my street to head down the alley, I realize that sleep is going to be postponed for a little bit.

Lauren is on a ladder half up to the second story with a long line of lights wrapped around the rungs of the ladder.

Jesus, if she's not careful, I'll be in an ambulance with her on the stretcher.

I park the truck and head to the front of the house where I admire her in her snug yoga pants with her short puffy jacket, which lucky for me does nothing to conceal her luscious ass. My mouth waters, wanting to bite down and accost her right here.

Now it's not just sleep on my mind. Being buried in Lauren for a few glorious hours and *then* sleep sounds like a much better plan.

"Whatcha doing?" I ask, calling up to her.

"What does it look like?"

There's no hello or my bed felt cold without you last night. Lauren's not really one for mushy conveyances of love, so I've purposely kept the red heart emojis out of our text exchanges.

She loves my dick though, because she can't stay off it. Her hands find a way to grab my ass or slide up my t-shirt. Her head finds a way onto my chest and her leg slides between mine in the middle of the night. I'm looking for assurances of her feelings for me through her actions, because I'm probably not going to get the words from her.

Like Mama says, action speaks louder than words, and I feel like a pussy for wanting her to tell me once how much... fuck, stop acting like a damn chick. Head in the game.

"Looks like you're about to go to the emergency room," I say.

I stuff my hands into my pockets and watch her. I have no doubt Lauren can accomplish getting the lights up herself. She prides herself on her independence, and I love dating a woman who knows who she is and what she wants. But sometimes a small stature is a limitation and that's exactly what's happening here because I'm not about to let her stand on the top rung.

"Do you doubt my ability?" She glances over her shoulder.

"Not at all, but I'd really like a good morning kiss." The string drops from her hand, hanging down the house from a plastic holder while she climbs down the ladder.

"Only a kiss?" She grins.

"Well, I was hoping I'd find you in bed."

She snuggles into my chest. "Welcome home." She presses her lips to mine and my body is so relaxed I could fall asleep anywhere as long as she was in my arms.

"Rough shift." I kiss her back, not getting too carried away because we're outside.

"I'm sorry." She tightens her arms around my torso.

I drop my bag by our stairs and circle her around. "Let's get this done so I can take you to bed." I kiss her forehead and then climb up the ladder before she has a chance to beat me.

She'd probably try to race me and we'd both end up on the ladder and then on stretchers.

"Luca!" she yells as I continue to climb.

"What? This is a man's job."

Sometimes it's fun to get a rise out of your girlfriend.

"I think I heard that wrong."

"You didn't." I take the string and her organized bucket of plastic holders, positioning and hanging as far as I can go.

The problem comes in when I have to climb down the ladder to get back on. She'll fight me for it. I know.

"I'd cover your balls when you come down."

God, she really is the best.

"Oh babe, there's kids in the neighborhood, you should really wait to teabag me until we get inside."

Unfortunately, I make this joke as I'm coming down the ladder, so I fully prepare myself for the smack on the back of the head.

"Oh, Luca, you don't know me at all."

I jump down once I'm four rungs from the bottom to escape Lauren's wrath, but she jumps on me.

"Teabag, huh?" she whispers. "You do realize I have other powers to punish you with, right? Like withholding sex."

"You're not a masochist." I pick up the ladder and slide it over. Yes, with Lauren on my back.

"Oh, believe me, you'll crack first."

She jumps off my back, but her hands slide up the hem of my jacket, under my t-shirt. I can easily ward off the hands on my stomach, but she ups the ante by sliding her hand down the front of my jeans.

"Kids, babe," I whisper without moving. What can I say,

if she can discreetly give me a hand job in the middle of the day I'll welcome her kinky side. I'm about to say screw the lights.

"Putty in my hands." She removes her hand and my dick is saluting instead of shrinking like he's waving his hand with a 'what about me?'

"Whoa!" I circle around.

She's laughing. "Still think you'd hold out?"

I climb the ladder. "Who brought up this whole juvenile challenge anyway?" Keeping my mind off my dick that is desperate for some love after twenty-four hours at a station without its drug of choice, Lauren Hunt, I string the rest of the lights. The sooner we finish, the sooner I'm in bed with Lauren.

"You did and you know I love challenges. Is this is your way of wooing."

"Wooing?"

"Instead of sending me flowers, you challenge me," she says.

I climb down the ladder, grabbing her with one arm around the waist and swing her around. "Is that what turns you on? Beating me?"

She laughs in my arms, the fallen leaves from the old oak in front of the house next door crumbling beneath my feet.

"I'm not incriminating myself."

"Hey guys." Victoria comes out with Jade and Snowball.

"Hey neighbor," I say.

I stop swinging her around and see Jade run down to hop on her bike to ride up and down the street.

Victoria zips up her coat and puts on her mittens.

"Finally putting on lights huh?" she asks. "Glad you got home, Luca because I tried to tell Lauren it wasn't safe but..." She rolls her eyes and shoots me a look to say, 'you know how she is.'

I put my arm around her waist because I know exactly how she is, and I wouldn't change one damn thing.

"Reed begged me to stop until he returned with Henry." Lauren clearly finds the fact that she could have killed herself hilarious and she squats down to pet Snowball. "Aren't you the cutest thing in your little argyle scarf."

"He was at the groomer." Victoria shakes her head. "I figure I'll never dress him up so, might as well leave it until it falls off."

"It suits him, being the dog of a lawyer and all." Lauren ruffles his white hair and Snowball pounces away to jump around the front lawn.

Speaking of lawyers, a minute later, Reed parks along the curb, an eager Henry running out with a football in his hands.

"Luca!" he yells and throws the ball at me. I run back and catch it.

I've met this little guy a few times when he's been next door. He's a great kid and I think I've gained a fan, humbly speaking of course.

"I think I need to change your name to Tom Brady." I throw it back.

Next thing I hear is a crash of metal on concrete and Jade's hands are out telling Henry to throw it to her.

Lauren stares over at them, half listening to Reed telling us how crazy traffic is already becoming with Christmas' approach. Complaining about all the people from the burbs clogging up the side streets to go look at the tree and shop downtown.

"It's my favorite part of Christmas," Lauren joins in, confirming women are paying attention at all times even when you think they aren't.

Reed gives me a handshake when I make my way over. "Hey, Luca."

"Thanks for trying to tell Lauren not to put up the lights."

Lauren narrows her eyes in my direction but keeps the conversation going in its previous direction. "I love the shopping at night with the lights and the tree up. Watching the ice skaters. All the red bows and green trees around. Christkindlmarket. It just puts that holiday spirit in you."

"I do love the window display at Macy's," Victoria adds.

Reed and I stare at one another and I'm sure we're thinking the same thing—football and turkey and cookies are probably the best things about Christmas.

"For Jade's first Christmas, I was a crazy mom. Thought I had to do it all. Decorate a tree with everything Mickey Mouse. I made cookies, bread, eggnog. Decorated the entire house. I crashed so early on Christmas I told myself never again."

"I think I'd be the same way," Lauren says. "You always feel like the firsts should be special."

Victoria looks at Reed and he looks at her, a knowing smile aimed at one another. "Seconds are good, too," Victoria says and Reed hugs her, kissing her on the lips.

"EW!" Jade and Henry say at the same time.

"It was the first time Reed had proposed," Lauren clarifies for me since I forgot Jade isn't his. Victoria was married before.

"True." Victoria and Reed don't stop touching each other.

"And I'm the best, so it nulls the first," Reed says.

All this talk about firsts makes me think about how I've already asked Lauren to marry me. What will happen the second time around when I actually mean it? She'll always remember the first time. The one that came with bargaining and stipulations. Why am I so stupid? How did I ever think asking my high school crush to pretend to be my fiancée would turn out anything other than disastrous.

"Hey." Lauren's arms wrap around my stomach. "You okay?"

I gaze down at her, the woman who's never out of my mind. "Just tired. Long night."

"Let us help. It will get done faster for you." Reed doesn't ask permission, but grabs a string of lights, starting around the two bushes next to the staircase.

"Next you guys need a tree!" Victoria grabs garland and some white hooks making our entryway look like Martha Stewart was here. "Aw, your first tree."

Lauren looks at me and I smile before climbing the ladder.

With Reed and Victoria's help, we finish the house decorations and after I crash in Lauren's bed because it's kind of ours lately. Lauren has some errands to do, so she heads out to let me catch some zzz's. Not exactly how I was hoping to spend my time in this bed but at least I get to smell her perfume on the sheets as I drift into dreamland.

Yep, I'm a total goner.

CHAPTER THIRTY-TWO

Lauren

Staring out the front window I admire the white lights decorating the trees on the street. I sip my cocoa and enjoy the quiet of the house for a little while before I get to work on my gifts for my patients.

Putting together Briana's gift is hard every year because it symbolizes the fact that I haven't done my job well enough to get her better. I know the statistics, that she'll probably need physical therapy most of her life, but I still hold out hope for her.

I spoke to my mom earlier and she invited us for dinner again in a couple of weeks. Said my dad should be easier to deal with by then. I was relieved to hear it though I didn't enjoy putting her off wedding planning by feigning being so busy with holiday plans that I couldn't even think of my wedding until the new year.

I set my mug on the coffee table and sit on the couch, looking at all the adjectives I've printed out and cut into strips. I pull out the attributes of her and them and the fake snow in the glass ornament that already has her name and the year written on it with glitter.

A Hallmark movie plays in the background and my hand almost reaches for the remote when I hear movement upstairs. Then I realize, Luca won't make fun of me for watching. Instead, he'll probably sit down next to me and critique how unmanly the guy is and how unrealistic everything that happens is. I kind of love it. He's willing to watch and we both pretend he doesn't enjoy them as much as he does.

The toilet flushes, some water runs and as his footsteps fall on the stairs, my stomach stirs in anticipation of seeing his face.

"Hey, you let me sleep way too long." He runs his fingers through his unruly hair and weaves through the two chairs over to me.

Luca is hot, that's undeniable. I've always noticed his strong jaw, his broad shoulders, and his perfect set of white teeth against his bronzed skin and dark eyes. This buzzing inside of me isn't from his level of attractiveness, it's for him as a whole and the fact he's mine.

"I think you needed it."

He slides in behind me on the couch, his arms around my middle and his chin on my shoulder. "What are we doing?"

Can I just say I love that he uses we, like whatever one of us is doing, we're in it together. I have to admit, Luca might've always been my biggest cheerleader, but he was so far back on the sidelines that it took me way too long to realize it.

"We're making ornaments for my patients."

He picks one up, shakes it making the show scatter within its limited space. "You made this?"

"Yeah. I do it every year. I usually get inundated with handwritten Christmas cards and homemade cookies. I want my kids to know I appreciate them just as much as they appreciate me."

He squeezes me harder, and inhales a deep breath, like someone does when they sip their morning coffee and it warms my insides.

His lips find my earlobe, his teeth nibbling.

"I gotta finish this." I lean my head in the opposite direction of his mouth.

Surprisingly he stops, picking up one of the words I've cut out of paper. "Beautiful," he says. "You're beautiful." His warm lips press to my cheek.

He drops that one and picks up another one. "Strong." And then another. "Fierce."

"This one is for Briana."

"Sounds about right."

I hold the ornament open for him. "Drop them in."

He does and then snags a fourth word from beside us.

"Priceless?" I ask.

"Briana is definitely one of a kind, but in a good way."

I lean back, allowing him to sprinkle kisses along my neck. "I love that you see her like I do."

He mumbles something against my neck, his hands sliding up my ribcage, and one hand pulls down the side of my V-neck t-shirt.

"Oh, I think I found something." Without wasting any time, he pulls the cup of my bra down and massages my breast in his big palm. "This is what I've been waiting for. I mean, I'd rather be laying on them like pillows but this will do." A long, contented sigh slips from his lips and he rests his head on my shoulder.

"You're horrible, I'm trying to make ornaments for a bunch of kids and you're doing that."

Of course, I judge, but I don't actually remove his hand

especially now that his thumb and forefinger are tweaking my nipple. I mean, what girl can really say no to that?

The ornament falls to the floor, thankfully staying in one piece, and Luca manages to get me on my back.

"Only a quickie because I'm taking you out tonight," he says as he's already trying to pull my leggings down.

"Where?" I ask, lifting my butt up off the cushion so he can make some headway.

"It's a surprise." His lips descend on my neck like he's a vampire and the bulge in his pants heats up my core.

I hate to tell him, I'm not sure quickie is a term either one of us knows the meaning of.

———

"Where are we going? We're walking?" I ask, my arm through Luca's, my head leaning on his arm.

Yep, we're the lovesick couple people either love or hate.

"We're not walking. And I'm not sure it will be a surprise in a minute."

He guides us around the corner.

"Public transportation?" I ask, spotting the train station up ahead.

"You're too smart for me to ever surprise you."

His newly showered scent intoxicates me and I feel like a koala bear to a tree, never wanting to release my grip.

"You surprised me with that candy delivery at work. And again, with the fact that you were hiding these intense feelings for me in high school."

He glances down at me while we wait to cross at the light. "I'm not sure I should've ever told you that information."

"Why? I love it."

"Because it makes me weak for never laying it all out on

the table for you. I mean, why wait all those years? Not to mention some of the things I said to you over the years."

We cross the street and walk through the entrance, paying and climbing the stairs to wait for the train. Luca's hand stays on the small of my back the whole time. My body hums with a giddiness I find hard to describe because it's new to me. I've never felt so hopeful or happy as I have lately. I'm in so deep with him, if we don't work out, I'll never free myself from the memories of us together.

"Don't tell anyone this." I rise to my tiptoes to whisper in his ear. "I kind of like the fact your feelings were so intense for me that you didn't know how to handle them." I laugh.

Luca's arms wrap around my waist, his head in the crook of my neck.

"Intense, huh?"

I tilt my head up to look up at him. "Don't be embarrassed. My feelings are pretty intense right now, too."

His lips fall to mine and his tongue slides into the opening of my mouth. Twisting in his arms, my fingers weave through his hair. The platform shakes with the rumble of the approaching train barreling down the track. The wheels squeaking to a slow stop behind me and even as I hear the doors of the train slide open, I'm not ready to leave his arms for even the small amount of time it would take me to get onto the train. I'm so over my head in this rush of emotions for Luca that he steals away my attention from everything else.

"Come on," he mumbles, grabbing my hand, pulling me onto the train right before the doors shut. As we round a silver pole, our lips find one another's again and he steadily supports me with one hand on my hip and the other gripping the pole behind his back while leans against it. My hero.

The train ride goes by in a blur and although I have my suspicions where he's taking me, I could be wrong, so when the train stops on State Street and he leads me off, I smile as we head up the stairs. Then it's me pulling him to go faster, the buzz of a Saturday night during Christmas on State Street bleeding into my veins.

We reach the top of the stairs and it's like we've transcended into our own Christmas snow globe. Busy shoppers crowd the sidewalks with armfuls of bags. A pair of little girls dressed in black velvet dresses with red bows in their hair run past. A crowd of people are enamored with the display in Macy's windows. The bells for the Salvation Army sound and the Santa's Ho Ho Ho's ring through the air. As if it's a Hallmark set of its own in this two-block section of downtown, a white dusting of snow falls all around from the dark sky. All of this is my favorite part of the season, but when I look up at Luca staring on at me instead of everything going on around us, it's evident that he makes it even more special.

"You've been here, right?" I ask, his hand in mine ready to pull him farther into Christkindlmarket, my mouth watering for the big pretzels.

"Yeah. But watching it through your eyes is so much better."

"I never knew you were such a romantic." I lean my head on his chest.

"Me either." His lips press to the top of my head, but we're pulled from our moment when horns honk and bodies behind us start moving around us.

For the entire night, our bodies were like magnets. If one of us strayed too far, we were drawn back to the other. We walk along the red and white striped tents, white string lights hanging above us as we enjoy eating pretzels and sausages. We browse the vendor tents, me buying some candles for my co-workers, while he weighs in with his opinion on which scent smells the best.

We stop with my back to his front, listening to the live German bands, drinking German beer.

As the vendors start closing up for the night, Luca buys a bag of cinnamon roasted almonds and we leave the feel of a small German village and head into metropolitan Chicago again where people hurry from place to place, ignoring what's around them.

"Up for some ice skating?" Luca holds a nut in front of my mouth and I open. The sweetness bursting inside my mouth.

"I'd rather put up a Christmas tree..." I say, a little unsure.

I have no idea why I'm worried to bring this up to Luca, but a tree feels like true coupledom. Like we bought a tree and decorated it together even though we've been together for months.

My thumb runs to the band on my left hand. Sometimes I forget that the ring doesn't really mean what it does to other people and I wonder if I should return it to him. In some ways, it feels more wrong to wear it now that we're actually a thing than it did when we were just pretending to play house.

As doubts plague my mind, Luca pulls something out of his shopping bag. He snuck off earlier to buy something and wouldn't tell me what it was.

"Partly naked?" he asks, showing me a cute yet revealing Santa-inspired teddy.

I push him lightly, but he doesn't budge. "Okay, I'll settle for skimpy lingerie."

"Looks like you have just the thing then."

He leads us back to the train. "Be careful. I have some very kinky taste. I played it safe this time."

"I figured, but just remember there is men's lingerie, too."

"I'm game."

$$\overline{\hspace{3cm}}$$

CHAPTER THIRTY-THREE

Luca

Christmas is next week and I've yet to buy Lauren's gift. Truth is I have no fucking clue what to get her. We haven't discussed the fact that everyone thinks we're engaged and now we've embarked on a real relationship. How the heck do you unengage the girl you're dating so that one day you can ask her again...probably, maybe? None of these thoughts occurred to me when I fell down on bended knee the first time.

As I sit in the ER for the fourth time today, thankful that my partner is handling the paperwork, my vision shifts to Lauren's Physical therapy office which I can spot through the windows. She's in there and I wish I was, too. I think back to weeks ago and how I thought she was a safe bet because she'd never want to actually date me. And here I am literally convincing myself not to walk over there and kiss her in the middle of her session with a patient. How did I get here?

My head falls into my hands.

"You're thinking hard over here," a woman's voice pulls me from my mini-anxiety attack.

Sitting up, I notice Keri. We didn't just bring in her patient in did we? Damn, my mind is only on that spunky brunette nowadays.

"Hey, Keri." I lean back, glancing over to Keith to see how far along he is with the paperwork.

"I stopped by your mom's room that night, but the lights were off and only an older gentleman was there."

She appears disappointed, but there's nothing between Keri and I that wasn't professional.

"Probably my dad. They have to do another ablation in a few months."

Her hand touches my thigh. I stare down at her mani-cured pink nails. Her fingers are longer than Lauren's, her palm bigger.

"I'm so sorry. I don't know much about that other than people can live with A-fib."

"Yeah, she's in good spirits and the doctor is hopeful."

My eyes won't stop staring at her hand on my leg. Why is it still there?

I shift in my seat, but she still doesn't move her hand.

I've had plenty of women touch me in more private areas than my leg, but nothing has ever felt this wrong. If anything, I welcomed the casual affection. Now, her hand feels like it's burning a hole through my uniform, but I have no idea how to get her to remove it. My vision shoots over to Keith once more, but he's busy chatting up the new young nurse.

"That's great. So, I was thinking..." Her hand slides farther up my thigh.

Fuck, do something idiot.

You'd think I swallowed acid the way my throat is burning as I watch her, but still, I sit there working out the puzzle in my head. Am I really ready for one woman to be the only one to touch me? My short time with Lauren flies through my mind like I'm flipping channels on the television. Us in the shower this morning, last night on the couch, two days ago when we were laughing so hard we ended up on the stairs. Her dark hair that lay like a veil over my face when we kiss. The slight squirm she does when I kiss the inside of her thigh right before I go down on her. It's not even all the sex, it's the Hallmark movie day when I fed her cookie dough well before I had a chance to taste the chocolate from her tongue. Her jumping in the end zone at a spontaneous game of touch football with my family. My mom showing her how to form tortellini.

A cool breeze from the sliding doors pulls me from my trip down memory lane of my short time with Lauren Hunt. My hand covers Keri's with one intent—to set her straight.

"Listen, Keri, I'm—"

"Luca?"

I twist my head in the direction of my voice and find Lauren standing there, her eyes not on my face and when I follow her line of vision, I know what she sees.

Fuck.

"Nope." I stand leaving Keri's hand to fall off my leg. "It's not what this looks like."

Lauren surprises me by staying in place and not fleeing. I would've been long gone and not waited for an explanation.

"Then tell me what this is." She crosses her arms.

"Let's go outside."

"Is she joining us?" She looks past me to Keri.

Circling back around, Keri's perfectly styled eyebrows are raised so high you might think she just got Botox. "Sorry, Keri, that's what I was about to tell you. I have a girlfriend."

"Fiancée actually." Lauren raises her hand and the overhead lights glint off her diamond.

I bite my bottom lip praying like hell I don't smile over

her staking her claim. Jealousy means she likes me. Jealousy means this isn't some fling to her. Jealousy means she's invested in a future with me. That thought alone elates me.

"Oh, I didn't know..." Color flushes Keri's cheeks and she shifts her weight from one high heel to another. "Congratulations."

"Thank you." Lauren lowers her hand.

"See you around, Keri," I say, but she's already turned around and disappearing down the hallway.

"I'll be outside, Keith," I holler.

He gives me a quick wave, never turning around because he could give a shit about me until we're back in the truck.

"You're with me." I link hands with Lauren and take her outside, but it's fucking freezing. Like snot in your nose dries immediately cold. Shrugging out of my jacket, I put it over Lauren's shoulders.

"So..." She shrugs, putting her arms through my jacket.

I pull out my phone and snap a picture.

"What are you doing?"

"I really wanted a picture of you with my jacket on."

"Like it's high school?"

"Well, you wore Cody's jacket all the fucking time."

She steps forward, her fingers digging under my belt loop. "Stop talking about Cody. I'm with you and if you want to dig up your letterman jacket, I'll gladly wear it." She rises on her tiptoes and kisses my jaw. A whimpering moan falling from her lips.

"So, what are you doing here?" I ask.

"Besides beating away all your admirers?" She raises a brow, but I don't respond. "I'm on lunch and I took a chance that you might be here."

"Can't get enough of me." Before she can protest, I slip my arms around her, capturing her mouth and sliding my tongue inside. Suddenly it's not so cold outside.

Stopping the kiss, she pulls back, staring up at me. "Is there anyone else I need to remind you're taken?"

"Nope but you can't expect me to put a sign around my neck that says I belong to Lauren Hunt."

"I don't know, I think I could."

Pulling her closer, I kiss the top of her head.

"So..." Her voice is muffled in my chest, but I know what's she's getting at just from the tone of her voice.

"I guess when you're the girl I'm with it's pretty fucking easy to say no to another woman's advance."

She lightly punches me in the stomach. "Still have all those worries about being a horrible boyfriend?" She stares back at me again.

I place my hands on either side of her face, our eyes only on one another. "I can't speak for all my faults, but I feel pretty damn confident right now."

She laughs rising on her toes one more time, pressing her lips to mine.

"Want to go make out in my truck?" I ask.

Taking my hand, she leads me to the open rig. "I have twenty minutes until my lunch is up."

"What about food?"

"I think there's a big meat sandwich that will fill me up at least until I get home tonight." She winks and rounds the rear of our truck, climbing up the bumper and into the bench seat.

"You really are the perfect girl."

I shut the truck doors, and her fingers fiddle with my pants. "Come on Romeo, let your Juliet give you one hell of a lunch break."

She takes me out and as I watch my cock disappear between her lips. I want to hammer down a gavel and yell SOLD! because I'm praying I'll never be on the market again.

CHAPTER THIRTY-FOUR

Lauren

Boxing up the ornaments for my clients while watching the Blackhawks has made it a tad dangerous with them not on their A game tonight. I've wanted to toss one across the room a few times. Hopefully, Luca and I can get to a game soon, but this is their last one before their holiday break.

The doorbell rings and I roll my eyes, standing up to answer. Maddie's the owner of the house, so I'm not sure why she doesn't use her key.

"Hey." I spring open the door to a smiling Maddie and Vanessa.

"What's going on?" Maddie says as they enter.

I sit back down on the couch, tying the ribbons on the boxes and placing them in a bag.

Maddie sets down her coffee and helps me out without any direction. She's been doing this with me for years.

Vanessa sits down and searches for the remote.

"I've had about enough of sports. Cristian watches it all

the time. Yesterday I found him watching a fencing competition." She sips her coffee and makes herself comfortable in Luca's ugly chair. I have a plan to have that reupholstered. "This is surprisingly comfortable."

"It's ugly and when I put this house on the market, it's going back to whatever dark hole it crawled out of." Maddie's fingers make quick work of the ribbons. She's always had a knack for the girly stuff like crafts and decorating.

"Cute tree. Why doesn't it have ornaments? Is that some trend I missed out on as a result of my life slowly being overtaken by all things man?" Vanessa looks at our big tree strung with colored lights. Luca insisted that white lights are classic and there's nothing classic about us. I tried to argue since the outside lights are white, but I lost. I think I'm losing my edge.

"No, it's just my family trees were always hung with homemade ornaments or ones that had meaning. I didn't want picture perfect high fashion tree, I want a homey one."

"So you'll have an empty tree until you and Luca have kids?" Vanessa asks with a groove in between her eyes.

"You could get an ornament for being engaged?" Maddie suggests because my friends are still in the dark about the whole fake engagement. "I have to say, you guys have really made a home here." She sits back on her legs and looks around the room. The Santas, trees, snowmen. Luca said screw a theme, we're going with a hodgepodge of everything. If you like it, we buy it. We've had fun decorating the past week, but still, our tree sits there empty.

"Yeah, maybe," I say.

"What's with the shift?" Vanessa asks, locating the remote and flipping to the Hallmark channel. The Blackhawks were probably going to lose anyway, and I'd much rather chat with my girls who I rarely see now that everyone has a significant other.

"Shift?" I pull my legs up under me.

"When you guys first announced your engagement, we all thought you guys were up to something. Cristian was convinced it was some ploy by Luca." She rolls her eyes like he never saw us in the right light. Van's been team Luca and Lauren since the beginning. "Now, you guys are always together, touching and kissing. Don't get me wrong, it's nice to see, but weird how it feels like we were witnesses to something evolving when you'd think we would have seen it before the ring was on your finger." Her gaze shoots to my hand, almost as if she's making sure the ring is still there.

Vanessa is way too observant, Is Cristian giving her some sort of lessons when he's off duty?

"I don't know." I shrug hoping to play it off and move on.

"Did you just feel uncomfortable because you said you hated him when you really looovveed him?" Maddie's body wiggles side to side.

"No. I really did hate Luca." At least I can tell the truth about that.

At least I think I did. It's all so confusing now. As much as I hated him, I loved pushing his buttons and challenging him. It was kind of a sick game I played when I look back on it. Like my feelings for him were right under my skin's surface, hibernating until he touched me. Maybe that's why I agreed to this whole thing in the first place.

"Well, you don't hate him now," Vanessa says.

The movie goes to a commercial and Vanessa with her poor attention span flicks through the channels.

"No, I don't."

Maddie leans forward. "We're going to be sisters-in-law." She places her left hand over mine, her bigger diamond outshining mine.

The hope overwhelming her eyes kills me inside.

I smile and luckily Vanessa interrupts us before I have to lie straight to my best friend's face again.

"No, not again." The remote falls to the floor and Vanessa digs into her hoodie's pocket, retrieving her phone. Pressing one button, she holds it up to her ear.

Maddie rounds the table, seeing the fire blazing hot, red and angry on the television. Neither of us listens to the reporter. Maddie goes for her phone, I go for mine.

Both Mauro and Luca are on shift tonight. At least my man stays outside the fire while hers runs into the building. And with all the warehouse arson fires lately, it makes his normal dangerous job even more hazardous.

She returns holding her phone in her palm, her eyes intent on the television. We've been here before. She scours the scenes, looking for a glimpse of Mauro while a camera guy shoots the scene. Nothing. There's nothing.

"Okay, let us know what you hear. I know. I know. I can't believe this either. Why aren't the police arresting anyone? I know, babe. Okay." Vanessa clicks end and stares over at us. "Another abandoned warehouse fire. Cris is going to try to find out what's happening. He said he'll let us know. He's calling Zia to make sure she's with Mama. We're to sit tight here."

Maddie gets up, walking back and forth in front of us.

Vanessa's phone rings and she mutes the television. "Hey. Okay. Thanks, babe. We will. Love you too." She places her phone in her lap. "Engine Fifty-Five are on the scene."

Maddie's eyes close and she inhales a deep breath, falling to one of the chairs. Her body rocks. Man, these fires have really shaken her up. "Sometimes I think I'm not cut out for this...to be a firefighter's wife. I mean every time he leaves for work, I'm terrified. Especially with these out of control warehouse fires someone is starting."

Vanessa stands and sits down in the chair next to her, her

hand on her knee. "He's smart. He's experienced. He knows what he's doing. With all the shootings in this city I fear for Cristian every day, too. It's a lot to handle."

I stare at them from across the room. I've never once been scared when Luca went to work. Not that I deem his job safe, he goes into uncontrolled situations a lot, but he does have a safer job than either Mauro or Cristian. Still, he's there in his ambulance right now waiting to help anyone who needs it. Maybe I'm underestimating the risks he's exposed to with his job. Should I be rocking like Maddie? If I cared more for him, would I be more worried?

Vanessa widens her eyes at me in question wondering why I'm not helping to reassure our friend that her fiancé will come home safely. What do I say? That I'm having a revelation here? I kiss him goodbye when he goes to work, never worried that he won't be returning to me twenty-four hours later. Am I naïve or do I just not care that much?

A phone rings and Van reaches for hers, but hers isn't ringing.

"It's yours," Van says.

I look down at the screen, where it lay on the couch and see Luca's name. "Hey," I say.

"You heard?" he asks.

"We did. Maddie and Van are here."

"Okay, Mauro is in the building. It's bad, babe. This fire is the worst of the ones I've been on shift for. But don't tell Maddie that. Mauro knows what he's doing but just stay by a phone just in case."

"Be careful," I say.

"You know me? I'm Superman. How else could I give you three orgasms in one night?" That light lilt of arrogance is in his tone and for some reason that puts the little uneasiness I have watching Maddie practically shatter in front of me at ease.

"Call me when it's over?"

"Yeah, once I'm back at the station. I'll call you if anything happens."

"Thanks."

"Sure. Bye, babe."

Neither one of us hangs up. I can hear him breathing. The words are on the tip of my tongue. Three little words most engaged couples say to one another hanging there in the silence, but what if I'm wrong? I mean even after this call, there's not one ounce of worry he won't call me in an hour either at the station or from the hospital.

"Talk to you soon," I finally say.

"Yeah...talk to you later." He hangs up the phone and the sourness in my stomach is the fact that I have no idea if I can trust my gut or not.

"What did he say?" Maddie asks, pacing again.

"He said they're there."

Maddie's eyes close again and she nods. Vanessa's eyes plead with me to come up with some sort of an idea, but I saw Maddie in this state a few weeks ago. Nothing other than Mauro calling or running through that door is going to get her to relax. So, all three of us sit and wait for the phone call.

Forty-five minutes later, it's Van's phone that rings. I've seen her hammering out text messages a few times and I'm guessing it was Cris telling her he was trying to get information.

"Hey," she answers and heads toward the front door for some privacy.

Maddie watches her intently.

Van swallows a lump in her throat and she turns to face the wall. Shit, something's happened.

I head over to Maddie and grip her hand in mine.

"Okay. Yeah, we're on our way. Love you, too."

She takes what seems like forever to turn around and I

squeeze Maddie's hand harder, letting her know that we're here for her, however she needs us. But Van's eyes fall to me instead of Maddie.

"It's Luca."

My stomach drops, and bile chases the involuntary cry up my throat. Everything around me swirls like a kaleidoscope and memories of my short time with Luca bombarded me and leave me gasping for breath.

"He's being rushed to County." Vanessa's voice startles me and it's like I'm being sucked backward through a wormhole until I'm back in the room with them. She tucks her phone in the pocket of her sweatshirt. "We're not telling Mama until Cris knows more. Mauro is in the ambulance with Luca." She swings her purse over her shoulder. "Come on."

It's then with Vanessa's urgent eyes pinned on me and Maddie's hand trying to slide from mine that I realize I was a fool to ever think I felt anything other than love for Luca because right now I want to rip the tree down along with the lights outside. Throw his sweatshirt hanging on the dining room chair out. Shred the Sports Illustrated magazine on the table because if none of that existed, it would mean my heart wasn't so invested that it could crumble to pieces like it is with the thought of losing him.

CHAPTER THIRTY-FIVE

Luca

"You fucking moron. What were you thinking?" Mauro yells at me as I lay on a stretcher with someone looking the burns over, taking my vitals.

"Shut up. I had to help. He was falling down. He needed oxygen."

"You know rules, Luca, you wait until we're over the line." He runs his hands down his soot-covered face.

Mauro was out of the building, trying to grab me when I ran over to help a firefighter down on the sidewalk with an oxygen mask. The mini explosion that propelled me fifty feet, landing me right on my back wasn't supposed to happen. At least in my mind.

"You always have to cross that line. Why can't you ever play it safe?"

"Mauro, this isn't calming him down. His pulse is skyrocketing. We have no idea about his back and I'm pretty sure these are second-degree burns on his legs," Javin, another paramedic, tells him.

"Cris is calling Lauren. She'll be here. You're not the one we're supposed to worry about." Mauro runs his dirty hands through his sweat-slicked hair.

"I'm good. I'm talking to you, aren't I?"

"You don't get it, Luca. You have a fiancée to go home to now. A future. Someone invested in you. Trusting you to keep the risks of your job to a minimum. Someone you have to put before yourself."

"Stop with the big brother lecture."

Javin puts an IV into the top of my hand to prep me for whatever they're going to do at the hospital. I know the drill well enough to predict what his next step will be.

"I don't think you'll ever grow up. Lord help Lauren because one day she's going to get a phone call that will destroy her."

Mauro's talking to himself more than to me now, but his words repeat over and over in my head. Destroy and Lauren the two prominent ones.

"You just can't do whatever you want. Why don't you understand that?"

I don't fight him anymore. Mostly because my mind is swimming with doubts again. Doubts about something happening to me and her not knowing how I really feel. Mauro can fuck himself if he thinks he's going to make me feel guilty for running to help someone. He would've done the same. It's what we do. So I really don't care what's up his ass now. My only concern is that I need Lauren to know that I love her.

I love her. I love Lauren.

I've never loved anyone before and accepting it feels like being bowled over by a tidal wave.

Telling Lauren is an urgent need inside me, like my heart is hammering with fists on my rib cage to get out.

"I need someone's phone. Where's mine?"

"In your own truck."

"Give me yours." I look to Mauro who narrows his eyes.

"Mine is in my truck. I had Trevor call Cris and he'll make the phone calls."

My mission is to memorize Lauren's number as soon as I get my phone back.

"She'll be at the hospital?" I ask my brother.

"Yeah." He doesn't look at me, like my face would sicken him.

In my mind, I figure out my list of tasks while Javin works on me. First is to admit my feelings to Lauren, Then I need to tell my family the truth. It'll be nice to have it all out on the table and then we can start our *real* life together.

Luca and Lauren forever.

CHAPTER THIRTY-SIX

Lauren

"We're here to see Luca Bianco." Maddie takes the lead at the nurse's station because I'm still in shock that of the three of us, I'm the one in this position right now.

"And you are?" the woman who looks to be in her mid-thirties asks, leaning back in her chair and crossing her arms over her chest.

"Maddie..." She looks behind at me. We all know the drill, family only more than likely. She grabs my shoulders and pushes me up to the reception desk. "This is his wife, Lauren Bianco."

The nurse looks me up and down and then laughs. "Luca Bianco has a wife?"

I nod. Again, with this lying business, but at least this time it's to a stranger.

"Luca isn't married. Honey, he's in here every other day. I'd know." She gives us all a smug look.

"Well, she's his fiancée." Vanessa holds up my left hand. "See! His ring is on her finger."

"That could be anyone's ring." She moves her attention to her computer screen and starts typing, seemingly done with us.

"Hold on, I'm calling Mauro." Maddie steps away with her phone in hand.

"If I let every girl in here who says they're engaged to Luca Bianco I'd be fired."

I lean forward. "How many girls?"

"He's not fucking Adam Levine. He's a paramedic," Vanessa snips.

The nurse just stares at Vanessa unimpressed. I'm not getting anywhere with this lady. I'm going to either have to make a run for it or wait for Mauro or Cris to show their face.

"Voicemail," Maddie says.

"I'll call Cris." Vanessa steps away, but the elevator dings and out walks that doctor from before.

What was her name?

I can't think of anything other than her hand on my fiancé's knee.

The one he flirted with in the elevator.

God, that seems so long ago now.

"Hey." She smiles politely over to me, while the nurse hands her some papers. She reads them and then she looks back at me. "Luca's, right?"

"Lauren. Yeah. Can you tell this nurse that I'm his fiancée?"

"I got voicemail, too," Vanessa says.

"She is his fiancée," the doctor says. "He's introduced me to her." The doctor smiles over to me and then goes back to reading her papers.

The nurse hems and haws but writes me out a visitor pass. "Room four fourteen."

I smack the sticker on my shirt and wait for the buzzer to allow me in.

"Thank you," I say to the doctor who gives me a little wave, probably secretly cursing my name.

A buzz sounds and the double doors open. Behind them, it's a bustle of activity. Wallows of pain can be heard, doctors talk to nurses about diagnoses and plans of care. Family members reassuring their loved ones everything will be okay.

I don't even know what condition Luca is in. He may not even be coherent for all I know. Oh God, what if he's in a coma or on life support? Someone probably would have told me, right? My heart is almost beating out of my chest. I want to hold him. I want his lips on the top of my head. If he's okay, we're so doing naked Christmas tree decorating like he suggested. I'll let him put up the lights because if I scared him this much when I was up on the ladder, I get it now.

I look up to the ceiling, praying for the first time in too long. "I'll let him win at everything. Competition doesn't matter as long as I have him. Please let him be okay. I'll be a better person, I promise."

The farther down the hall toward his room number, my gut locks up like heavy chains tying knot above knot as I struggle to walk.

One thing is certain, I don't care if he doesn't feel it yet, I'm telling him I love him. That sometime during this fake relationship, something real emerged and I've fallen head over heels in love with him. We'll be like one of those cheesy couples from the Hallmark movies and I can't wait. He just has to be okay.

I pass room number four twelve and decide that even if he's not awake, I'll hold his hands so I'm the first person he sees.

My footsteps slow as I approach his door, taking one last deep breath for courage.

Lay it all out there, Lauren. Be honest with him.

"It wasn't real." The sound of Luca's voice sends a thrill through me until I process his words.

I stay where I am, unshed tears burning in my eyes.

"I knew it!" Cristian's conviction rings clear in his voice. "Just because Ma was sick, right? What were you thinking? Did you think about what would happen when she found out? How she'd feel then?"

"No," Luca says.

"If you weren't in a hospital bed right now, I'd beat the shit out of you," Mauro chimes in.

"You guys know how Ma was always on my case about not growing up. She wanted her three boys settled down. So I gave her what she wanted."

"And what now?" Cris asks. "What are you going to tell Ma now?"

"I don't know. I haven't figured that out yet."

"Of course you haven't. You probably want Cris to tell her," Mauro says, and I can hear the fury in his voice.

I hear a sound of slapping hands. "I wipe my hands of that responsibility. It's about time you own up to your mistakes."

Is that what I was to Luca? A mistake?

"Maddie's already planning us moving into side by side houses, having bar-b-cues and having kids around the same time. On second thought, I'm going to kill you because you didn't just fuck with your own feelings, you're fucking with other people's—most importantly the one person I put in front of my own."

There's a light scuffle and I wonder if Mauro really is kicking his ass.

"Stop it. This isn't going to help." Cristian, the peacemaker, intercepts whatever's happening. "I think the important question is, what are you going to tell Lauren?"

"She knows. She agreed to the plan. I just have to tell her

it's over. That we're not going to play future bride and groom anymore. Laying on the stretcher made me realize I've been an idiot for ever coming up with that plan."

"Finally, some sense," Mauro says.

"Just relax," Luca bites out.

"How will she handle that? You two seemed really close lately," Cristian asks.

She'll understand. We get each other. I owe her two more Blackhawks games but..."

Those three words I was intent on speaking are swept away like dust in the wind.

"Are you going in, dear?" A nurse touches my elbow startling me from my eavesdropping.

"No, not anymore." I start to turn back the way I came and stop.

Luca was using me as his fiancée...but he slept with me. Was that always part of his plan? All those stupid lines that I fell for... 'I wasn't a romantic until I met you.' He played me, using everything at his disposal, even Briana. Giving me that word priceless to describe her and put in her ornament. He knew exactly what he was doing.

Mauro's right, he needs a little lesson of his own. "Actually." I touch the nurse's arm who's about to go into the room. "Could you give me one minute?"

She smiles. "Sure. Do you want me to kick the other two out?"

I smile back. "No. I can handle that."

She pats my hand where it still rests on her arm. "I'll give you two some time then."

Once she disappears into another room down the hall, I look both ways like I'm about to commit a felony.

I walk in and all six eyes shift to me.

Mauro looks hesitant.

Cristian appears sorrowful.

Luca... well, I wouldn't know because I'm not actually looking at him. If I did, I don't know if I could keep from strangling him.

"Baby," he coos.

I inhale a breath to settle myself before I pick up the chair and throw it at him.

"You think you fooled me? Joke's on you, Luca."

"What?" His forehead scrunches up.

"Lauren." Cristian comes to my side, touching my elbow.

I wrench it out of his grip. "I heard your little confession to your brothers." I look at both of them. "Yes, I agreed to play his fiancée and I'm sorry. Mostly to your mom, but I did it and I can't take it back." I look toward Luca, but I'm really just looking over his head, still not able to stomach making eye contact with him. "Did you think what was between us was real?" I let a caustic laugh loose. "You were a convenient lay. That's all. But I'm glad we're on the same page. It makes our fake break-up easy. Have a nice life, Luca."

I turn to leave, praying the tears pricking my eyes don't fall.

"Hunt!" he hollers, and my feet stop at the door's edge. He uses the name he used all through high school. How convenient. "It was really a joke? You didn't feel anything?" I hear the crack in his voice and he almost has me. Almost. But I know it's just his ego that's feeling the sting of my rejection right now.

"I felt nothing. Have a nice life, Bianco." I walk out the hospital room, down the hall, push open the doors, and run out of the hospital and into the ice-cold night.

He doesn't try to stop me by running after me like it's a Hallmark movie. Hell, this feels more like a Nicholas Sparks movie.

I slip into the first cab I come across, finally letting the tears fall down my face. I always knew heartache was inevitable and I curse myself for giving my heart to that man.

I'll allow myself one night of regret before I pick myself up and get on with my life, free of Luca Bianco.

CHAPTER THIRTY-SEVEN

Luca

The morning glow seeps into the front room of the house as I walk in after being discharged. The decorations are still up, the tree bare without a single ornament still stands. Everything is where it's supposed to be. I half expected my shit to be in a pile at the curb, our tree to be tossed on the front lawn and any decorations I purchased broken into pieces.

I guess I feel like the space Lauren and I shared should resemble what my hollowed out heart feels like—broken and destroyed.

I walk up the stairs, hoping she's still asleep so we can hash out the truth. Lauren can say whatever she wants but I know what she felt for me and it was love. The way her body quivered under my touch and she always leaned into me, we were on our way to a record-breaking start.

I understand why she did it, turned the tables and tried to play us off like we were nothing to her. She wanted to save face.

What she didn't wait around to hear with her eavesdropping in the hallway was me telling my brothers how deeply in love I am with her. That I've fallen so hard and fast for her that I don't want to be without her by my side. How I wanted to come clean because one day I want to ask her to be my wife for real, with a new ring and a new start.

I never got to that part because Lauren is a reactor. It takes one to know one and I'm sure I would've done the exact same thing she did—stormed in and tried to hurt the person who hurt her.

Hell, I struck back by calling her Hunt before I realized what was really going on.

So now I have to make her see that she didn't see the whole picture with what she overheard, just a small part of the canvas. But my girl can be stubborn. This is going to take some work.

Stepping up to her room, I knock lightly and slowly open the door.

I'm greeted with a lifeless room and a made bed. Heading to the bathroom, I see that all her toiletries are gone. A squeezing sensation constricts my chest—she's trying to run from me. From us.

Limping my way back into her bedroom, I check her closet and see that her clothes are all still hung up which means she plans to come back at some point.

"Luca!" Ma calls out from downstairs.

Shit, what the hell are they doing here?

I walk down the stairs, trying not to put too much pressure on my right leg. The painkillers the hospital gave me are starting to wear off and the burn hurts like a bitch. The only good thing about any of this is that I've gotten medical leave through the holidays so there will be plenty of time for make-up sex with Lauren—after we make-up that is.

When I reach the bottom of the stairs, Ma places her hands on my cheeks, staring at me like I might turn to dust at any moment. After she seems content that I'm alive and well, she wraps her arms around me.

"Hey, Ma." You're never too old to feel safe and loved from one of your mom's hugs and I sink into her and squeeze her back.

"I'm so happy you're okay."

"Okay, Maria, let the boy be." My dad taps her arm and she finally releases her hold.

"I don't know why you boys have to pick these jobs. Your cousins are all safe in offices." She shakes her head and makes her way over to the couch to sit down.

Little does she know the crazy ass shit those three do outside of those offices, but those aren't my stories to tell.

"You good?" my dad asks, shaking my hand, his eyes inspecting every inch of my body.

"Just a little sore, but okay."

"Where's Lauren?" Ma asks, looking around. She picks up a snow globe of Christkindlmarket I found two days ago and surprised Lauren with.

"Can I come by your place in a little bit? I have somewhere to go."

Ma puts the snow globe down and studies my face. As though she's a psychic who can sense when I've done wrong, her lips tip down.

"Where's Lauren, Luca?" This time the question isn't asked with curiosity, it's with a finger pointed right at my chest.

I let out a deep breath which seems like all I've been doing recently. "Sit down."

My dad's face grows serious, but he does as I ask.

I sit as well then pull out my phone, sending Lauren a

quick text before this conversation starts. That way by the time my parents disown me, I'll know where to find her.

> Me: Where are you? (A gif of Superman looking everywhere in the sky)

"Put the phone away," my mom says, clasping her two hands in her lap like she's a priest waiting for my confession. The problem is I could say a million Hail Mary's and it wouldn't make this right in Ma's mind.

Tucking my phone into my pocket, I'm hoping like hell I feel it vibrate in a second.

Yeah, I'm totally smoking crack thinking she'll respond.

"Talk," Ma says.

I worry about Ma. This was all to help her, but now that it's come down to me confessing I can only hope that I don't do her more harm.

"I don't know where Lauren is."

My mom nods, waiting for more.

"She's mad at me."

"Why?" my dad asks.

My mom continues to stare at me, her mouth shut. She's waiting for me to fess up. This has always been her way and although I haven't had to experience it since high school, I forgot how intimidating she is when she does this.

"She overheard me talking to Cris and Mauro..."

"What did you say?" my dad asks. He's still calm. Maybe this will go smoother than I thought.

"Just that..."

"Spit it out, Luca!" my dad yells.

My mom smacks his leg. "Give him a minute, Tony."

My dad springs to his feet, walking over to the window. I think about the figure eights Lauren does when she's upset. A small smile almost comes to my lips until I see my mom. Sitting and waiting.

It's now or never. "Ma, our engagement was a fake." I rush out the words and there's a certain amount of freedom now that I've said them out loud, but I also feel sick waiting for her reaction.

And then...she doesn't react. I half expected her to pass out and I'd be doing CPR while my dad called nine-one-one.

"Did you hear me?" I ask.

"I did." Her face is blank.

"Did your brothers get all the brains? What the hell did we do wrong, Maria?" My dad looks at my mom, completely bewildered. Though I'm mildly offended about him calling me stupid, I can't argue with him because right now because I've lost the only woman I want to spend my life with.

Ma holds up her hand for my dad to stop his ranting, her eyes poised on me, waiting for me to continue.

"Before your surgery I wanted you to know that all your boys were happy and would be taken care of, so I asked Lauren to pretend to be my fiancée."

A low grumble floats over from my dad.

"She agreed to do it because I convinced her it was what was best for you and it helped her solve an issue she was having at work."

She nods.

"What did you think would happen? Did you think you'd marry her just to save face? When are you ever going to grow up? I've let you off too easy. This is all because he was the baby, Maria."

Ma raises her hand again and my dad stops. I take nothing he says seriously, it's the Italian temper and I can hardly deny that this wasn't my brightest plan.

"We announced the engagement and I bought her the ring, but she was never my girlfriend," I continue.

Well, she kind of was for the blink of an eye.

My mom's hand falls to my knee. "She was."

"No Mom, it was all an act."

She shakes her head. "No."

My dad takes a few steps closer to us. "Maria, he's admitting it. She was like those girls who call the deli."

"No, she wasn't." Ma's voice holds the conviction that she's right.

My head swivels to my dad. "She wasn't, Dad. She was never one of those."

"Did you sleep with her?" he asks.

I really don't want to answer that in front of my Catholic mother. But I do. I nod, hoping my confession doesn't make my mom go to church asking for my forgiveness.

"Then?"

"Lauren was never like those other girls."

"You both deceived us. You slept with her with no intention of being her boyfriend or marrying her. How is she any different Luca?" My dad steps even closer.

"Because she's my everything," I whisper. My chin falls to my chest in shame as the realization dawns on me—she really is everything good in me. She finds everything that is right with me and draws it out.

"Then why the hell are you here?" He grips my shoulder and squeezes.

"Because she heard me say she was nothing."

Ma's squeezes my hand between both of hers. "Then you go convince her she's your everything." Ma's hand moves to my cheek. "Time for you to grow up, Luca."

"I love her, Ma." She pats my cheek once more.

"I know that, but I'm not the one who needs to hear it."

I spring up off the couch and grab my coat before I realize that I have another problem. "I can't drive." I stare down at my injured leg.

"Come on, Maria, let's help our boy get his girl." My dad takes his keys out of his pocket.

I'm locking up the door when a hand whips me across the back of my head.

My hand covers the injured spot. "Ma?"

She shakes her head and walks down the stairs to my dad's car.

I guess I deserved that one.

CHAPTER THIRTY-EIGHT

Lauren

"*I* think you should answer his text." Maddie sits next to me on my parents' couch, pretending to flip through a magazine.

I've confessed my sins to everyone—my two best friends, my parents—everyone now knows what an idiot I am. Thankfully, they've decided to take the approach of being a support system to the down and out rather than lecturing me on my wrongdoings. I think they all feel sorry for me, which is probably pretty easy given my state of being at the moment.

I spoon myself up another heap of cookie dough. Somehow the gooey chocolate doesn't taste nearly as good as it did the last time I had it.

"I don't care to hear his rehearsed bullshit excuse."

Van sits down in the chair by the door, crossing her legs. "I'm not sure that when it comes to Luca, anything's rehearsed."

"Van!" The magazine drops into Maddie's lap.

"What? You know it's true. He isn't one to talk it out before he says whatever's going through his mind. If he was, we probably wouldn't be sitting here."

"Why's that?" Maddie asks.

"Because he would've started by telling his brothers how in love with Lauren he was. Not how the whole thing was fake."

"Why are you so insistent to believe we have some special bond?" I ask around my spoon. "He admitted to his brothers that it was all a game."

Vanessa remains quiet, her eyes on mine. For the first time in a while, I can't figure out what's behind those blue eyes.

"What?" I ask, spooning another cookie's worth of dough into my mouth.

"Okay, I'm just going to pull the plug on the dough." Maddie takes the bowl, but I steal it right back.

"I'm afforded twenty-four hours to eat whatever I want." Spooning another extra big helping into my mouth, I mumble. "I still have at least ten hours left."

"I'm making your favorite." My mom rushes in from the kitchen, picking up the candy wrappers from the glass table by my feet. "Chicken and dumplings." She squeezes my ankle. "After that night here, I never would've thought he'd break your heart."

"He didn't break my heart."

My mom stops cleaning, Maddie stops reading, and Vanessa stops fidgeting.

"You guys think he broke me? He didn't break me. I knew the score when I signed on."

It's bullshit and they know it, but how can I admit that I fell for the biggest playboy in Chicago and actually thought I meant something to him? I believed the lies he spewed. I invited him into my bed and unfortunately, my heart.

God, he did break me.

Twenty-four hours is a joke. I wouldn't be over him if I ate ten bowls of cookie dough.

"So, maybe I kind of liked him."

Maddie's hand covers my knee. "Maybe even love?"

I point the spoon at her. "That's taking it too far, Mad."

I'm lying, and they all know it, but I need to save a little face here. Pride has long been one of my downfalls.

The doorbell rings and I tense up and still like it's Michael Myers and he's about to murder us all. I want to whisper, tell them not to answer the door, there's nothing good on the other side.

But Vanessa stands, and her hand covers the doorknob before I can speak.

"Well, look who we have here." Vanessa slips through the door and shuts it behind her.

I glance over to Maddie. She bites her lip.

My mom disappears into the kitchen, hopefully, to bake a pie we can throw in Luca's face.

Vanessa is the worst bouncer ever because when the door opens again, it's Luca himself walking through it. He scours the room until he finds me on the couch.

I'm regretting the fact that I'm wallowing while wearing sweats and a sweatshirt with my hair piled on top of my head and my face stripped of any makeup. Way to let him see what he's leaving behind.

Maddie stands up, the magazine long forgotten. Surely, she won't let him get to me. She'll shove him out the door and kick him in the nuts for me.

All that angry energy she had earlier dissolves when Mr. and Mrs. Bianco walk through the door.

He brought his parents? Dumb move, I'll still annihilate him.

"Ma. Pa?" Maddie asks, confused as I am as to what they're doing here.

I unhook my ponytail, my dark hair falling down my shoulders.

My mom walks into the room. "Maria? Anthony?" She hugs each one of them, placing a kiss on their cheeks. "FRED!"

Luca cringes when my mom calls my dad.

Good because the tables are about to turn. Luca might have helped my dad see the light, as proven by my team picture now on the Hunt wall of fame, but he hurt me, and my dad is going to nail him to the wall for it.

The creak of the stairs alerts everyone that my dad is on his way up from the basement. He appears in the doorway and when he spots Luca it's clear that my dad would love an hour in the basement alone with him so he could try out his new tools.

Just as I'm expecting my dad to lay in on him, his eyes catch Luca's parents and his scowl turns into a smile. "Tony. Maria."

They all shake hands and stare back at Luca.

"Your boy did wrong," my dad says.

"He's here to make it right," Anthony says.

"He better because my daughter deserves the best. A man who will protect her and take care of her."

A small smile creeps onto my face seeing my dad stick up for me.

"I can take care of myself." I desert the cookie dough and head to the kitchen. I don't want any part of whatever Luca's here for. It's not my job to help him clear his conscience with his parents.

"I know you can," my dad says, making me pause for a second. He's done a one-eighty and I wonder if it will last forever.

"Lauren," Luca says.

My eyes close with the sound of my name coming from his lips.

"Let me explain," he continues.

I turn, my eyes falling to my parents first. It wasn't pleasant telling them when I woke on their couch this morning that I had agreed to be someone's fiancée in exchange for some Blackhawks tickets and a date. I'm really hating Luca more for making me go through this again in front of everyone.

"There's nothing to explain. It was an act. From the fact your parents are here I'm guessing everyone knows our little secret now. Let's just move on with our lives." I turn around with the intent on hiding in the kitchen until he leaves.

"That's bullshit, and you know it. I was not the only one who felt something."

The front door opens and closes. Great, more witnesses here to enjoy my embarrassment.

"Sorry," Mauro mumbles.

"Oh shit, thank God we didn't miss it," Cris says to Mauro, but we can all hear him.

"This isn't the fucking Maury Povich show," Luca spits out. "Give us some privacy."

"No." My dad's deep voice is the only one who answers.

Luca rolls his eyes. "Well?"

I swallow down the lump in my throat and stomp over to him. "Well, what? What exactly do you want me to say?"

Getting me face-to-face almost pulls a cocky smile out of him. Bastard.

"I want you to say you love me because I sure as hell love you."

I suck in a startled gasp. At his words, yes, but also from the ferocity he delivered them with.

"Luca!" his mom scolds him.

Luca continues as though no one said anything. "Do you think if I had a choice, I'd pick you, Lauren? Newsflash, I wouldn't. We'll probably kill one another before we reach the "til death do us part' promise in our vows. But the choice isn't mine because my heart is yours. You've held it since I was fifteen and I never want it back."

All the women in the room simultaneously put their hands over their hearts and sigh. Traitors.

My bottom lip quivers, betraying myself so I bite down on it with my teeth.

"I love you," Luca whispers, placing a hand on my cheek.

My tears having nowhere to go, trickle down my face.

"We went our separate ways after high school, but fate brought us back together because our story wasn't finished. It hadn't even begun." He swipes away one of my tears with his thumb. "I know you love me, too. If you would've waited at the hospital a damn second, I was about to tell my brothers the truth."

Tears tumble out of my eyes like an overflowing sink now. I hate that he's so easily able to convince me that I'm wrong. I hate being wrong. But the truth is, I've never been so happy to be wrong in my life.

When I don't speak, he continues, "The truth is that I fell so hard for you, I can't find the ground under me. I know you didn't mean those things you said last night. You just didn't want me to be the one to hurt you. But we can't be like that, Lauren. That might've been us at one time, but not anymore. Win or lose we do it together. No more competition. You and I are a team now."

I desperately want to trust his words. My gaze falls over him. His sunken eyes and grayish face. The way his hair sticks up in all directions. His mismatched outfit. Has he been hurting as much as me?

"Having you be in a committed relationship would be like

fencing in a wild horse. At some point, I won't be enough for you. You'll want to bust out to see what you're missing in the world."

That right there is my biggest fear. That I won't be enough for the free spirit that is Luca Bianco.

He winces at my words as though I slapped him, but he keeps his eyes fixed on mine.

"Don't you see? You freed me. Wild horses don't roam alone. There's so much out there in the open fields for both of us to explore—together."

A small smile turns up the corners of my lips. Luca raises his index finger up and digs into the pocket of his jeans, pulling out his phone.

"Maybe this will convince you that I never really forgot about you, even when I was out grazing with other mares."

Holding his phone up, he hands it over to me.

There's a picture of me asleep on his childhood bed. I don't even remember when this would have been taken, but my chin length hair tells me it was high school at some point.

"I know it was wrong, but I couldn't help myself," he says, looking adorably sheepish.

"What is it?" Van asks Cristian.

"I don't know," she whispers back.

"You took this?" I could see Cody doing it, but not Luca. Luca barely tolerated my existence in high school.

He nods. "It was a party at my parents' house and you weren't feeling well. I argued with Cody about putting you in my bed, told him to take you home. That I didn't want you puking in my bed. I only said that because I couldn't handle the thought of you sleeping in my bed. Your scent all over where I slept would be the cruelest form of torture for me. Cody insisted though because he didn't want to leave the party. I snuck up there to check up on you and..." He glances over his shoulder at all the bystanders. "I snapped the picture because well...I like to torment myself, I suppose. I was used to the two of us going at it all the time and you looked so sweet and innocent laying there."

I giggle because I'll give it to him. That took guts to share that.

I've been so stupid. Stupid for second-guessing him. I know him better than that. Luca shows he doesn't tell, and I allowed words to put us where we are now.

"Don't you see, Lauren, I'm not too proud to admit, you've always been the one I really wanted."

"Luca."

His hands cup my cheeks. "What? I'll do anything." The desperation in his eyes almost undoes me.

I take a step back and slide the ring off my finger. "Take your ring back." I press it into the palm of his hand as a look of horror overtakes his features. "And ask me out on a proper date."

Luca's arrogant smile appears, and he tucks the ring into his pocket for safe keeping. Then he falls down to bended knee, taking my now empty hand in his. "Lauren Hunt, will you go out with me tonight?"

I pretend like I have to think really hard about it when all I really want to do is kiss him. "Sure. Knock on my bedroom door at seven?"

"Knock on our headboard?" He stands up, winding his arm around my waist and pulling me into his body, where I fit perfectly.

"That works, too."

He bends his head down and even though we're in front of both our families, our lips crash together. Every deal should be sealed with a kiss.

EPILOGUE

Luca

Four Months Later

The lights in the arena and the red carpet is extended out to mid-ice. It's been months since Lauren gave me that ring back, but now I've got a shiny, bigger one in my pocket as the announcer comes over the speaker.

Mauro and Cris bring a blindfolded Lauren out to the ice's edge.

"This is ridiculous and I want you both to know that payback is a bitch."

Mauro shoots me a look to say I owe him one, which I do.

He and Cris convinced her that she needed to appease me because I was able to score tickets that let us meet the team, but I wanted to do a lame birthday surprise for her.

I had no choice but to tell one little white lie because it's Lauren and she's not a girl who's willing to be blindfolded unless we're in the bedroom. In which case she quite enjoys herself.

Wanting to make me happy she agreed to pretend to be blindfolded for the last stretch, but what she doesn't know is that I'm in the middle of the United Center, on bended knee in front of thousands of people.

The last four months have been amazing. I got to unwrap her at Christmas, kiss her at midnight on New Year's, pretend to shoot her with cupid's arrow on Valentine's Day and watch them dye the river green with her on St. Patrick's Day. It's not just the holidays that Lauren has made sweeter. It's every day that I get to come home to the woman who keeps life interesting and fills me with joy.

Since my mom's last ablation two weeks ago was successful, and they caught the arsonist—which by the way was the Osmond Brothers, who kept stealing properties from Mauro and Maddie—I count my blessings every day. Ma might not always remain A-fib free, but we'll take what we can get while we have it.

Maddie and Mauro are planning their wedding for this summer and Cris has yet to ask Vanessa, but I can't wait any longer. Staring at Lauren's empty left hand nauseates me every time.

The Jumbotron lights up with a slideshow of the two of us with "Speechless" by Dan + Shay playing in the background. Lauren's shoulders droop when the song starts, and she strips the blindfold off, which I kind of expected from her. Her eyes find me and her face scrunches into that expression right before she's about to cry.

The crowd roars to life and I hold my hand out for her to come to me.

The closer she gets, the more I see the scowl through her tears and I can't help but chuckle.

I know what she wants, but I'm a 'go big or go home' guy.

She said so herself. Since I can't announce to every single person in this world that I love Lauren Hunt, this is the closest I'll get.

The song finishes, and I pick up the microphone. Jesus, I never thought I'd be this stressed about it when I was putting it all together. I'm pretty confident of her answer, but I've been wrong before.

"Luca," she says my name in a mock scolding way.

I chuckle. "Sorry, babe, but you love me anyway, right?"

Laughter rings throughout the arena.

"What are you doing?" she asks.

"I'm telling all these people how much I love you."

Again, the crowd laughs and I'm second guessing my decision to call in a favor after saving the general manager's life a couple months ago.

"Nice, babe."

She's in her ratty Blackhawks jersey and jeans. Her hair is thrown up in a ponytail and her flawless face has little makeup on it. Exactly how I love her most.

"Oh, but one more thing." I pull the ring from my pocket and take her left hand in mine.

"Luca." She sighs.

"Lauren Hunt, you make my life worth living. If I was a poet or a writer, I'd probably make all these people swoon with oohs and aahs. But I'm not. I'm just the man who can't live without you. Who wouldn't even want to try. Without you, my heart will be just as cold as my bed at night. What do you say? Torture yourself for the rest of your life and agree to be my wife?"

Laughter falls down from the rows of seats.

Lauren smiles and nods, tears in her eyes. "I do love to hate you."

I slip the ring on her finger and applause rings out.

"I'm just thankful you love to love me more."

Her arms wrap around my neck. "You know it."

"Forgive me for all this?" I glance around at the thousands of spectators.

"I have a feeling I'll be doing that for the next fifty years or more."

I chuckle. "You know it."

———

Later that night we get home and though I know she's excited that we're really, truly engaged this time, I've sensed something else below the surface.

Once we're in our house, I'm ready to give her one more surprise, but I want to figure out what's going on first. If she thinks it's too soon to be engaged, I want to hear it. No more keeping our feelings bottled up inside.

"Hey, babe, I have one more gift for your birthday, but are you okay?"

She nods, sitting down on the couch. "I'm good."

"You're not acting good."

Her fingers play with her new adornment on her left ring finger. She stares down at it. "It's really pretty."

"It is." I should know, I'll be paying for it for a few years.

"Is it returnable?" she asks.

My heart stumbles over a beat. She's kidding me, right?

"I suppose I could be one of those schmucks who have to return a ring." I put my palm out for it.

"Luca, I..."

"Spit it out, Lauren."

"Do you have the other ring still?" she asks like I'm about to go off and she's worried about my reaction.

"What ring? The first one?"

She nods.

My forehead wrinkles. "Why?"

She stares down at the new and improved ring on her finger. "When I gave it back to you, it was so you could give it to me again."

"But that ring was when everything was a lie?"

"It really wasn't. It's the first ring you gave me and you know how I am about firsts." She smiles.

With my heart lighter now, I run up the stairs, digging into my sock drawer and running back down.

"You really want this one?"

She holds out her left hand for me. "Yeah. It's ours. That first engagement was just the beginning of us falling in love with each other. This one means so much more to me. Do you know how many times I stared down at this ring wishing it was real?"

I sit down beside her pushing the small box aside.

"No."

"I did, Luca. Not at first, but later on. It's what first gave me the thought of what it would be like to be Mrs. Lauren Hunt-Bianco."

"Okay then. I'll happily be one of those poor schmucks who returns an engagement ring then." I slide off the big diamond and put on the smaller diamond and she's right, that's her ring. "We need to talk about the whole hyphenating your last name thing by the way."

She chuckles and lays her head on my chest, staring at her outstretched left hand. "I'll go with you."

I reach around and pull out the box I'd stashed behind the couch cushion earlier. "One more thing."

"You're really upping your game here. I don't think I can top this for your birthday."

She rips off the paper and opens the box. "How sweet, papers."

"Read the papers, babe," I say with a laugh.

She looks them over, her jaw dropping the farther into them she gets. "You bought the house...from Maddie?"

Pride fills my chest. "I did. She did give a pretty big brother-in-law discount, but it's ours. Just like that ring, this place is ours. It's where we're meant to grow our love and build our family."

"I love you." She leans in and wraps her arms around my neck.

"I love you more," I say and kiss the top of her head.

She pulls back and stares at me with joy in her eyes. "I love you until infinity."

"I love you to infinity plus infinity."

"I love you..."

"Babe, shut up and kiss me."

Our lips crash together, and I'm lost in her orbit. Screw that, this is our orbit now.

The End

COCKAMAMIE UNICORN RAMBLINGS

That's it. The end of the Blue Collar Brothers series. We're sad to see the Bianco brothers go, but we have a feeling we'll be revisiting them often.

This series was so much fun to write and we couldn't be happier with the way you've opened your hearts for each one of our Italian brothers. All three of them are like our unicorns, magical and unique, making us love them all equally. Just like Mama Bianco.

The story for Luca's book started with us trying to figure out a title that worked with EMT that had an alliteration to it. (Insider Tip: Piper is a HUGE sucker for alliteration.) When we thought of the word engaged, it worked perfectly because the fake engagement/fake relationship is a storyline we haven't attempted yet.

From there we had to think of a reason WHY Luca would want to enter into a fake engagement. Since we are writing romantic comedy, we knew we had to tread carefully and not make the book too sad. This is where Mama Bianco's heart arrhythmia was born. Rayne's dad has been living with Atrial Fibrillation for over five years now. Although her family is comfortable with his diagnosis now, those early years and surgeries were scary times. Which made it easy to see why Luca, the baby of the family, would be the perfect hero to do something crazy like fake an engagement for his Ma's benefit (or so he believed). Of course, the only girl he'd want to do it with is the one he loves to hate...or at least pretends to.

We enjoyed giving Luca and Lauren a run for their money. She loves to call him on his shit and he loves to pull reactions out of her. Hopefully you agree with us, that these two were only meant for each other.

It takes a village and we'd be remiss if we didn't give thanks to ours:

Letitia from RBA Designs
    Wander Aguiar
    Ellie from Love N Books
    Shawna from Behind the Writer
    Dani Sanchez and the whole Inkslinger PR gang
    All the bloggers who carve out time to read and review our books.
    All our early ARC readers
    And of course, all our unicorns. <3

Thanks to each and everyone of you for helping get this book out in the public. We literally could not do it without all of you.

A huge thanks to all the readers who embraced these characters and want to join the Bianco family as honorary members! Hey – maybe we should put that on a t-shirt or something? LOL

Next up for us, is the start to a brand new series in a brand new world, The Baileys. BUT after the first three books from that world are released, we're heading to NYC to spend time with the Bianco's NYC cousins. That's right! Remember

Enzo? All three of the Mancini brothers will be getting their own book in our White Collar Cousins series. And just wait until you meet the three ladies who get these Italian men hot under the collars! ;) Look for the first book, Sexy Filthy Boss, out in June 2019.

Until then unicorns, stay fabulous!

Xo,
    Piper & Rayne

ABOUT PIPER & RAYNE

Piper Rayne is a USA Today Bestselling Author duo who write "heartwarming humor with a side of sizzle" about families, whether that be blood or found. They both have e-readers full of one-clickable books, they're married to husbands who drive them to drink, and they're both chauffeurs to their kids. Most of all, they love hot heroes and quirky heroines who make them laugh, and they hope you do, too!

ALSO BY PIPER RAYNE

Blue Collar Brothers

Flirting with Fire

Crushing on the Cop

Engaged to the EMT

White Collar Brothers

Sexy Filthy Boss

Dirty Flirty Enemy

Wild Steamy Hook-up

The Modern Love World

Charmed by the Bartender

Hooked by the Boxer

Mad about the Banker

The Single Dad's Club

Real Deal

Dirty Talker

Sexy Beast

Hollywood Hearts

Mister Mom

Animal Attraction

Domestic Bliss

Bedroom Games

Cold as Ice

On Thin Ice

Break the Ice

Box Set

Chicago Law

Smitten with the Best Man

Tempted by my Ex-Husband

Seduced by my Ex's Divorce Attorney

The Rooftop Crew

My Bestie's Ex

A Royal Mistake

The Rival Roomies

Our Star-Crossed Kiss

The Do-Over

A Co-Workers Crush

The Baileys

Lessons from a One-Night Stand

Advice from a Jilted Bride

Birth of a Baby Daddy

Operation Bailey Wedding (Novella)

Falling for My Brother's Best Friend

Demise of a Self-Centered Playboy

Confessions of a Naughty Nanny

Operation Bailey Babies (Novella)

Secrets of the World's Worst Matchmaker

Winning My Best Friend's Girl

Rules for Dating your Ex

Operation Bailey Birthday (Novella)

The Greene Family

My Twist of Fortune

My Beautiful Neighbor

My Almost Ex

My Vegas Groom

A Greene Family Summer Bash

My Sister's Flirty Friend

My Unexpected Surprise

My Famous Frenemy

A Greene Family Vacation

My Scorned Best Friend

My Fake Fiancé

My Brother's Forbidden Friend

A Greene Family Christmas

Lake Starlight

The Problem with Second Chances

The Issue with Bad Boy Roommates

The Trouble with Runaway Brides

Hockey Hotties

My Lucky #13

The Trouble with #9

Faking it with #41

Sneaking around with #34

Second Shot with #76

Offside with #55

Kingsmen Football Stars

You Had Your Chance, Lee Burrows

You Can't Kiss the Nanny, Brady Banks

Over My Brother's Dead Body, Chase Andrews

Chicago Grizzlies

Something like Hate

Something like Lust

Something like Love

Standalones

Single and Ready to Jingle

Claus & Effect

www.ingramcontent.com/pod-product-compliance
Lightning Source LLC
Chambersburg PA
CBHW020133310726
48970CB00006B/1851